AUTUMN SOFTLY FELL

An evocative and charming Edwardian family saga

DOMINIC LUKE

The Brannans Family Trilogy Book 1

JOFFE BOOKS

Revised edition 2021
Joffe Books, London
www.joffebooks.com

First published by Robert Hale in Great Britain in 2014

Cover art by Jarmila Takač

ISBN: 978-1-78931-835-7

. . . after Spring had bloomed in early Greece,
And Summer blazed her glory out with Rome,
An autumn softly fell, a harvest home,
A slow grand age, and rich with all increase . . .

1914
Wilfred Owen

CHAPTER ONE

A clock struck twelve.

Dorothea Ryan turned and twisted in her sleep, the sound of the clock haunting her dreams. Each stroke came from an immense distance, grew louder, reverberated in her head, and then dissolved to make way for the next. It was only after the twelfth and last stroke that she woke with a start and sat up.

Her dream shredded, disappeared. She looked around. This was not home. It was nothing like Stepnall Street. The bed in which she was lying was huge, the mattress springy, the sheets crisp and white. Such a bed had never been known in Stepnall Street. Even more startling was the profound and uncanny silence.

Where was she? And why was she here?

She knit her brows, thinking back. They had set off on a journey, she remembered, her and her papa.

'Where are we going?'

He had not answered. He was like that sometimes, shut away inside himself.

'Mrs Browning will wonder where we've gone.' They had left without a word to anyone. It had troubled her.

She cast her mind back to the railway station, a cavernous place with an echoing roof and crowded platforms. She had run, following her papa's coat tails, dodging the people who towered over her. There had been a metal monster — that was how she had put it to herself — hissing, belching steam, giving off an acrid smell. She had never seen a locomotive up close before, had never travelled by train. She had found that she did not like it. The railway carriage jerked and jolted, rattling, trundling, while outside the winter dusk closed in. She had pressed her face against the cold glass, looking for lights; but there had been nothing, just the reflection of their compartment and — beyond that — a black emptiness. Her papa had not spoken as the journey went on and on. In the end, she had curled up on the seat and gone to sleep.

Sitting now in the plush bed, she wondered where her papa was. Why did no one come for her?

She pushed back the bed clothes and slid out of bed. The air was chill. She shivered. But she was used to the cold, took no notice. Someone had undressed her last night, she discovered, and had put her into a nightdress. It was several sizes too big for her. She had to hold up the skirts as she walked across the carpeted floor (carpet!).

No one lived in this room, she felt sure. It was too clean, too silent, too impersonal. The furniture was old, just as the furniture in Stepnall Street was old; but this furniture did not look as if it was about to drop to pieces. There was a wardrobe (empty apart from a pair of men's shoes), a wooden stand with a pretty china basin (no water) and a long table against the wall with drawers and a mirror. No fire burned in the fireplace; but then there was never a fire in the room in Stepnall Street either.

She pulled aside the heavy curtains (such curtains!) and looked out of the window, not knowing what to expect. In Stepnall Street, if you peeled back the brown paper and looked through the window frame, there was a view of soot-stained walls, gaping windows, slanting roofs. Chimney stacks were etched against the smoke smudged sky. Down below was the courtyard with its puddles, its piles of rubbish, its slimy cobbles.

But here . . . Her eyes widened as she tried to take it all in. A cold grey morning. A vast cloudy sky. Wintry fields stretching into an unguessable distance. Trees. Hedges. No houses, except far off and to the right there was a glimpse of a tower: a castle? a church? To the left was a hill, leafless trees on top like spiky hair on a big round head. Directly below her was a circular space of gravel surrounding a tall spreading tree. The sight of the gravel nudged her memory: a crunching sound as she walked, the feel of it beneath her feet, the way the little stones worked in through the holes in her boots . . .

They had left the train, walked a long way. It had been cold and dark. She had been dead on her feet. Her papa had picked her up and carried her and she had slept again. What had woken her was the sound of a bottle falling — *chink!* — to the ground. Her papa had stopped, sank to his knees, and she had rolled out of his arms onto loose stones and cold compacted earth.

Sitting up, rubbing her eyes, she had looked around. No street lamps, no buildings, no people; just a row of trees on either side, the tops of them like black spikes jutting into the paler black of the sky. It was then — she remembered — that the clock had struck, the clock that had haunted her dreams. The sound of it had been faint, distant, but had carried clearly in the terrible silence. Twelve o'clock. Midnight. It had seemed somehow ominous. As the last stroke died away she had sat on the cold ground shuddering. The wind seethed in the trees. Her papa gasped for breath as he groped for the fallen bottle. When he found it, he shook it. Liquid sloshed.

'Papa? W-where are we?'

'Not far now, Dotty. Not far to go.' He had tipped the bottle back, gulped. She had smelt gin, the smell she most hated; but out in the silent, empty night its familiarity had almost been comforting.

'I'm cold, Papa.'

'Cold, are you? And we've forgotten to bring your coat.'

'My coat's in the pawn shop.'

'So it is. Well, then, we couldn't have brung it anyhow.' Another swallow of gin. 'Gee up, Dotty. We must be nearly there now, if the man at the station told us right.'

He had scrambled to his feet, pulling her up after him, and they had walked up the long path or track or road between the sighing trees until they came to the gravel.

Those little stones, she thought as she stood by the window, *will still be in my boots*. But when she looked around the room her boots — and the rest of her clothes — were nowhere to be seen.

She turned back to the window. Her breath steamed up the glass. She thought about the house she had seen as she stood in the cold and dark on the gravel: a house so huge that she had for a moment believed it must belong to giants. The low branches of the spreading tree had seemed to be reaching to grab her as she followed her papa, stumbling towards the steps that led up to the front door. A golden glow had spilled out from the fanlight. She had heard faint sounds from within: music — a piano, perhaps? — and voices, many voices.

Her papa had banged on the door as if he had no fear of the giants. She had shrunk against him, clutching his threadbare coat. He had swigged gin, waiting.

She found herself shivering. She was actually here, inside the big house, the house that had filled her with foreboding. She was here — and she was alone.

Trapped?

She turned away from the window, faced the door. Was it locked? Was she a prisoner?

She fought back panic, tried to be sensible. *One step at a time*, Mrs Browning always said, and whatever else Mrs Browning might be (one could not call her a motherly woman), she was eminently practical. One thing at a time. First: try the door.

She crossed the room, took a deep breath, put her hand on the handle. The door opened, squeaking faintly. She looked out into a gloomy anteroom. There was a door to the left, closed. There was a door to the right, ajar.

Dorothea hesitated. What next? Think of Mrs Browning. One step at a time. Find her clothes, then find her papa. After that, they could go home together, back to Stepnall Street.

It was a sensible plan, quite within her limits. But . . .

She hesitated, looking apprehensively at the ajar door and the glimpse of corridor beyond.

There had been a man. An angry-looking man. She did not want to meet him again — even if he was her uncle. (Could it be true? Was he really her uncle?)

She shut the bedroom door, leant against it, her heart beating. The angry-looking man had not been alone last night. There had been lots of people — hundreds of people, it seemed, all gathered around Dorothea and her papa, and all of them neat and polished and wearing the most wonderful clothes. But it was the angry man her papa had pointed out to her: a tall, burly man with streaks of grey in his black hair, and a great bushy moustache that all but hid his mouth.

'Gee up, Dot! This here's your uncle what I told you about. A very fine gent. Did I not say as much?'

If he had been anyone else, she would have called him a fibber, for her papa had never said a word about any uncle. Perhaps he had forgotten. Grown-ups often were forgetful — especially after they had been drinking gin. Gin made them forgetful and clumsy and quarrelsome.

She remembered the way her papa had looked at her last night, shaking his head and talking to himself (that was due to the gin, too). 'Breaks my heart, so it does. But I can't see no other way around it, and that's the truth.'

There had been tears in his eyes, which had been the most frightening thing of all — more frightening by far than the giant house or the angry man or the hundreds of watching eyes. She had never seen her papa cry, had not believed it possible, for he was the bravest man in the world.

The memory of the tears galvanised her. She straightened up, wiped away tears of her own, turned once more to face the door. It was no good *shilly-shallying* (as Mrs Browning would say). It was time to be as brave as her papa. ('Him? Brave? Ha!

I'd as soon call a mouse fierce!' Mrs Browning's words. But what did Mrs Browning know? She was only the landlady. That was what Papa called her, anyway: *the landlady*.)

Dorothea opened the door — it squeaked again — picked up her skirts, crossed to the door on the right, the one that was ajar. She looked out.

A long, wide corridor stretched ahead. There was a carpeted floor and painted walls, the carpet clean, the walls without a stain. There were pictures — such wonderful pictures — beautiful landscapes. She would have liked to examine them but now was not that time. All seemed quiet and deserted at first but as she stood hesitating in the doorway there came from a remote distance the sound of a door closing. So she wasn't alone. There were other people (who?). But what a vast place this house must be! It would take her days — weeks! — to find her way round. If she wanted to track down her clothes — and her papa — then she would have to start looking at once.

She slipped past the door and hastened along the corridor, her bare feet making no sound on the carpet. Soon she came to a wide flight of stairs going down. She remembered the stairs. Last night she had been half-dragged, half-carried up them by a girl in black-and-white clothes. On and on they had climbed, as if climbing the Tower of Babel up to heaven itself. But at least she now had some idea where she was. If she followed the stairs down she might — might! — come to other places from last night: the hallway with the front door, or the big room where the hundreds of people had been.

Her foot was poised to take the first step when a sudden sound made her freeze: the sound of footsteps, coming up. Without stopping to think, Dorothea dashed back along the corridor to hide behind a cabinet. Peeping out, she saw a bald, elderly man come puffing and panting up to the landing. He was carrying a black bag, seemed preoccupied. He did not pause to look round but went away along the corridor, turning into a room on the left. He shut the door behind him.

All was quiet again. Dorothea let out her breath, eased herself out of her hiding place. It was time to press on.

She set off down the stairs, trailing one hand along the banister. After a time she came to another landing, a different corridor. This one was more luxurious than the one above, the carpet thicker, the paintings even more grand. The stairs carried on, however, and down she went with them.

On the next half-landing, her courage failed. She had come a long way from the room where she had slept — miles, it seemed. She could not have felt any lonelier and more exposed had she been standing in the middle of a moor. And as she shilly-shallied — she couldn't help it — she noticed a picture on the wall above her: a red-faced man in a white wig staring out across the centuries — staring, she was sure, directly at her. She cowered, but the self-important eyes seemed to follow her, seemed to demand to know who she was and what she was doing in this house — *his* house.

Tears pricked her eyes again. She was ashamed to be crying like a baby when she was as old as eight. But this was an awful place, an unfriendly place. She could not imagine why her papa had brought her here.

She was not sure how long she spent shilly-shallying but suddenly she heard noises below. Wiping her eyes on the sleeve of her oversize nightgown, she crawled to the edge of the half-landing and then slid down first one step then another until she could peer between the banisters and see what was happening.

Below her was a wide, tiled hallway. An ornate clock was slowly ticking. There was a table with a vase of flowers. Her eyes were drawn, however, to the front door — the door with the fanlight, the door through which she had entered the house last night. It was wide open and people were coming in. There must have been a dozen or more, all wrapped up against the cold, wearing hats, scarves, gloves, boots. The ladies had furs, the gentlemen Norfolk jackets. There was much rubbing of hands, stamping of feet, puffing out of cheeks. As they began to divest themselves of their outdoor things, two girls in black and white came running to assist. They were dressed in exactly the same way as the girl who had taken Dorothea up to bed last night.

Servants, Dorothea said to herself: *maid servants*. And there was a man servant, too, tall and smart. But taller still was the daunting figure of the gentleman who — by all accounts — was her uncle. Those dark, angry eyes, that deep booming voice: she remembered him clearly from last night.

Several people were talking at once but Dorothea's attention was drawn to someone else she recognised from last night, a gracious lady who was getting on in years: she had to be forty at least.

'It's far too cold to be outside on a day like this,' she said as she unwrapped herself; 'but you men *will* have your sport. How did you get on, Henry?'

'Best not to ask!' A noisy young man interrupted. 'Fitzwilliam's the most awful shot, you know!'

'As you can tell, Alice,' said Dorothea's uncle to the gracious lady, 'young Harding here has had a most pleasurable morning. I am not sure which he has enjoyed more: shooting pheasants or making sport of your son!'

'Fitzwilliam has been telling us all about that contraption of his,' yelped the noisy young man. 'Apparently it's gone lame!'

'A spot of bother with her hind wheels, that's all,' said the man named Henry. 'I'll soon have her running smoothly again, you'll see.'

'Ha! You heard him! He calls the thing *she*. I rather think he's cracked!'

Dorothea, peeking through the banisters, decided that she did not care for the young man called Harding. How dare he make fun of Henry! Of all the people in that big, glittery room last night, Henry was the only one who'd been kind to her. Indeed, he was the only one who'd even spoken to her. He had gentle eyes, she remembered, and bony knees.

She shivered on the stairs. There were details about last that she would rather not remember. She'd fund herself isolated, shaking with fear, surrounded by strangers all watching her. It had seemed an age before the tableau was broken. People at last had begun to drift away. There'd been a murmur of voices. The voices had grown louder as the piano struck up once more in the next room. There'd been laughter, the sound of singing. But Dorothea had stood frozen in place, fighting the urge to burst into tears, her face working with the effort.

Without warning, a young man had loomed up in front of her. 'Hello there! You're a funny little thing, aren't you!'

She had flinched, raising her hands to protect herself, and the shock had opened the flood gates she'd been struggling to keep shut.

'Hey now! Don't cry! There's no need to cry! Come to Henry, that's the way!'

She had been terrified to begin with as the young man scooped her up and carried her to a chair where he sat down, perching her on his knee. She had swallowed her sobs in alarm, wondering what on earth he wanted from her and in what way he thought her *funny*. But as she looked down at herself, she'd been struck by the great difference between her clothes and the lavish clothes of the people all round. Her smock was decidedly grubby — the bright gaslight made it glaringly obvious — her bonnet was too small and her boots had holes in: she had actually been able to see a little white toe peeping out. To the jolly young man holding her, whose big shiny shoes looked brand new, she must have seemed *funny* indeed.

He had passed no further comment on her clothes, however, and had given her instead something to drink — something fizzy in a tall glass. It had tasted most peculiar. The bubbles had gone up her nose and made her sneeze.

'Is that wise, Henry, feeding the child champagne like that?' The gracious lady who was forty at least had appeared at their side.

'It's a good old nannying trick, Mother,' Henry had said, looking affably up at the lady. 'Give the baby some spirits to keep it quiet.'

'I hope you are not suggesting, Henry, that any of your nannies ever did such a thing! In any case, champagne is not spirits, and this child is not a baby.'

Henry had grinned. 'What's the matter, Mother? Someone has provoked you, I can tell.'

'Oh, it's nothing. Just Arthur Camborne, as usual.'

'What has the good doctor said to upset you this time?'

'He talks such *nonsense*. To insist that we are still in the nineteenth century is simply absurd — and I told him so. Half an hour ago it was *eighteen* ninety-nine. Now it is *nineteen* hundred. The century has changed. That is clear enough, even to me.'

Henry had laughed. Dorothea had felt the tremor of it running through her body, oddly comforting. 'Impeccable logic, Mother.'

'Well, I think so.'

'But Dr Camborne does not?'

Henry's mother had pursed her lips. 'He merely said — in his most condescending manner — that he never gainsays one of the fair sex; and then he made some remark in Latin in that irritating way he has: *sed fugit* — oh, I forget what it was.'

'*Sed fugit interea, fugit irreparabile tempus*: meanwhile time is flying, flying never to return. It's Virgil.'

'Nonsense.'

'Not nonsense, Mother. It is a genuine quote from Virgil.'

'I mean that *he* talks nonsense: Arthur Camborne. I'm afraid I was quite short with him. And then there's Viola Somersby—'

'Mrs Somersby too! Golly, Mother, is there anybody here tonight with whom you *haven't* quarrelled?'

'Don't be silly, Henry. You know I never quarrel with anyone. All the same, if I have to hear once more how old-fashioned Clifton is, how Victorian it's décor . . . But one bites one's tongue. One makes allowances.'

'Because her son is in South Africa?'

'Yes, Henry. Precisely. The news has been so bad lately. One can only imagine what she is going through.'

'I'm sure no measly Boer will dare lay a finger on Mark Somersby. They will all be too afraid of what his mother would do to them!'

'Oh, Henry! How very wicked you are!'

But Henry's mother had been smiling, as if she didn't think him wicked at all. She seemed to enjoy being teased, had not shown him the back of her hand for his sauce as Mrs Browning would have done. Not that Henry was cheeky in the same way as Mickey; he was not so blunt, had much better manners. Dorothea had felt safe with his arm round her — even if it was rather beneath her dignity to be sitting on someone's knee at her age (eight-and-a-half!).

Crouched now on the stairs, Dorothea found herself wishing that Henry was her uncle and not the angry man with the bushy moustache. But she would much rather not have an uncle at all — not if it meant she had to lose her papa. This thought reminded her of her quest: it was high time she found her papa, then the two of them could set off for home.

Taking her courage in both hands, Dorothea stood up, but the people below were too engrossed in their own business to notice her. They were still discussing Henry's *contraption*, whatever that might be.

'I don't really approve of these horseless carriages,' Henry's mother was saying.

Several people agreed with her.

'But we must move with the times!' exclaimed Henry. 'Autocars are the future!'

'Nonsense, nonsense!' A bluff and blustery old man spoke up, jerking his arm as if to sweep away all such poppycock as horseless carriages. 'They are nothing but an infernal nuisance, raising all that dust in summer, splashing mud everywhere in the winter — knocking people down, too. And those ridiculous pilots, done up like monkeys! There ought to be a law against it. A law, I say!'

'There was a law,' said Henry, 'the Red Flag Act.'

'What's become of that law now, eh? Tell me that!'

'It was an outdated law. Stood in the way of progress.'

'Ah, now,' rumbled Dorothea's uncle, 'I'm all for progress as a rule. But I'm not convinced that . . .'

The voices faded as the whole party moved off along a passage that led towards the back of the house. The last of the servants scurried away. All was suddenly quiet, except for the ponderous ticking of the clock.

Gathering her skirts, Dorothea walked down the last flight of stairs and stepped into the hallway. The black-and-white tiles were cold against her feet, made her toes curl. She looked along the passageway where the people had gone. At the far end was a door with glass panels, a white wintry light coming through. There was no sign of the people, just a faint murmur of muffled voices. She looked round, wondering what to do next. The big house was bewildering.

All at once she stiffened. She could hear another voice, a woman's voice, getting ever nearer. There must be another corridor, she realised, leading off from the main one. She hesitated, wondering if she could ask this woman about her papa, but she didn't like the sound of the voice at all, sharp and complaining. She decided instead to make a dash for the stairs.

But it was too late. The voice was upon her.

'. . . and it's almost more than mortal can bear. I'm sure that *you* appreciate the problems, Mr Ordish. Cook says it's like old times, with so many guests and the carriages rolling up morning, noon and night. But I said to her, I said, "If all the old times were like this, then I'm glad to be living in normal times." Needless to say, I don't get any cooperation from Cook *at all*.'

With that, a woman dressed entirely in black came sweeping out from the unseen passage, a short, deferential man trotting at her heels. The woman paused, half turning so she could address her companion head on. Dorothea shrank against the newel post, hugging it.

'We need a deal more staff, is all I can say, if we're going to have this sort of performance on a regular basis. I'm sorry, but there it is. I can't be expected to do the jobs of three people at once. I've hardly had a wink of sleep, and—'

The voice came to an abrupt stop. All this time, as she was speaking, the woman's eyes had been darting about as if she was looking for something (something else to complain about, Dorothea said to herself). Now — suddenly, terribly — her gaze came to rest on Dorothea. Several different expressions — none of them pleasant — passed across her face. Finally she turned to her companion with a meaningful look.

'The Abandoned Child!' she enunciated.

This was too much for Dorothea. To be given a dressing down was one thing — nothing less could be expected from such a woman — but to be called *abandoned* wasn't just an insult, it was a slur against her papa. He would never abandon her, never.

She drew herself up. 'Please, I can't find my clothes.'

The woman ignored her. 'You see how it is, Mr Ordish? One can't rely on *anyone* to do *anything*!'

Suddenly, with a darting movement, she came swooping towards Dorothea like a great black bat, a bunch of keys jangling at her belt.

'What *is* Nanny thinking of, letting you wander all over the house practically *naked*!'

'But my clothes . . .' stammered Dorothea.

'*Those* pestilential rags were fit only for the fire!' An arm darted out, strong bony fingers clamped onto Dorothea's wrist. 'Come *along*. Back to the nursery.' She yanked Dorothea up the stairs, sweeping on ahead, black skirts swirling. 'As if I hadn't enough to do . . .'

Dorothea felt that her wrist might snap off at any moment as she was jerked and dragged back the way she had come, lashed by the woman's displeasure.

'Mrs Brannan wants you in an orphanage,' the woman said coldly. 'It's the best place for you, in my opinion. There's enough work as it is, without taking in waifs and strays. But there's no knowing *what* the master will do. He's a law unto himself.' She sniffed, as if being a law unto yourself was not to be encouraged.

They crashed through doors and came back to the room where Dorothea had slept. Here, a maid was kneeling on the hearth, lighting the fire. It was the same maid who had taken Dorothea upstairs the night before. She looked rather startled as they whooshed into the room. Her eyes widened at the sight of the woman in black.

'Well, so here you are, miss!' The girl got to her feet, brushing down her skirt and apron with the backs of her hands. 'I was wondering where you'd got to.'

The woman glared at the maid in a way that made Dorothea quake. 'I found her wandering in the hall. In her *nightgown*!'

'I'm sorry, Mrs Bourne. I was only gone for a moment. I—'

'It's not good enough, Turner. Not good enough at all.' The voice was like a whip, slashing. 'I shall be having words with Nanny.'

Mrs Bourne pursed her lips, gave them both — maid and child — a look of infinite contempt, then turned and swept off. The door slammed. The sound of jangling keys faded.

'Oh dear,' said the girl. 'Now I shall catch it hot from Nanny. She does hate it so, when Mrs Bourne has anything over her.'

Dorothea stood rubbing her wrist, her head spinning. She wished she could wake up and find it had all been a terrible dream. This giant house with its seemingly endless number of inhabitants did indeed seem the stuff of nightmares.

But then a slow smile spread across the face of the rosy-cheeked maid and Dorothea felt a tiny bit better.

'Well, miss, you're back now, any road. We can get you washed and dressed. How would you like that?'

'I've no clothes. That lady said she burned them.'

'I'm afraid that's true, miss. But look at this, how about this? It's only an old frock of mine, but it will serve for now.

Our Billy fetched it up from the village. And here's some nice hot water and a bit of soap. The fire's lit now, so the room will soon be nice and snug. I ought to have lit the fire first thing, but it's been one thing after another this morning, and I've had to help out downstairs and all.'

As Dorothea listened to the maid's chatter, she found herself being eased out of her nightdress, scrubbed with soap and water, dried on a soft clean towel, dressed in the borrowed frock. It seemed that she was required to nothing for herself, not even speak.

She did not like having her nightgown removed. It felt wrong, having nothing on. She had never taken all her clothes off at the same time before. It was bad enough that someone had undressed her when she was half-asleep last night; but to be left exposed in broad daylight was shameful. The maid, however, seemed to think nothing of it. She was gentle but insistent, worked quickly.

'That's the way, miss. Let me do up those buttons.' The maid's flow of chatter was unceasing. 'As I said, I've had to help out downstairs today, but normally — Well I never, this fits a treat! Who'd have thought it? Now for your hair — normally I spend all my time in the Nursery. That's my position, miss: I'm the nursery maid. Why, what lovely curls you've got! But they're all in knots. I'll be as gentle as I can. There now!' The maid stepped back, looking at Dorothea with approval. 'Pretty as a lily!'

Dorothea was taken aback. She was sure the maid meant well, but nobody had ever called her *pretty* before, not even her papa. Sometimes he called her 'my pumpkin' or 'my piccalilli', but a pumpkin was hardly the same as a lily. (What a 'piccalilli' might be was anyone's guess.)

This reminder of her papa brought Dorothea back to more pressing matters.

'Please, do you know where Papa is?'

'I don't, miss. I'm sorry. But there's no need to look so down-in-the-mouth! I'm sure your Uncle will be able to tell you.'

'Is that man really my uncle: the tall, angry man? I didn't know I had an uncle.'

'Well, we knew nothing about you either, miss. It was ever so much of a surprise when you showed up as you did last night. Even the mistress — that's your aunt, miss — even she was taken aback, and she's never caught napping!'

The maid's smile was infectious. Dorothea found it impossible not to smile back. Even though Henry had been kind to her last night, she had still been rather in awe of him. The nursery maid was more down-to-earth, like an ordinary person: she was someone you could talk to.

'Please, I don't know your name.'

'I'm Turner, but you can call me Nora if you like.'

'And that lady . . .' Dorothea hesitated, feeling pain in her wrist. 'The black lady. Is *she* my aunt?'

'Heaven bless you, no! That's Mrs Bourne, the housekeeper. As miserable a piece as ever lived. But don't go telling her I said so, or she'll have my guts for garters!'

'I don't like her.'

'You're not alone, miss.' Nora winked.

Dorothea warmed to the nursery maid, found that her tongue was loosened. She could now ask some of the questions that were piling up inside her head. Nora did not seem to mind being asked. She answered cheerily and at length as she flitted round the room, scooping up the night dress, making the bed, tending the fire. Dorothea learned that most of the people she'd seen downstairs did not belong to the house. There had been a party last night, with lots of guests. Some of the guests had stayed over.

'Which is why we are all at sixes and sevens today,' said Nora. 'The party, the house guests — I've been run off my feet!'

'There was a lady, a nice lady, and a man called Henry.'

'That will be Lady Fitzwilliam from Hayton Grange, and her son.'

'He's got knobbly knees.'

Nora laughed. 'I daresay he has. He's a funny one, Mr Henry, scooting along the horse roads in that machine of his.'

'This house . . .' Dorothea paused, not sure how to put it, the way she felt about the place: the dark facade seen the night before, the dazzling lights of the party, the long corridors, the endless stairs, room after room, walls lined with pictures, the eyes in the portrait staring with disapproval. 'It's like . . . like a palace!'

'It's a big place, miss, I'll grant you that — much grander than Hayton Grange, for instance. But Clifton's not a palace: not a palace that would be fit for the Queen.'

'Clifton?'

'That's the name of the house, Clifton Park. Didn't you know? But listen to me going on, and it's gone twelve already and you've not even had your breakfast! Let's go through to the day room. I'm supposed to be watching Baby, as well as seeing to you. They expect me to have eyes in the back of my head, I'm sure!'

The day room was next door, a large place with a glowing fire and barred windows, shelves stacked with toys and games, a rocking horse, a mournful parrot in a cage.

Nora peeped into a cot. 'There's Baby, miss, sleeping like a log. And over here . . .' She took Dorothea's hand and led her to a big sturdy table in the middle of the room. 'This young gentleman is your cousin, miss. Aren't you going to say "hello", Master Roderick?'

Dorothea, rather self-conscious in her borrowed frock and combed curls, looked shyly at the boy sitting at the table. He was about her own age, perhaps a little younger, scrubbed and spruce in knee breeches and a shirt with a wide collar. He had been playing with tin soldiers. A great many of them were lined up on the table. But now he abandoned his game and slipped off his chair, and advanced on Dorothea with a brazen, inquisitive look, grey eyes staring from under black brows.

'Who are you? Why are you here? I've not heard about you before!'

'My . . . my name is Dorothea.'

He scoffed. 'That's a silly name!'

Dorothea stood her ground. It was all very well being frightened by her tall uncle or by the fierce housekeeper, but she would not allow herself to be browbeaten by a mere boy — especially a rude little boy like this one.

'*Dorothea* is not a silly name. It is no sillier than *Roderick*.'

'*Roderick* is a warrior's name.' The boy puffed out his chest.

Showing off, thought Dorothea. Just like the boys in Stepnall Street. Just like Mickey. *Look at me! Look at me! Aren't I brave/smart/strong!* But Mickey, for all his faults, had always looked out for her, even though he wasn't her brother or her cousin or any other sort of relation. This boy Roderick, she sensed, didn't look out for anybody other than himself.

'Now you leave poor girl alone, Master Roderick,' said Nora, brushing the boy aside and leading Dorothea to the far side of the table. 'She's going to have her breakfast!'

Breakfast was the word Nora used to describe a feast fit for the Queen. There was porridge, a boiled egg, toast, butter, marmalade and a huge glass of milk. It was more food than Dorothea was used to eating in an entire day, let alone for breakfast. But she was ravenously hungry. She could not remember when she had last eaten. She set to work with gusto — even if it was slightly off-putting having Master Roderick watching her every move. Like the people at the party last night, he had obviously never been taught that it was rude to stare.

'Are you going to eat *all* of that toast?' he demanded at length.

She shook her head, watched as he grabbed a slice, spooned great dollops of marmalade onto it, gobbled it up. A word formed in her mind: greedy. But she told herself not to be so hasty. Maybe he was hungry. Maybe he had not had a breakfast fit for a Queen. And perhaps he was rude because he didn't know any better. He might be quite a nice boy underneath. Papa often said, 'The world judges by appearances, Dotty — and it's wrong. It's plain wrong.'

She couldn't eat another morsel. She had never felt so full in her life. Getting down from the table, she explored the big room — far bigger than the room where she lived off Stepnall Street. The baby was awake now, kicking and gurgling in its cot. The parrot, rather moth-eaten, was unresponsive. Flames leapt over the coals. Such a pile of coals, too! She had never seen the like.

At that moment, a plump, prickly-looking woman came bustling into the room. She had a black bodice and skirt, and a big red nose. Locks of greying hair were escaping from under her cap. Dorothea's heart sank. How many more people would she have to meet in this hectic house?

'So. This is the forsaken child.'

Abandoned, forsaken. Dorothea gritted her teeth as the plump woman looked her up and down. She resented such words.

'Well, my lady,' said the woman haughtily. 'What a spectacle you made of yourself last night, by all accounts, turning up out of the blue like that! Mrs Brannan was very cross that her party was spoiled. Quite beside herself, she was — or so I've heard. Cook says they had words this morning, the master and the mistress. Not that they haven't had words before, mark you. It's only to be expected when a woman marries beneath her. But where was I? Oh yes. Stand up straight so I can look at you!' The piggy eyes raked over Dorothea once more but seemed to lose focus half way. The woman groaned, clutching her temples. 'My head's that bad today I can barely stand it! But listen now because I don't want to have to repeat myself. I'm Nanny and I'm in charge. You're to mind your Ps and Qs and do as you're told. I don't want a peep out of you, do I make myself clear?'

Dorothea nodded. The cosy feeling that had grown inside her after meeting Nora and eating the big breakfast was rapidly withering away, but there was one question that could not wait. She took a deep breath. 'Please, where's my papa?'

A look of irritation crossed Nanny's blotchy face. 'Now what have I just said? I don't know where your pa is and I'm sure I don't care. Hold your tongue now! And that goes for you, too, Master Roderick! The next person to open their mouth will get a good hiding!'

Nanny settled herself in a chair by the fire. She soon fell asleep, snoring. Nora was called away to help downstairs. Roderick went back to his toy soldiers. Dorothea inched her way towards one of the windows. She felt that if she could just see outside, she might not feel so hemmed in. But there were bars on the window which only increased her sense of being trapped, and the world outside — the fields and trees and the great grey sky — seemed very remote and unfamiliar. It was not at all like the world she knew and gave her no clues as to where her papa might be.

Time ticked by. The trees and fields faded into an early dusk. Dorothea's eyes filled with tears as she leant against the bars. She felt as if everything was drifting away from her. Her whole life — everything she had known — was being swallowed by the grey gloom. But crying got you nowhere. Mrs Browning, back in Stepnall Street — a million miles away, as distant as the moon — boxed their ears if they started 'bawling and carrying on', Dorothea and Mickey and Flossie. But Dorothea wouldn't have minded having her ears boxed — wouldn't have minded gong without that glorious breakfast — if only she could have been home again.

With nothing to do and nowhere to hide, she found she could no longer keep back the memories of last night: all the bits she had tried so very hard to forget. She saw in her mind's eye her papa and her uncle confronting one another in the midst of the lavish room, growling and snapping their teeth like half-starved dogs in the narrow courts back home.

'Well, Albert, so this is where you're holed up now. Very nice. Very nice indeed. Landed on your feet and no mistake. Though it's a bit off the beaten track, you might say. I had a devil of a job finding the place.'

'You are drunk, Frank.'

'I've had a nip or two, to keep out the cold. Only a nip.'

'A bottle or two, I should say, by the state of you.'

'Now then, Albert: there's no call for that sort of talk! But why should I expect any different? You always did have it in for me. You always did try and blacken my character.'

'Is it any wonder, after what you did?'

'You're no better'n me, Albert, that's the long and short of it. There's only one difference between us. My old man didn't have a business to pass on. That's where you struck gold.'

'I built up my own business, Frank. I didn't need my father's.'

'But his money helped, Albert, you can't deny that. You had all the luck, see? You had all the luck, whereas I fell on hard times.'

'Took to drink.'

'That's a lie, that is! Nor I didn't, neither — not till I'd lost everything, not till it was all gone.' Her papa had stopped short, had looked down at her. He'd smiled, the special smile that was hers alone. 'No,' he'd murmured. 'Not everything. Not quite everything. I've still got one thing left. One precious thing.' But then the smile had faded and tears had come into his eyes, the tears that had so frightened her. 'Breaks my heart, so it does, but it's for the best, it's all for the best . . .'

Her uncle had said nothing. When she'd glanced up at him she'd realised that he wasn't looking at her or her papa. He'd been watching instead a lady on the edge of the crowd: a very stiff, upright lady in a sumptuous gown trimmed with miles of lace, a huge flared skirt sweeping out behind her. Seeing the lady's icy blue eyes, Dorothea had known that she was very angry, but the anger had been all shut up inside her and had not shown on her face, which had been as cold and blank as a statue's. She was beautiful like a statue, too, immeasurably dignified, somehow timeless. Dorothea had sensed that her uncle was more aware of this lady than of anyone else in the room, as if the frost in her eyes was piercing him to the marrow.

But she had forgotten all about the beautiful lady when her papa began speaking again. She had watched in dismay as he retreated towards the door, bowing and scraping when he'd always said, *Just remember, Dotty, we're as good as anyone, me and you; we've nothing to be ashamed of. Hold your head up, Dotty: always hold your head up . . .*

'I'll not presume on your 'ospitality no longer, Albert. And I do hope—' (bowing) '—that all you fine ladies and gents will 'scuse the interruption. It was family business, you must understand: family business. But now—' (bowing again) '—I'll leave you to get on with your party. And you, Dotty: you be a good girl for your uncle, do you hear? And just remember that your old Pa loves you and . . . well . . .'

With that he had gone. Her uncle had followed him out. A low buzz of conversation had broken out in the room, but Dorothea had only had ears for the faint voices in the hallway. Only brief snatches of the angry exchange had been audible.

'. . . can't you do this one thing, for *her* sake, for Flo . . . ?'

'. . . dare you talk of my sister—'

'My wife!'

'. . . regret the day she ever clapped eyes on you!'

'. . . we belonged together . . . but it was the child what did for her . . . she made me promise . . . *do your best, Frankie* . . . but my best ain't good enough . . .'

Standing by the window in the day room, the metal bars pressing into her forehead, she tried to make sense of the remembered words.

'She's your niece, Albert, your own flesh and blood. It's what Flo would have wanted.'

'Do you seriously imagine you can palm your brat—?'

Dorothea had heard no more as the piano began to tinkle and the hum of conversation grew louder, and Henry Fitzwilliam had appeared and scooped her off her feet just as she felt her wobbly legs could not hold her up any longer.

She looked out of the Nursery window. It was growing dark. Hours and hours had passed, and her papa had not come.

He was not going to come. He had abandoned her. Forsaken her.

It seemed suddenly very cold in the big room, despite the glowing fire. She was shivering, her hands pressed against the cold window, the icy metal of the bars digging into her head.

'Will I ever see him again?' she whispered to her dim reflection in the glass.

But the winter dark gave no answer.

CHAPTER TWO

Dorothea lay forlorn between crisp sheets listening to the rain beating against the window and trying to count the days and weeks since she'd arrived at Clifton Park. It was impossible. One day blurred into another. Time dragged, yet seemed to pass her by. It had been weeks and weeks since she'd last left the confines of the nursery — since she had seen her fierce uncle or kind-hearted Henry or the black bat-figure of Mrs Bourne. Did any of them even remember her, after all this time? She felt as if she was being slowly suffocated.

Nanny had sent her to bed early this evening. 'I can't be doing with you, fiddling and fidgeting.'

'But I didn't—' (She hadn't.)

'None of that! I won't have you answering back! Now off you go, and be quick about it!'

Dorothea did not really mind. It was all the same being bored in her bedroom as bored in the day room. It was Sunday, too, which made things even worse. Sundays were days that lagged, dreary days when the Nursery seemed more like a prison than ever. Nothing was allowed; even reading was forbidden on Sundays.

'The Sabbath is a day of rest,' said Nanny. 'Whoever doeth any work on the Sabbath, he shall surely be put to death.'

But this did not seem to apply to Nora who did as much work on the Sabbath as she did on any other day — not that Dorothea dared point this out to Nanny who, she felt, was more than capable of putting people to death. Nanny reminded her of Mrs Browning with her short temper and cuffs round the ear. They even had the same red nose; but Nanny never smelt of gin.

The Nursery was a lonely place. Baby was no company at all, Nora was often too busy to talk, and Roderick had gone away. Dorothea was not entirely sure that she liked Roderick, but he was better than nothing. He had, however, been sent off to school. There were schools where boys went to live for weeks at a time without ever coming home. That was where Roderick had gone. The way he'd described it sounded horrible, another kind of prison, but Roderick had stuck out his chin and said, 'It's not as awful as all that, not really.' Afterwards she wondered if he'd been telling the whole truth. There'd been a look in his eye that she remembered seeing in Mickey's when he was telling fibs.

So Roderick had gone, and even Nora escaped the Nursery each evening when she went home to the village.

'I wish I could go with you, Nora! I'd much rather live in your cottage than here!'

'Whatever for, miss, when you've a room to yourself and your own comfy bed? What a funny one you are! Why, there's no room to swing a cat at home, and six of us to share two bedrooms. You'd not like it at all.'

But Dorothea felt it was exactly what she *would* like. Had not five of them shared just *one* room in Stepnall Street? Nora's village, she was sure, was a place where real people lived — ordinary people: not like this house, full of the strangest, most objectionable people you could imagine.

Dorothea shivered, listening to sleet pummelling the window and the sound of the wind seething amongst the branches of the big tree (a cedar tree, it was called). Whatever Nora might say, Dorothea could not get used to a room of her own. It made her think of the old woman in Stepnall

Street — the old woman who'd lived in a basement room in the same court where Dorothea lived. The old woman had hardly ever been seen. No one had noticed when she'd stopped being seen altogether. And then one day she'd been found dead. Mickey had known all about it, of course. Someone had come looking for the rent, he said. When their knocking went unanswered, they had broken down the door. The old woman had been found the old woman sitting in her chair dressed in her old rags, covered from head to foot in lice. She had been dead a week at least. Mickey had laughed. He was like that.

Lying in the dark of the deserted room, Dorothea wished she had never known about the old woman. She wondered if she would end up forgotten too. She wondered if she might die and no one would know.

When at last her eyes shut and she slid into sleep, it seemed to her that she woke up again almost at once; but somehow she knew that she wasn't awake in truth. She tried to ignore this because she wanted the dream to be real. She was at home, in Stepnall Street, in the room on the third floor, lying in the ramshackle bed with only one blanket. The wall beside her was cold and damp to the touch, but Mickey was there to cuddle up to, warm as toast. He was fast asleep, gently snoring, dribbling too. The way spittle leaked from the corner of his scabby mouth always made her queasy but for once she didn't mind a bit. She was just glad to be home.

The room was in darkness. The others were sleeping too. Flossie was gurgling faintly in her banana crate cot. Beyond the pinned-up curtain, Papa and Mrs Browning were breathing noisily out of sync, Mrs Browning whimpering every time she exhaled. Dorothea listened happily to these familiar sounds. There were others. Rats were scrabbling under the floor boards; there were muffled voices and the sound of thumping and bumping from other rooms. Outside, cats were fighting on a nearby roof, mewling and hissing, their claws scraping and sliding on the tiles. Faint footsteps came from the street; someone was singing out of tune; down in the court a man and a woman were arguing, their voices shrill, their words slurred. After so long away — weeks and weeks — these well-known noises which had so often disturbed her sleep sounded more like a favourite lullaby.

She smiled drowsily and tightened her grip on Mickey, pulling his warm body close. Her eyelids fluttered and closed. She felt herself drifting, drifting . . .

She woke with a start. There was still a smile on her lips but this time she was *really* awake. She was not in Stepnall Street. She was lying in the big bed in her room at Clifton Park and it was morning. Another dreary day had arrived.

The sense of disappointment was crushing.

Slowly she sat up, wiping away the tears that had sprung into her eyes. As she did so, she suddenly realised what she had to do. Her papa had not come back for her, so she must go to him. Stepnall Street was not just a dream, it was a place, it existed, and maybe — just maybe — her papa would be waiting there for her.

She reached a decision. It was like a weight being lifted. She would go to London. She would go to Stepnall Street. She would go home.

* * *

Dorothea sat at the big table in the day room fingering carved wooden objects that Nanny called 'chess pieces'. Chess was a game, Nanny said. Dorothea did not know anything about it. She moved the black-and-white counters across the scrubbed tabletop, putting her plans into place.

'Nora . . .'

'Yes, miss?'

'When Roderick goes to school, does he go by train?'

'He does, miss.'

'And is the station far from here?'

Nora paused in her scrubbing of the floor, sat back on her haunches. 'It's not far at all, miss. I've walked it many a time.'

The station, Nora said, was on the main line down from London. It was at a place called Welby.

But where was Welby? How did you get there?

That was easy, Nora said. She knew the country hereabouts like the back of her hand, could find her way to Welby with her eyes shut. From Clifton you went down the drive, turned left at the road, headed for the village. Once in the village it was straight on at the Green and out the other side. You crossed the turnpike and took the road to Welby. The station was on the right, just before you reached Welby village itself. 'You must have come that way yourself, miss, the day you arrived. You came by train, you said.'

'I don't remember. It was dark. I was asleep most of the time.'

Nora looked at her curiously. 'What's brought this on, Miss Dorothea? Why are you so interested in the railway all of a sudden?'

Dorothea sidestepped the question, wrinkled her nose instead. 'That smell . . .'

Nora laughed. 'Carbolic, miss. Helps keep the place clean. Never mind, I've nearly finished. You can help me put the rugs back, if you like.'

* * *

One step at a time, Mrs Browning said. The first step of Dorothea's escape was to get out of the house. She called it her *escape* because, although no one really seemed to want her ('A plague and a nuisance,' Nanny muttered, casting dark looks at her, and hadn't Mrs Bourne said something about an orphanage?), she felt sure that *they* (Nanny, her Uncle) would never agree to her going off on her own and would probably veto any idea of returning to Stepnall Street under any circumstances. She had no choice but to keep her plans under her hat. This troubled her. Was it the same as telling fibs? Mrs Browning maintained there was nothing wrong with a *little white lie*, but Papa thought differently. He had taught her that all lies — white or otherwise — were wrong. But what else could she do? She just hoped Papa would understand.

Mulling things over, she took considerable heart from the experience of her first morning. She had managed to get all the way to the front door without being caught. Would she be able to do so a second time? And when would her chance come?

* * *

'Now then,' said Nanny, looming over the table. 'Eat your breakfast. I want it all finished by the time I get back. But I must just have a quick word with Cook.'

Off she went to the Kitchen (wherever that might be in this labyrinth of a house) for yet another of her 'words' with Cook: words which, Dorothea had learned by now, were never 'quick'. At first she thought nothing of it, carried on eating. But Baby was being particularly fractious that morning and Nora had her hands full. 'She's teething, poor thing.' Cradling Baby, gently rocking her, Nora looked round the day room and sighed. 'I just can't get on today, no matter how I try.' There was always so much for Nora to do, cleaning, tidying, dusting, scrubbing, polishing, laying and lighting the fires, making the beds, feeding and bathing Baby, but Nora rarely complained. It was Nanny who felt hard done by. 'I'm nothing but a slave, and never a moment to rest my weary legs.' But what Nanny actually *did* was something of a mystery.

As Nora stooped over the cot, laying Baby down, Dorothea suddenly remembered her plan. Swiftly, she slipped two pieces of toast into her sash and stood up. As she edged towards the door, Nora didn't so much as give her a glance.

In her room, Dorothea pulled on her coat and tam o'shanter, her heart thumping. The coat was a boy's and rather too small for her; the hat was too big and kept slipping down over her eyes. All the same, she would be leaving Clifton in better clothes than those she'd arrived in. She had the toast, too, to sustain her on her journey.

She took a last look round. It was then that she had her first wobble. She would not have said until now that she had grown fond of her room, but it seemed something of a wrench to be leaving it forever. She trailed her hand over the old wardrobe (still mostly empty) and over the dressing table with the three-folded mirror. She looked at the big bed, so soft and comfortable. Must she really give it all up?

She took a deep breath. She was just being soppy. Mickey would have jeered at her. He was never soppy and not afraid of anything. He took on boys twice his size in the blink of an eye. But even Mickey would be bowled over when she walked into their room in Stepnall Street after so long!

If she ever got there.

But she mustn't think like that. She mustn't get too far ahead of herself. One step at a time.

She left her room and opened the green baize door which marked the frontier of the Nursery. She took one step, then another. Now she was beyond the pale. She was trespassing. She was at large in the forbidden parts of the house. The endless maze of stairs and corridors was a daunting prospect, but she knew that if she kept her head she wouldn't get lost. She just hoped she wouldn't run into the menacing figure of Mrs Bourne. She was in no hurry to meet *her* again.

She was tiptoeing along the corridor to the stairs when the sound of a voice made her jump out of her skin. She half expected to see Mrs Bourne sweeping towards her to grab her arm, drag her screaming back to the Nursery. But nothing happened. The corridor was empty. There was no footstep on the stairs.

The voice came again, faintly. 'Nurse! Nurse! Where are you?'

It was not Mrs Bourne or even Nanny. It was not an alarming voice at all. Just the opposite: rather feeble and peevish. A child's voice. It was coming from a room away on the left: the very room, Dorothea now remembered, into which the bald man with the black bag had gone on her first morning. The bald man was Dr Camborne. He had called to examine her soon after her arrival. She had not liked him much.

'Nurse!'

Perhaps the child in the room was ill. It would explain the doctor's visit. Nobody had mentioned a sick child in all the weeks she had been here, but then nobody told her anything. They wouldn't even tell her about her papa. 'Ask me no questions and I'll tell you no lies,' Nanny said.

Dorothea hesitated at the top of the stairs. She felt an urgent need to get on, to make good her escape. But what if the child needed help? You couldn't ignore a cry for help. Mickey would no doubt say that she was being soppy. But what about the Good Samaritan? Papa had told her that story many times. People should help one another, he said. It was the Christian thing to do.

Reaching a decision, she walked quickly along the corridor and pushed open the door on the left.

She found herself in a room like her own, or perhaps a little bigger. It was very gloomy. The curtains were closed. Lying in a large bed — dwarfed by it — was a pasty-faced boy with deep-sunk dark eyes and coal black hair. He did indeed look ill, as feeble and peevish as his voice, his head lolling and listless. His expression changed when he caught sight of Dorothea. His head jerked up, his mouth fell open. His big dark eyes were as round as saucers in his thin face.

'Hello.' Dorothea found her smile had deserted her.

'Who are you?' the boy whispered.

'My name is Dorothea. I . . . I heard you calling for a nurse.'

'*The* nurse. My nurse. Where is she?'

'I . . . I don't know.'

Dorothea glanced over her shoulder. Every second's delay increased the danger of being caught but for some reason she could not tear herself away just yet. Perhaps it was because the boy looked so helpless. She felt sorry for him.

She took a step nearer, managed a smile at last. 'What's your name?'

'It's Richard.'

'Are you alright? Why were you calling for the nurse?'

'My pillows are out of place. I'm not . . . not comfy.'

She wondered why he couldn't rearrange his pillows himself. Perhaps he was too weak. He certainly looked it.

'Let me help,' she said. She moved his pillows as he directed, holding him up as she did so. He was limp in her arm, very warm, with a bony back. She was close enough to see herself reflected in his big dark eyes.

As she stepped back, he said, 'You have your coat on. Have you just come, or are you going?'

'I'm going.' There were questions on the tip of her tongue, but time was pressing. She could not afford one question, let alone the dozen or more piling up in her head. 'I have to leave now. I'm sorry.'

'Must you? Will you come back? I wish you would.'

'I can't. I'm going away. I'm going away forever. I have to.'

She felt it was mean of her to leave him like this, ill in bed, all alone. And to think she had considered herself hard done by in the nursery! But the escape was more important than anything. For once, she had to put herself first. Even the Good Samaritan would have done the same.

'It was nice to meet you. Goodbye.'

'Goodbye,' the boy whispered. His dark eyes followed her as she left the room.

As she returned to the head of the stairs, Dorothea heard another door open behind her and quickly dodged down before peering back round the corner. A strict-looking woman appeared in the corridor, entered the sick room. She shut the door firmly behind her. Dorothea wondered if that was the Nurse. She would never know.

Hurrying down the stairs, treading softly, her mind was in a whirl. Who was the poorly child? Why had no one spoken of him in all the weeks and weeks she had been here? It was almost as if he didn't really exist, as if he were a ghost.

She was so busy with her thoughts that she reached the ground floor almost before she knew it. There in front of her was the big front door. It was shut. She knew that it was only kept locked at night, but would she be able to open it?

To her relief, the handle turned easily. The door moved smoothly and soundlessly on well-oiled hinges. Cold air came shivering into the hall — cold, but fresh. It was wonderful! She breathed deeply as she slipped outside, pulling the door to behind her. Her heart leapt as she skipped down the steps. Out in the open again after so long, she really felt that she was on her way now.

Her joy was short-lived.

Away to the left, across the space of gravel, there was a high red-brick wall with a doorway set into it. Through the doorway came a crusty old man wearing an apron and a weatherworn cap and pushing a wheelbarrow. He saw her at once.

Her shoulders slumped. She hung her head. To have got all this way, right out of the house, only to be caught on the doorstep! All her plans lay in ruins.

'Morning, miss.'

Something in the old man's tone made her look up. He was looking at her with deep brown eyes as he passed, but there was no sign of disapproval or vexation on his face, just mild curiosity. He nodded, touched his cap, went on his way. Before she'd had time to gather her thoughts, he'd gone, wheeling his barrow round the corner of the house.

She could hardly believe her luck. She was still free, her escape still possible. Quickly, she set off across the gravel — not without a twinge of guilt, for she had been rather rude, had not said 'good morning' in return. ('Good manners cost nothing,' as Papa often said.) She felt that she might have liked the old man if she'd got to know him. She never would now. She would never even find out who he was.

She reached the far side of the gravelled space. The driveway led off sharp right down an avenue of evergreens. Here she had her second wobble. Her feet slowed and stopped. She wondered what Nora would think, finding her gone. And the boy in the bed, the old man with the wheelbarrow: would she really never see them again?

She looked back; and in doing so she saw the house properly for the first time.

It was a very big house, square and symmetrical with a great grey facade. There were many windows. High on the roof were rows of chimneys with smoke curling up into the overcast sky. The front door was still ajar as she'd left it. The steps swept grandly down. To the right of the door, ivy climbed the wall. Adjoining the house on this side was a sort of add-on in red brick with an archway leading to a courtyard. This was where the old man had gone with his wheelbarrow (she could see no sign of him now). To think of all the rooms behind all the windows made her dizzy. There was so much to discover, so many mysteries and secrets hidden away. The poorly child, for instance. She could not see his window, of course. It would be round the other side of the house (there would be more windows round the other side, more!), but one of those high windows on this side must be hers, the room she'd left behind. She looked up again at the spiralling smoke. It made her think of the nursery fire and the warm, snug day room.

She shook her head. The nursery had been a prison. She must remember that. And she couldn't afford to dawdle. She had to go now, immediately, before anyone else saw her. Any number of people might be looking out of the windows — Nanny, or Mrs Bourne, or even that remote presence Aunt Eloise.

She turned hurriedly away and set off down the drive at a run. The wind buffeted her. Stones and clods of earth flew up as her booted feet hit the hard ground. The evergreen trees seethed and swayed, their branches dipping down as if to grab her. She ran and ran. At last, at long last, puffing and blowing, she came to the end of the drive. Here she stopped to catch her breath and gather her thoughts. There was a road in front of her running at right angles. To the right it sloped down to where there was a glint of water amongst the fields and trees. But Dorothea remembered that she had to turn left. That was what Nora had said.

There was some sort of little house half-hidden in the trees nearby which made Dorothea uneasy, as if she hadn't yet quite escaped the clutches of Clifton Park, so she took to the road and set off once more. The road ran up a gentle incline. She could not see very far ahead. Alongside on her left was a crumbling sandstone wall. This soon faded away and the road ran on between hedgerows where new leaves were growing, with fields beyond, green with bitten grass or ploughed brown. She was too puffed to run anymore so she walked briskly, listening to the birdsong that trilled and rippled down the wind. But that wind was bitter, stinging her face (it was only March, after all) and the sky was grey and wintry-looking. There had been recent rain. Water lay in the ruts in the road. More rain was on the way by the looks of things. She was determined to reach the station before it came.

She quickened her pace.

Up she went then down again — and there now was the village ahead, Nora's village, the place she'd heard so much about. She hurried towards it. Though she knew she must have passed this way with her papa, she had no memory of it at all.

She tried to recall everything she'd learned in the last few weeks. The village was called Hayton. Nora had lived there all her life. Which was Nora's house? The first house that Dorothea saw was empty, half-ruined and overgrown; then came some rather grand houses with garden gates and gleaming windows — far too luxurious to be Nora's two-up, two-down cottage. After that Dorothea came to a meeting of three ways with a space of grass and a tall tree. To the left, set back from the street, was the church with the crenulated tower which she could just see from her window at Clifton. The clock was chiming the quarter hour — the very sound which had haunted her dreams on her first night.

'This must be the Green,' Dorothea said to herself, recalling Nora's words: *straight on at the Green, cross the turnpike, and take the road to Welby*. What was a *turnpike*? She would soon find out. It couldn't be far now.

On one side of the three-cornered Green there was a little shop. As Dorothea passed near it, the door opened with a jangle. An old woman in a black bonnet came out. She was carrying a basket. Standing on the doorstep, she stopped and stared. Dorothea hung her head, tried to be as inconspicuous as possible. Keeping close to the wall of the churchyard, she hurried on, didn't dare look back.

The village straggled to an end. Just past the last house, she met a man in a cap coming the other way, leading two enormous horses. She had no choice but to face him, did her best to look as if she was minding her own business. It seemed to work. The man barely gave her a glance. Her spirits soared, she hopped and skipped along the road. She had got all this way — right through the village — and no one had stopped her, no one had even asked where she was going. The railway station had to be very near now. Perhaps she would be able to see it from the next rise!

She broke into a run, holding her hat with one hand as the breeze tried to whip it away. Puffing and panting, she reached the top of the slope — only to meet with disappointment. There was no sign of the railway. The road ran on and on, curving gently down into a wide shallow valley under the enormous grey sky. Fields, trees, hedgerows stretched away into an unguessable distance. There were perhaps some far-off buildings, but they were so remote as to fill her with despair. She would never have guessed how incredibly vast the countryside was — so lonely and unfriendly, too! London seemed hardly more than a dream, so distant she could scarcely believe it had ever existed.

Crushed by her sense of despair, lashed by the wind up here on the exposed hillock, she took shelter by the hedgerow, sitting down on the damp grass, her plan in tatters. What next? Go on — or go back? But she didn't dare go back, too frightened of what they might do to her. As for going on, where would this endless road take her? She might wander lost in the wilderness for evermore. She sat in a hopeless daze, staring at the muddy road, hearing the wind hissing through the grass and seething in the hedge.

Suddenly her head jerked up. There was something else, another sound — not the wind, not the birds — quite the oddest noise she had ever heard in her life, a growling, chugging, buzzing sound. And it was coming rapidly nearer.

She scrambled to her feet, pushing the tam o'shanter out of her eyes. Swooping up the road out of the wild blue yonder was a most extraordinary machine. Wheels spinning, black bonnet gleaming, it raced up the incline so rapidly that she had no time to hide. She cowered against the hedge as the terrible apparition bore down on her.

The machine slowed then came to a stop right in front of her, juddering and growling. An outlandish figure was sitting on it, swathed in coat, cap, scarf and goggles.

The figure spoke. 'Good grief! Dorothea, isn't it?'

A gauntleted hand pulled down the scarf, pushed up the goggles, revealing surprised green eyes in a plain yet pleasant face. It was a face she recognised. The voice, too, she knew.

'You're the last person I expected to meet,' the voice said. 'What are you doing all the way out here?'

The cat had got her tongue. All she could do was shake her head.

'Don't you remember? We met on the night of that party. It's me, Henry Fitzwilliam!'

Of course she remembered. How could she forget? She'd sat on his bony knees. There'd been a fizzy drink with a nasty taste. But what stuck in her mind most was his soothing voice and gentle smile. The smile was the same out here in the wild, but his face rather different. He had a black eye that even Mickey would have been proud of.

Finally she found her voice. Pointing to the machine, she said, 'What is it?' She had to shout above the preposterous noise.

'What's what? Oh, you mean my autocar! Have you never seen one? They're all the rage!'

'But it's . . . it's . . . What makes it go?'

'That'll be the combustion engine. It's, er, all rather complicated. I'll explain it sometime, when you've a few hours to spare.' He rubbed his chin with his gloved hand. 'Would you like a ride? I could take you to wherever it is you are going. Where *are* you going, by the way?'

Dorothea bit her lip. She was reluctant to tell him her plan. He might think it silly. She did not want to look silly in Henry Fitzwilliam's eyes.

He jumped down from the autocar. 'You look perished, poor thing. Here, put on my dust coat. That's the ticket. And my hat too. It's warmer than yours. Look! It's got these little flaps to keep your ears snug. Now, up you get!'

He lifted her onto the shuddering machine then swung himself back into the seat beside her. Reaching for a big lever, he said, 'Right-oh. Where is it I'm taking you?'

She had to tell him now. It didn't matter whether he thought her silly or not. 'I'm going to London. I'm going to find my papa.'

Henry looked at her circumspectly. 'London, is it? I say. That's rather a long way on your own! How were you thinking of getting there?'

'On the train, of course.'

'Ah yes, of course. You've got the money for your ticket, I suppose?'

Dorothea felt her cheeks burning. Henry had seen the flaw in her plan at once. Even if by some miracle she had reached the railway station, she wouldn't have got any further. She didn't have a farthing to her name.

So much for Mrs Browning and taking one step at a time.

Henry was rubbing his chin again. He looked thoughtful, wasn't laughing at her. 'London's a bit far for a jaunt. I doubt Bernadette would make it.'

'Who's Bernadette?'

'This is Bernadette. My Daimler.' He patted the contraption fondly. 'Listen. I've an idea. Why don't I run you back to Clifton? You can get warm in front of a fire and if you decide you still want to go to London, it can all be arranged properly. What do you say to that?'

What could she say? She had no plan now and no choice. She nodded glumly. Did Henry realise he was taking her back to gaol?

He set the machine in motion. At once, Dorothea forgot everything else, was consumed by terror. She clung to her seat as the autocar bowled along, bumping and jerking over the ruts in the road, the roar of its engine and the noise of the wind deafening. There was an oily, smoky smell that made her feel sick and the hedgerows flashed past in a way that made her giddy. Yet all the time Henry kept up a flow of chatter as if he hadn't a care in the world.

'. . . quite a decent little machine . . . speedy too . . .' (Many of his words were blown away by the wind.) '. . . twelve miles per hour is the limit . . . the police hide in ditches with stopwatches . . . quite ridiculous, but there's nothing one can . . . Oh rats, what's up with her now?'

The last words came out loud and clear as, without warning, the engine coughed, spluttered, and died. The autocar ground to a halt, one wheel lurching into a rut. Dorothea's head was still spinning. All those miles and miles she had walked — through the village and up the rise: and they had covered them in just a few minutes. They were almost back at Clifton already. She recognised the crumbling sandstone wall on the right.

As she collected herself, Henry jumped down, tore off his gloves, threw up the bonnet. He began poking around inside with an oily rag.

'Come on old girl. Don't let me down today of all days.'

He was speaking to the machine as if it was a person. Dorothea remembered that someone had said Henry was cracked. Perhaps they'd been right. But just at that moment he looked up at her and grinned and at once she knew that he wasn't cracked at all. He was, in fact, the nicest grown-up she had ever met — apart from Papa, of course.

'Now don't you worry, Dorothea. This often happens. It's only a glitch. I'll have her going again in no time.' His grin broadened as he looked her over. 'That coat is far too big for you. It's like a marquee.'

But he'd been right about the coat being warm. It was much better than her own coat. She felt warm inside, too, just as she'd felt all those weeks ago sitting on his knee with his arm around her. She wanted him to know all this. She wanted to tell him that she didn't think he was cracked, that he was nicer than anyone, that she too believed in autocars — because if Henry believed in them, how could you not? But when she opened her mouth to speak, the right words wouldn't come out and all she could manage, stammering and blushing, was, 'You . . . you've got a black eye.'

'Yes. A real shiner.' He touched it gingerly. 'Someone threw a stone at me. Well, more of a rock, actually.'

'But why?'

'Because they want autocars kept off the roads. They don't think autocars belong there. A lot of people get very angry about it indeed. Most just shout and wave their fists, but one or two throw things too. Luddites, I call them.'

'There was a man who wanted a law against it,' said Dorothea, thinking back to her first morning, the overheard conversation in the hallway.

'That would be Colonel Harding, the chief of all the Luddites. I drive past Newbolt Hall every day to annoy him!' Henry chuckled, then ducked back down inside the machine. His muffled voice came floating up to her. 'No news about your father, then?'

'He hasn't come back. That's why I have to go and look for him.'

But even as she was speaking, she suddenly wondered why. Why hadn't he come back, why should it be down to her to go looking for him? How dare he bring her here and just leave her! How *dare* he! It was wrong. It was cruel. It was . . . *selfish*!

She was choked with rage, knocked off balance by it, flooded with guilt too because Papa wasn't cruel or selfish, of course he wasn't. He was the kindest, the best man who'd ever lived! But just at that moment she couldn't quite believe it.

It was as if the world had been tipped upside down.

Tears sprang into her eyes. The wind whipped her. The big, grey, empty sky made her want to cower and hide.

'Why did he leave me? *Why?*' Her voice was little more than a whisper but Henry must have heard because his head reappeared and he regarded her thoughtfully.

'Who can say why parents do anything?' he said at length. 'Take my mother, for instance. She'd forever trying to marry me off. She won't let it lie. I've told her time and again that it's too early for all that. I'm only twenty-two. I've no intention of getting married until I'm thirty at least. But she won't have it. Says I need a steadying influence. Can't imagine why.' He wiped his hands on the oily rag, put it aside. 'Hey now! Don't look so glum! I'm sure your father only wanted to do right by you. He wouldn't have left you at Clifton if he didn't think it was for the best. And I don't suppose he's gone for good. I daresay he'll turn up again sooner or later. Which is more than can be said for my pater. *He's* dead and buried.' She caught her breath at this and he glanced up and smiled. 'Don't worry, it all happened long ago, I'm over it now.' But as he closed the bonnet and climbed back into the seat beside her, a faraway look came into his eyes. 'Funny thing, really. I haven't thought about it for years. It hits one hard at the time. I'd almost forgotten. Cried my eyes out, I seem to remember. But I was only ten.'

Dorothea looked at him — his plain but affable face, his thin moustache, his deep eyes. He looked so grown up that she couldn't imagine him aged ten. Had he really cried for his father? Mickey would have died of shame at the very idea. But Henry was not like Mickey. He was not like anyone she had ever met.

'I wish I could live with you, Henry, instead of at Clifton!'

He smiled. 'That wouldn't work at all. I'd drive you up the wall. I do Mother. Me and my fads, as she puts it. She thinks it's high time I took a more serious view of life. But why ever would you want live with me when you've an aunt and an uncle and all the comforts of Clifton Park?'

'Nobody there wants me. They keep me locked in the nursery, I never see anyone. Roderick has gone away and Nanny is horrible and — and—'

'Well I never! What a life! But it can't all be bad, surely? As for your nanny, I wouldn't take too much notice of *her*. It's her job to be horrid. All nannies are. Mine used to lock me in a cupboard for misbehaving. It didn't make me a better boy, but I'm jolly well terrified of the dark even now!'

Was it true, she wondered: could someone as brave and wise as Henry *really* be scared of the dark? She watched him rubbing his chin. There must have been a speck of oil on his fingers because when he took his hand away, there was a black smudge on his jaw.

'I'm sure your aunt and uncle will be wondering where you are. They'll be worried about you, mark my words!'

'But I never even see them. And my uncle — he and Papa — they had the most terrible argument—'

'Don't take it to heart. Grown-ups are always having disagreements. It never amounts to anything.'

'But why does my uncle hate Papa so much?'

'Well, let me see. I'm no expert of course. I've not had much to do with your uncle — I've been away at college and so on — but it's true to say that some people in these parts consider him an interloper. He's *not one of us*, as Mrs Somersby would say. But Mother's always got on with him, and she's no fool, so . . .'

'But the argument: what was it all about?'

'Well, now, what can I say?' He caressed the steering wheel absently, weighing his words. 'I only know what Mother's told me. She says it's all to do with the elopement.'

'What's an . . . elope . . . ?'

'An *elopement*. It's when two people run off together without telling anyone. That's what your parents did, or so Mother understands. I suppose you can see that your uncle might be angry about it, when it was his own sister and it was your father she ran off with.'

Dorothea looked at him in astonishment. 'Why did they do it? Why did they run away?'

'For love, I suppose. People do the rummest things for love — so I've been told.'

'And now I've run away and Uncle Albert will be angry with me, too!'

'I'm sure he won't be angry. He'll be glad to have you safe and sound. You're his niece when all's said and done. Blood is thicker than water, as Mother always says.'

Dorothea looked at Henry from under the hat with the ear flaps and wondered what it was like to have a mother. She thought of the sister who'd eloped, someone she had never known, a stranger. You couldn't call a stranger *mother*. Mrs Browning was the nearest thing Dorothea had ever had to a mother but it had never crossed her mind — it wouldn't have seemed *right* — to call Mrs Browning *mother*. Not that she'd ever felt she was missing out, not having a mother. She had her papa, and that was enough.

Except that now Papa had gone.

She shivered inside Henry's dust coat. Grey clouds scudded across the vast sky. The cold wind gusted round her. The road stretched ahead, rutted, muddy, empty. Fields receded endlessly in every direction. It was a wild and cheerless place and Henry her only friend in all the world. He looked rather comical with his black eye and the matching smudge on his jaw. She smiled but the smile faltered and tears came into her eyes as she thought how Henry was afraid of the dark, how he'd cried as a boy for his father, how people called him cracked because of his enthusiasm for autocars. Why did she feel so miserable? Why did the world seem so topsy-turvy and beyond repair? And all she had to look forward to was returning to the big house, being locked in the nursery again. It filled her with a sense of despair. No one would ever come for her, no one cared, she would end up forgotten, discarded, like the old woman in the basement.

'Hey now!' Henry was watching her anxiously. 'Why the long face? It can't be as bad as all that, surely?'

But it was. It was hopeless. All the same, she swallowed her sobs and put on a brave face for Henry's sake. And she thought of her papa, too. *Gee up, Dotty. Look on the bright side. There's always a bright side, no matter how well hidden.*

Henry was the bright side — meeting Henry. Nora, too. Perhaps Roderick, if she ever saw him again. And what about the boy with the big dark eyes? Might he become a friend as well? But she didn't even know who he was! Perhaps Henry might know.

'What boy's this?'

'He said his name is Richard.'

'Ah. That boy.'

'I didn't know he was there until today.'

'He often seems to get overlooked, one way or another.'

'But who is he? Why is he in bed?'

'He's Richard Rycroft, your aunt's nephew. A delicate creature, they say, but I don't really know what is wrong with him. You'd have to ask Mother.'

'He wanted me to stay but I couldn't. I was running away. I felt mean, leaving him.'

'Why was that?'

'He looked sad. I wanted to . . . to make him smile.'

'Did you, now?' Henry gave her a curious glance. 'You're quite something, Dorothea, do you know that?'

'Is . . . is that good?'

'Yes. Very good. Very good indeed.'

'I . . . I think you're *something*, too, Henry.' She felt it a great cheek using his name so freely but he didn't seem to mind.

'My word! You certainly know how to make a chap blush!' He laughed, looked rather bashful, but then rubbed his hands together briskly. 'We should get going, before we catch our deaths. If Bernadette will oblige . . .'

Bernadette did oblige. In the blink of an eye, it seemed, the Daimler was juddering up the long driveway between the tall evergreens. Huddled in Henry's dust coat, Dorothea couldn't ignore the sinking feeling inside. Her escape was over. The big house was waiting to claim her once again.

* * *

Uncle Albert put in an appearance. Dorothea had never seen him in the nursery before. He did not look best pleased.

They left her alone with him. She felt all trembly, as if her legs might give way at any moment. It didn't help that she was still giddy from Nanny's cuffs and blows. Not that she was a stranger to such treatment — Mrs Browning was none too gentle — but Nanny seemed to take a particular pride in that aspect of her work. Dorothea did not like to imagine what Uncle Albert would have in store for her. She wished she had run along that endless road as far as her legs could carry her. She might have been curled in a ditch by now, starving, but anything would be better than this.

'Why did you go off like that?' Uncle Albert's voice was an angry growl. 'Eloise — your aunt — is very cross. Very cross indeed.'

Dorothea stood frozen, couldn't speak a word.

'I don't know what to do,' he murmured after a pause. 'I don't know what to do for the best.' His big, thick fingers tapped impatiently on the table but he wasn't looking at her, which was a blessing. 'Ellie would prefer it if you were sent away, but . . . well . . . I don't like the idea of . . . of *those* places.' He turned to look at her. 'Don't you like it here, eh? Eh? Is that why you ran away?'

Dorothea quailed. His fierce eyes seemed to burn into her. But it was important to tell him the truth. 'Please, Uncle, I just want to go home.

'And where is home? Where did you live before you came here?'

'In . . . in Stepnall Street.'

'Stepnall Street?'

'It's in London.'

'Big place, London.'

'There's a house, a court, cobbles . . .' She tried to put her thoughts in order. 'There's a road nearby where the trams run. Mickey likes to race the trams.'

'And who is Mickey?'

'Mickey is . . .' Who exactly *was* Mickey? She'd thought of him as a sort of big brother, but he wasn't really her brother. He belonged to Mrs Browning. But who was Mrs Browning? Papa called her *the landlady* but he gave a strange sort of laugh when he said it, as if it was some sort of joke. Their room, though, *was* Mrs Browning's, she'd been there first. Dorothea found herself wondering who Mickey's papa was, and Flossie's. She'd never thought about it before.

But it wasn't important. All that mattered was her own papa. 'Please, Uncle, can't you find him? Can't you find my papa?'

'It's like trying to find a needle in a haystack, child. He could be anywhere by now. Anywhere.' Her uncle turned away, crossed to the window. His broad shoulders seemed to blot out the light, as if a shadow had fallen across the day room. But Dorothea drew comfort from his words which seemed to suggest that he *had* made an effort to find her papa even if the search had been, up to now, fruitless. She wanted to tell him to go on looking, not to give up. It was more important than anything.

But at that moment he turned to face her and the words died in her throat.

'Come here, child.'

It was the last thing she wanted, but Uncle Albert was not the sort of man you dared disobey. Her feet dragged, her legs were like jelly, she hung her head because she could not bear to look into his eyes but there was no escape. His big hand tilted her chin and she had to look up at him.

Her head was spinning. She felt faint. He was so tall and grim and angry that she couldn't bear it. But as he moved her head from side to side, she realised that the angry glare was fading from his eyes. He was looking at her now with a curious expression, half wonderment and half something else — pain, perhaps?

'Yes,' he muttered to himself. 'It's quite definite. I can't think why I didn't see it before. It's Florence all over. Florence reborn.'

She found her voice. 'Who . . . who is Florence?'

'Eh? What? But surely you know, child? Surely you know! Florence was your mother. My sister. And you are the spit and image of her.'

He let her go and turned away. A shudder seemed to pass through him. The shadow in the room had gone. Dorothea could breathe again.

'I think,' he muttered, 'I think for now it would be best if you stayed here, with us.'

'Until . . . until Papa comes back?'

'Yes, yes. When — if — he does. Or maybe . . .' He cleared his throat. 'It's not a bad place, once you get used to it. Not bad at all.'

He sounded almost as if he was trying to convince himself, and Dorothea remembered Henry's words: *he's an interloper . . . he's not one of us . . .*

'No more running off, now, do you hear me, child? There's no knowing what might have happened if young Fitzwilliam hadn't come along. Do you promise?'

'I . . . I promise, Uncle.'

'Good. Good. And now, well, talking of Fitzwilliam, he had rather a bright idea. A governess, he said. To keep you in line. To *improve* you.'

A governess? What was a governess?

Dorothea did not have chance to ask. Uncle Albert, with one last keen glance, departed as abruptly as he'd arrived.

She was to have a governess. But what did that mean? If Henry had suggested it, surely it couldn't be too bad.

Nanny soon put her right on that score.

'It's no more than you deserve, my girl. If you'd behaved yourself properly, it needn't have happened. Running away like that! Mrs Brannan was most put out. Spoke very sharply to me, she did. Well, I can't be everywhere at once. I haven't got eyes in the back of my head — which she doesn't understand, seemingly.'

Nanny glared at Dorothea. (*Don't take any notice*, Henry had said: *it's her job to be horrid . . .*)

'Wilful disobedience, is what I call it. And see what's come of it! You've been such a naughty, wicked girl that only a governess will do. You needn't think that a governess will be all kindness and charity like dear old Nanny! Gracious me, no! A governess will beat you as soon as look at you. Why, I knew one as used to hold her boy's head under water for two whole minutes at a time, to teach him his manners. So just you watch out, little madam! You'll soon be put in your place, make no mistake!'

CHAPTER THREE

'Whatever shall I do?' Dorothea was in despair. She had just been given the terrible news. As if it wasn't bad enough that all governesses were monsters, the one who was arriving at Clifton Park tomorrow was a *foreign* monster. Nanny had been breathless with horror, having heard it from Cook who'd got it from Mrs Bourne who knew every last detail of the business of the house.

The boy Richard, propped on his pillows, looked at Dorothea with his big dark eyes, guarded. 'Tell them to send her away. That is what I would do.'

'No one will listen. There is no one to tell.' Only Nora, who had no standing at all, or Nanny, who never took heed and who might either brush you aside or lash out, give you a hiding. Dorothea knew she'd not been forgiven yet for her *wilful disobedience* in running away. 'You don't understand,' she told Richard. 'You don't know what it's like. I'm no better than Polly, locked in a cage.'

'What about me?' said Richard sulkily. 'How would you like it if you weren't even allowed to get up? How would you like it if you had a withered leg?'

Very proud of it he was too, thought Dorothea bitterly as she sat there on the edge of Richard's bed unable to focus on much else other than the terrible governess. But she was being unkind, she told herself. Richard might be a misery at times and he did tend to *wallow* in it (as Mrs Browning would have said). But wasn't it enough to make anyone a misery, suffering as he did? Most of the time she enjoyed his company. Being permitted to visit his room was the only lasting advantage of her failed escape. She had a duty to cheer him up, not to wallow in troubles of her own.

'Is your leg really so bad? Can't you stand on it at all?'

Richard lowered his voice. 'Sometimes I try, when Nurse isn't looking. Sometimes I can stand up for just a second, if I hold onto the bed.'

'Try now. I will help. You can hold on to me instead of the bed.'

But Nurse as always seemed to have a sixth sense and came striding into the room at just the wrong moment. 'Now that's enough. Master Richard is tired. He needs his rest.'

'But I don't *like* resting, Nurse. It is resting that makes me tired in the first place.'

'What sort of talk is that?' Nurse plumped his pillows, felt his forehead, manhandled him like a rag doll. 'All this to-do is making you peaky. Miss Dorothea must leave you in peace.'

As she was ushered from the room, Dorothea heard him call anxiously after her, 'You will come again, I suppose?'

'Of course I will come. As often as they'll let me.'

But Nurse said, 'I'll have the last word on that score,' and she shut the door in Dorothea's face.

'And where have you been, my girl?' said Nanny as Dorothea returned to the day room.

'I was talking to Richard. Nurse sent me away.'

'Humph! Well! Isn't that Nurse all over!' Nanny glowered, sitting in her chair by the fire. 'Such an uppity creature. My word, isn't she! All out for herself, too. I know *her* game. There'll be rich pickings, she's thinking, when Master Richard comes into his own. That's what *she's* after, mark my words! Artful madam!'

'W—what do you mean, Nanny? What will Richard come into?'

'Never you mind, my girl. It's none of your business. I'll have no more of your questions. You can save your breath to cool your porridge. Now, you just sit quiet like a good girl and don't go waking Baby while I pop and have word with Cook. I haven't told her yet what *that woman* said to me this morning.'

Dorothea sat meekly at the big table, anxious not to get in Nanny's bad books. But once Nanny had gone Nora winked and said cheerily, 'Take no notice, miss. She's like a bear with a sore head today. She's had words with Mrs Bourne again.'

It was scant comfort, however, to be reminded of the bickering and squabbling which seemed to be the stock in trade here. Nanny never had a good word to say about anyone except her ally Cook. What was it, exactly, that she had got against Nurse? What sort of rich pickings Nurse could ever hope to gain from so thin, puny and pasty-faced a boy as Richard? It was yet another mystery. At times, Dorothea felt as if she was being kept in the dark about *everything*.

Nora went off to 'do' Nanny's room, leaving Dorothea alone in the day room, the fire crackling, Polly biting the bars of her cage. How dreary it was! Dorothea yawned, tracing the grooves in the table, found herself wishing that Roderick was here, even though she'd been only too glad to see the back of him at the end of the Easter holidays.

He'd arrived from school to express surprise at finding her in the nursery. 'I thought you'd have gone back where you came from by now.' He had gone on to tell her loftily that he had no time for her — no time for mere *girls* — even if she *was* his cousin — which, he'd added, looking down his nose at her, he very much doubted. Dorothea had done her best to keep the peace by staying out of his way but every time she'd turned round, he seemed to been there — for all the world as if he was following her.

'What are you doing now, Dotty Dot-dot? What game are you playing?'

'I'm not playing any game, I'm just minding my own business like Nanny said I should. Please won't you leave me alone? And don't call me Dot. Only Papa calls me Dot.'

'Then what *am* I to call you? Cuckoo in the nest? Answer me! Answer at once! If you don't, I shall pull your hair!'

He had pulled so hard it had made her cry out.

'What's all this? What's this hullaballoo?' Nanny had suddenly loomed over them, had swatted Dorothea aside with one clout, had grabbed Roderick by the ear. 'Master Roderick! If you *won't* behave yourself then you must be taught a *lesson*!'

She had given Roderick such a leathering it had made Dorothea's eyes water. The fact that Roderick gritted his teeth and didn't utter a sound had only served to spur Nanny on.

'You were very brave!' Dorothea had whispered afterwards when Nanny was safely out of the way and Roderick was lying under the table on his belly with his head in his hands. Mickey had liked to be called *brave*. It had made him puff out his chest.

'I don't care about being brave,' Roderick had said in a voice which made Dorothea wonder if he'd been crying. 'But she shan't catch me again. I shan't let her. You'll see.'

Now Roderick had gone again. He was back at school. And Dorothea's heart sank as she sat at the big table and thought about tomorrow and the arrival of the monster. After tomorrow, long, dreary days would seem like paradise. Things were about to take a turn for the worst, she had no doubt.

* * *

'Oh, but Dorossea, zis is very bad! Did your previous governess teach you *nothing*?'

Dorothea's blood ran cold. Was this the moment when the monster struck?

They were sitting at the big table, books spread out in front of them. The lesson was called *arithmetic*. It was impossibly complicated. Dorothea would not have understood it even if her head had not been spinning with fear. What made it worse was that the governess did not *look* like a monster. She was tall, thin, quiet, self-contained. She came from France and her name was *Mademoiselle Lacroix*. Without Nanny's warnings, Dorothea might easily have been taken in. As it was, she'd been on her guard for over a week since the Mam'zelle's arrival, waiting for the moment when the monster would show her true colours. That moment had perhaps arrived at last.

'Dorossea, I ask you a question.'

Dorothea shook, her teeth chattered. 'I've n-n-never had a governess.'

'Then school. Have you not been to school?'

'I went to the board school b-b-but only the b-boys did arithmetic.'

'And the girls?'

'S-sewing.'

The monster smiled. 'Sewing is a noble art. But we need to do our sums too.'

The smile, the gentle voice — such deception! Any moment now the governess would pounce.

Day after day of waiting for the worst had taken its toll. Dorothea could stand it no longer. 'I can't do sums! I don't want to do sums!' She flung the book away from her. 'I don't understand, I don't understand!'

She stopped, appalled, her chest heaving. What had she done?

Mlle Lacroix leaned forward. Dorothea cowered.

'If you do not understand,' the governess said in her strange sing-song way of speaking, 'then we will start again at the beginning. But first—' She reached out. Dorothea shied away, hunched up in her chair, but there was no escape. The governess caught hold of her hand across the table. 'But first, Dorossea, tell me, why are you always so desolate? What can be so dreadful that you never smile?'

Dorothea looked at the hand holding hers, the long pale fingers, the soft skin. Was such a hand really capable of the cruelties that Nanny had described?

The fingers stroked. The voice soothed. 'Dorossea? Will you not tell me?'

What did it matter, Dorothea thought, what did anything matter anymore? She might as well speak. It wasn't as if she had any choice. The monster had her trapped.

But once she started to talk, it all came out in a rush, everything. How much she missed her papa, how she was angry with him, too, for leaving her (oh, the shame of feeling like that, the shame!). How the Nursery was a prison and the days dragged on and on and nothing ever happened and she felt trapped and stifled and lost and hopeless. The monster listened, did not interrupt, did not become angry or impatient — did not, in fact, behave much like a monster at all. Her expression softened, her eyes became moist, and all the time her fingers went on stroking, stroking, stroking.

'Oh, *ma petite*, what a sad story you tell me!' she said when Dorothea finally fell silent. 'You love your poppa very much, I think.'

'There's no one else. I don't have anyone.'

'Ah, but zis is not true, Dorossea. Do you not have your aunt and your uncle? Is not Nora always kind to you? Is there not Richard, too?' (She pronounced his name strangely: *Rishar*.) 'And there is someone else, someone you have forgotten, someone who watches over all of us.'

'I d-don't understand.'

'God, *ma petite*. God watches over us. We are all in His hands.'

Dorothea was bewildered. She had been expecting a beating, to have her head held under water until she nearly drowned. Instead — was it possible? — the governess was offering words of comfort. And now, to complicate matters further, there was talk of God. Dorothea did not know much about God. She remembered a man once coming to Stepnall Street to tell them they should go to church, it was their duty. Mrs Browning had given him short shrift. 'Go to church? I've never heard such rubbish! Do you think we've got time to waste, praying on our knees? Church is not for the likes of us! We've a living to earn! Be off with you!'

What was the truth of the matter? Did God really have everyone in his hands, as Mlle Lacroix said? Whatever the case, even God's hands could not be as soft and comforting as those of the governess. Dorothea was beginning to doubt Nanny's words. There must be some mistake. Not all governesses were monsters, they couldn't be.

'Now,' the governess said with a gentle smile. 'We shall try the sums again, yes?'

* * *

She wanted to tell Richard the extraordinary news — that not all governesses were monsters — but Nurse turned her away, said that Richard was too poorly for visitors, she must come back another day. Was Nurse being entirely honest, Dorothea wondered, or was she using her authority to keep them apart? There was nobody you could appeal to. Nobody was interested in Richard. He was, as Henry had said, often overlooked.

Lost in her thoughts as she wandered slowly back along the corridor, a sudden noise brought her back to herself. Her heart was in her mouth as she looked round in fear, half expecting to see Mrs Bourne looming up — but it was only one of the housemaids on the stairs with a duster.

'Oh my days, Miss Dorothea! You did give me a turn! I thought it was Bossy Bourne, checking up on me!'

The maid's name was Bessie Downs, a friendly girl if something of a chatterbox. Nora, however, called her *slovenly* and *a slouch* and said you couldn't believe half of what she said.

'I'm keeping out of everyone's way, miss.' Bessie Downs flicked her duster around in a desultory manner as she sidled up to the landing. 'They're all as miserable as sin today, I can't tell you. Cook's got a face on her that would curdle milk and as for Bossy Bourne— But when is she any different?

Such a slave-driver and always finding fault! Do you know, miss, I've never met such a quarrelsome crew as this lot in all my born days. But they do say that it's the mistress that sets the tone of a place, so what chance do we have with Old Sourpuss?'

Bessie Downs paused, looking at Dorothea expectantly while tucking her hair under her cap on one side as it fell out on the other.

'Old Sourpuss? Do you mean Aunt Eloise? Why do you call her that?'

Bessie Downs seemed pleased by the question. She lowered herself down to sit on the top step, patted the place next to her for Dorothea to sit too. 'I call her Old Sourpuss because she's as sour as old milk. I reckon her face would crack in half if she ever tried to smile. But then again, what has she got to smile about? They do say—' Bessie leaned close, lowering her voice. 'They do say as she only married the master because no one else would have her. Her family wanted better for her than a factory man but beggars can't be choosers. Twenty-seven she was, when she got wed, if you can believe it! Near enough an old maid! If I get to such an age without a ring on me finger, I'll slit my own throat, I swear!'

Dorothea shivered at the gruesome turn of phrase. Bessie Downs was what Mrs Browning would have called *a saucy piece*, but there was something about her that held you enthralled. She ventured to say things that no one else Dorothea had met in the house would dare to.

'Not that I'll have much trouble finding a husband,' Bessie Downs continued, tucking her hair in again, 'not with my looks. Nor will you, miss, when the time comes, with your curls. But if you ask me—' She lowered her voice again. 'If you ask me, it's the house that Old Sourpuss pines for more than she's ever pined for any man. It eats her away that it'll never be hers, for it's the only thing she has ever cared about!'

'What do you mean, Bessie? I thought this was Uncle Albert's house?'

'Bless you, no! Mr Brannan has no connection here! He comes from up Coventry way. It's Old Sourpuss who was born here and she's lived here near all her life. But she'll never own the place because it belongs to Master Richard!'

'*Richard*!' Dorothea gaped at Bessie in astonishment. She remembered what Nora had said, that you couldn't believe half of what Bessie Downs said. This without doubt must be the tallest of Bessie's tall tales. 'Richard! But how, why?'

'Surely you know, miss? Well I never, so you don't! But it's true. True as I'm sitting here. Master Richard is the *real* master — or will be once he's twenty-one. Funny, ain't it, to think of a wizened little cripple like him owning a big place like this! But they do say that—'

Bessie stopped short as they heard footsteps behind them. They jumped to their feet in alarm.

'So this is where you've got to, miss. I've been looking all over!'

It was Nora, only Nora. Dorothea breathed a sigh of relief, although she wished Nora hadn't appeared at precisely that moment. She had a hundred and one questions buzzing inside her head which only someone like Bessie Downs would answer. Nora, however, took Dorothea's hand firmly.

'Come along, miss. The mam'zelle says it's time for your walk. You must put on your coat and shoes.' Glancing over her shoulder as they walked away, Nora added tartly, 'I'd watch what I was saying, if I was you, Bessie Downs.'

Bessie laughed, flicking her duster, her hair hanging loose on both sides. 'You're such an old fuddy-duddy, Nora Turner. You want to let your hair down once in a while.'

Nora pursed her lips as she opened the green baize door. 'She's no more sense than she was born with, that one. She'll be for it, no mistake, if Mrs Bourne catches her idling and scandal-mongering.'

'But Nora, Bessie said—'

'What? What did she say, miss? I'm surprised at you, I must say, listening to the likes of *her*. But there, you're only young and you don't know no better. It's Bessie Downs who's at fault. She'll come to a sticky end one of these days, mark my words! But never mind all that. We must hurry. The mam'zelle is waiting!'

* * *

Fresh air, said Mlle Lacroix, was *efficacious* (a French word, perhaps?). A daily walk in the gardens (weather permitting) was part of Dorothea's new routine. But today her head was in too much of a muddle to enjoy it. She was going over and over what Bessie Downs had said. Did the house *really* belong to Richard? It was so big and solid and deep-rooted that it seemed impertinent to think of anyone *owning* it. It would be the other way round, if anything — the house would own *you*. Was that how Aunt Eloise felt about the place?

Leaving the governess sitting with a book under the pergola, Dorothea wandered off with her secret thoughts. She had felt from the first that the house was somehow *alive*. It might permit you to lodge within for a day or a year or a lifetime but when you'd gone, the house would carry on. It would carry on forever.

Looking up from the cinder path on which she was walking, Dorothea saw ahead of her the old gardener Becket clipping a privet hedge. Becket was none other than the crusty man she had met on the morning of her failed escape. She had met him often since. He had worked at Clifton for years, which he was quick to tell you. 'I was just a nipper when I started. It was Mr Jephcott as took me on. He was head gardener in them days. It must be fifty year back if it's a day. Since then, I've worked for four different masters and seen head gardeners come and go. Now I'm head gardener myself. Leastways, that's how I see it, for there ain't no one but me.'

Dorothea skipped along the path. If anyone would know about the house, then Becket would. He could be crotchety at times but he didn't mind answering questions.

Becket stopped his clipping and tipped his cap back, listening to her eager enquiries. Well, he said when she'd finished, Bessie Downs was nothing but a flibbertigibbet, but in this case she was quite right. The house was Richard's. Not just the house, either, but the grounds too, and lots of land around — what Becket called *the estate*. It would all be Richard's when he came of age.

'I don't understand, Becket. How did Richard come to own *everything*?'

'Well, miss, now let's see. Where shall I begin?' He laid his shears aside, took off his cap, scratched his head, making his fluffy white hair stand up in tufts. Dorothea knew it was no good trying to hurry him. Becket did everything in his own good time. 'When I started here as a nipper, Sir Edward was guv'nor, the last of the Massinghams, them what had owned Clifton Park from time out of mind. Titled folk, they were. Baronets. But Sir Edward had no son so the estate passed to his nephew — the estate, but not the title. *Mr Harry Rycroft*, this nephew was named. Title or no, he was a gentleman proper and he loved the gardens here. Ah, but they was kept spic and span in his day! There was a whole troop of us back then, head gardener, under gardeners, no end of boys — everything was done as it should be.'

Hopping with impatience — what had all this got to do with Richard? — Dorothea nonetheless knew better than to interrupt. To interrupt was to invite even more humming and hawing.

Becket paused, giving her a sharp look as if he knew very well what she was thinking, and then he pursed his lips, staring into the distance as if he was trying to see back to days gone by.

'Now Mr Rycroft, he was guv'nor here for forty year and more. Two kiddies he had, a boy and a girl. The girl growed up to be Mistress Brannan — your aunt, that is to say. But the boy was Master Fred — Mr Frederick Rycroft, to be precise. He was the one who became guv'nor when Mr Rycroft passed on. He *inherited the estate*, as they say.'

Dorothea couldn't let this pass. 'Why did the estate go to him? Why didn't it go to Aunt Eloise? Why couldn't she be guv'nor?'

'Because Master Fred was the elder. Besides, it's sons what inherit, not daughters.'

'But that's not fair!'

'Fair or no, it's the way things are.'

'And do girls get *nothing*?'

'Girls get to rule the roost. You ask Mrs Becket if you don't believe me.'

'But what has all this got to do with Richard?'

'Ah, well, I was coming to that, wasn't I, if you'd just hold your horses.' He gave her another hard stare from under his bushy brows. 'Master Fred's wife was Lady Emerald, Lady Emerald Huntley — an earl's daughter, so they said. But that's summat else you'll have to ask Mrs Becket about. She's the one what knows about earls and dukes and all manner of royalty.'

'But—' Dorothea stopped herself just in time, and Becket nodded solemnly, as if he approved of her self-restraint.

'This Lady Emerald—' He sniffed as he said the name, as if he didn't think much of her. '—was a girl who liked to rule the roost in every way. Very distinguished, as I never doubted, but there was no *sense* there, if you take my meaning. She never fitted in here. Not like you, miss, you've taken to it like a duck to water. But then again, Lady Emerald was never happy anywhere, if you ask me. Couldn't settle. Always gadding about. Spent a lot of time in foreign parts, her and Master Fred, after they was married. And time was marching on, and there was no sign of a kiddie and folks were beginning to think there never would be. And then, out of the blue, they came back one day from abroad (or thereabouts) and Lady Emerald was in a delicate condition at long last. My word, but wasn't there was a fuss and a palaver when that little lad was born!'

'What little lad?'

'Why, the one you've been harping on about, of course, that poorly mite up at the house.'

'You mean Richard?' Dorothea's head was spinning as she tried to untangle the web of names. 'So Master Fred is Aunt Eloise's brother, and he is Richard's papa as well?'

'Master Fred ain't anything anymore. He's been dead these five years. And that's how the poorly mite came to inherit the estate: he inherited from his father, the way Master Fred inherited from old Mr Rycroft.'

'Poor Richard! But how did his papa come to die?'

'Ah, well, now you're asking. Some folk say one thing, some say another. It's not my place to judge. But it was his wife as went first — her that had never been ill in her life afore. Something she picked up abroad, like as not. And Master Fred, he loved her even if no one else didn't, and nobody nor nothing could console him once she'd gone. If ever a fellow died of a broken heart, then it was Master Fred. It were a great pity to my way of thinking. He'd been something of a rapscallion in his younger days but he growed out of it. He growed some sense. He had all the makings of a half decent guv'nor. But that's as maybe. Twas not to be. He passed on not three year after his old dad, and that sickly lad you're so fussed about was left all alone in the world. There it is. Some misfortunes can't be mended. You just have to make the best on it, be you rich or be you poor. Not that it was any hardship for Mistress Brannan to come back to Clifton. She never took to life in Coventry, by all accounts.'

'Why did she go to Coventry and why did she come back?'

'She went when she was married and she came back because she was needed. A young lad like the one up the house needs *guardians*. Mistress Brannan is his guardian, Master Brannan too. But that's enough talk for now, miss. I must get on. Nothing'll ever get done if I stand here chopsing all day.'

He picked up his shears and set about the hedge again, clippings piling around his feet. Dorothea hardly noticed. She'd been given plenty to think about. Poor Richard! Her own misfortunes paled next to his: the terrible illness which had left him with a withered leg, the deaths of both his parents, and now the house — a heavy burden for such frail shoulders!

Mlle Lacroix appeared on the cinder path and took her hand. As they walked back towards the house, she said, 'You have been talking to Monsieur Becket. A very clever man, I think.'

'But how can he be clever, Mam'zelle? He can't even read!'

'Being able to read does not in itself make one clever, Dorossea. Books open one door to knowledge, but there are other doors too. Often experience is the best teacher of all. And no one in the world knows everything. Even a professor of the Sorbonne might have something to learn from an English girl in a country garden!' And she laughed, a light trilling sound which invited you to join in even when you weren't exactly sure what was so funny.

* * *

In his room later, Richard answered Dorothea's eager questions somewhat irritably. 'Of course the house is mine. Everything that was Father's comes to me. I thought you knew. Everyone knows.'

'And your papa and mama? What were they like?' She wondered why she had never asked before. She had known they were dead, but that was all. When she thought how often she spoke about her own papa, she was filled with remorse. It was as if she'd been rubbing Richard's nose in it, that her father was alive (albeit missing), whereas his was dead.

Richard could tell her very little about his parents. His father sounded a restless sort of man, always fidgeting, never sitting still. It had worn Richard out just watching him. As for Richard's mother, she'd worn jewels and long white gloves, she'd always been going out or going away, she'd never looked Richard in the eye when she spoke to him.

Richard squirmed beneath the bed clothes. He pulled a face. 'I don't want to talk about her. I don't want to talk about Father, either. I don't like to remember them.' He looked at Dorothea with a sullen expression. 'I expected you to come earlier. I was waiting for you. I've been waiting all afternoon.'

'I had to take my walk, and then I met Becket and—'

'I suppose you like Becket better than me. I suppose you like everyone better than me. You don't care about me at all. Well, soon I shall be dead and then you'll be sorry!'

'What a horrible thing to say!'

'It's the truth. I am ill, getting iller all the time.'

'Such fibs! You aren't ill at all! There's your leg, of course, and I'm sorry about that, but it can't be helped so there's no point in crying over spilt milk!' The words were out before she could stop them. It didn't sound like her at all. It was more like Mrs Browning, hard as nails. If only Richard hadn't made her so angry, saying that she didn't care! It wrung her heart, looking at him now, sunk in his pillows, so flimsy, as if a puff of wind would blow him away. It wrenched at her heart, angry with him though she was.

'You hate me!' he gasped. 'Everyone hates me, Aunt Eloise most of all. She despises me because I'm a cripple!'

'That's not true, I don't hate you, nobody hates you, and you're not a cripple, not really!' If only he could get up once in a while, get away from this mournful room with its half-closed curtains and bare walls! If only he could go into the gardens! It would make all the difference, she was sure of it, just as it had made all the difference to her.

The sound of their raised voices brought Nurse into the room, demanding to know what all the noise was. Richard was delicate. Such excitement was not good for him. But when Dorothea ventured to suggest that Richard might not be so delicate if he was allowed out now and again, Nurse stamped on the idea at once. No, no, no: it was out of the question! Fresh air would have the most terrible consequences! Richard would deteriorate, would get pneumonia, would die. Did Dorothea want *that* on her conscience? Look at the trouble she'd caused already. (Richard had started coughing.) Wasn't that enough mischief for one day, without all this talk of *outside*?

It was no wonder Richard was so obsessed with death when the word was so often on Nurse's lips, but Dorothea didn't dare say as much, and she was rather frightened by the fit of coughing which was wracking Richard's thin frame.

Nurse thumped Richard on the back — none too gently, it seemed to Dorothea. 'Haven't I enough to do, without all your bright ideas? I don't need the bother of it! I'm not here as some sort of skivvy. I'm a professional, I am! Now run along, miss, and leave me in peace, before I lose my patience!'

Dorothea hesitated in the doorway. But Richard looked so thin and scraggy, coughing and retching and being thrown around by Nurse as if he was nothing, that she couldn't bear to watch. She turned and fled.

* * *

She had never quarrelled with Richard before. She didn't like it. Some people you quarrelled with and it didn't matter, it was forgotten in an instant. You could say anything to Mickey, for example, and he never took it to heart. Richard was different. He didn't have a hide as thick as an elephant's. But was he really quite as delicate as Nurse made out? There was only one person who would know.

As Dorothea expected, the doctor was called after Richard's coughing fit. Taking her life in her hands, she slipped out into the corridor and waylaid him as he was leaving. Was it really out of the question, she asked in a breathless rush, for Richard to go outside? Would it really get pneumonia and die? Only Nurse had said—

Dr Camborne interrupted. 'What's this? What has Nurse been saying? Oh, she has, has she! Well, well, so *she's* the expert now, is she? I can tell you, young lady, that in my *qualified* opinion a bit of fresh air would do the boy no harm at all. Indeed, it may — *may* I say — do him some good. But he must only go out when the weather is warm and only for a short time. Never mind what Nurse says, this is what I say, and *I'm* the doctor. I am putting you in charge, young lady. You must see to it that my instructions are followed to the letter. I am sure I can rely on a clever little girl like you!'

He smiled at her — a smile she did not particularly care for. Nurse did not like the doctor's smile either, but she made it rather more obvious. This, however, was beside the point. What mattered was Richard and making things better for him. Nurse would never dare to go against the doctor's orders.

But later, Nanny came bustling into the day room in high dudgeon. 'Well! Aren't you a busy-body, sticking your nose in where it's not wanted, talking to Dr Camborne and I don't know what else! Nurse is most put out, let me tell you! Said I should keep more of an eye on you. Humph! As if I need advice from *her* about how to do *my* job! But it would never have come about if you didn't meddle in things that don't concern you! I've a good mind to box your ears, my girl! You need to be taught a lesson!'

Dorothea flinched as Nanny bore down on her, but at that moment there was a discreet little cough from the governess who was sitting by the window reading, seemingly oblivious.

Nanny glanced at the governess then slowly lowered her hand. 'Well,' she said, backing away, 'that's what you *deserve*, a good hiding. But as I'm such a tender-hearted creature, I shall let you off just this once. *Just* this once, mind. And now, let's have all this mess cleared off the table, all these books and whatnot. Unsightly, I call it. It'll do you no good, either, too much reading. It ruins your eyesight, don't say I didn't warn you.' (She cocked an eye at the governess.) 'Really, what stuffy old books they are! Take this one. I can't understand a word of it. It's all in foreign. And that's not right. It's not right at all. I can't abide foreigners — and I don't care who knows it!'

* * *

A letter arrived out of the blue. Dorothea had never received a letter in her life. To receive one now from Roderick of all people was baffling.

A chap must compose letters here on a Sunday, he wrote, *so I thought I may as well write to you as anyone.*

Was this the same Roderick who'd wanted nothing to do with her at Easter? Though he had, to be fair to him, made one overture back then, asking if she'd like to go looking for birds' eggs with him. Dorothea had not been at all sure that she wanted to steal eggs from the nests of poor unsuspecting birds but she had shown willing by agreeing to the plan. However, when she had said that she had to visit Richard first, Roderick had curled his lip.

'Richard! What do you want with a duffer like Richard? He's such a wet blanket!'

'No he isn't! He's—'

'I don't care what he is. I don't care about him at all.'

'Why must you be so horrible? I shall be glad when you have gone back to school!'

'That's a fine thing to tell a chap, I must say! How would *you* like it if *you* had to go to school?'

'I should like it very much!'

'That's what you think! You'd soon change your mind if you knew what it was like — if you had to get up at six o'clock every morning and bathe in freezing cold water and then spend the *whole* day construing Latin with hardly a *bite* to eat. School is beastly, a beastly hole. But never mind. I shan't bother you again. I shall never ask you to do anything. I *had* thought you might like to climb a tree or two, or ride my pony, or swim in the canal, but if you'd rather talk to *Richard* . . . !'

He'd stomped off with his nose in the air, only to reappear in the doorway a moment later.

'By the way, you needn't tell Mother I swim in the canal. She'd only make a fuss.'

Then he'd taken himself off again.

And now this, a letter, the last thing she'd expected. She was not sure what to think. It was easier to put the letter aside and leave it until later. Indeed, she had no time to consider anything just then, for there were more important things to think about. Not only was Richard going outside for the first time today, but — almost as exciting — Uncle Albert was bringing some bicycles from his factory in Coventry, the factory he travelled to every morning to take charge of things. Today he was coming home early, especially.

Dorothea put the letter in a drawer and ran to watch Richard being carried downstairs by the footman John (his real name was Tomlin, but Nora said the footman was always called John at Clifton). Settled in his bulky bath chair, Richard looked small and frail, blinking in the daylight like a hatchling in a nest. But it wasn't long before he was laughing out loud as he watched Dorothea and the governess trying to master the art of riding their bicycles — for Mlle Lacroix had been given a bicycle too, despite her protestations.

'Oh, *Monsieur*, I do not want a bicycle, do not make me! I shall fall off and bump my 'ead! They are 'orrid things, these bicycles, with their hard seats and bumpy wheels. And those unspeakable horrors — *mon Dieu*! How is it you call them? Penny-farthings?'

Uncle Albert had laughed. 'Things have moved on rather, since the days of the penny-farthing, Mam'zelle. Modern machines are built for comfort. They have indirect gearing, pneumatic tyres, all the latest developments. You'll see!'

They certainly looked the part, brand new and shiny in pale blue and deep red with the letters *B.B.C.* stamped on them for the Brannan Bicycle Company. Dorothea could never have imagined such affluence in the dour precincts of Stepnall Street, owning a magnificent machine like this! But owning it was one thing, staying on was quite another — even with Uncle Albert acting as instructor. It was quite a performance, Dorothea admitted, as she and the governess wobbled round on the gravel in front of the house, losing their balance and falling off and despairing of ever getting the knack. But it didn't matter how silly they looked, because it made her heart swell to see Richard laughing as he sat in his bath chair in the shade of the cedar tree, the footman in attendance (Tomlin was unable to keep a straight face either). Nor were these the only spectators. Becket with his wheelbarrow was watching from the doorway into the gardens and Bessie Downs was peeping out of an upstairs window when she ought to have been seeing to the bedrooms.

In the end, Dorothea managed to cycle right round the cedar tree without putting her foot down once. She had never felt such a sense of achievement. But when she came to put her bicycle away in an empty loose box round in the yard, she saw Roderick's machine in the gloom waiting for him, and she remembered the letter and felt a twinge of guilt. Was school really as terrible as he made out? Poor Roderick! And there she'd been, laughing and joking all afternoon as she hadn't a care in the world!

She made up her mind then and there to ask Mlle Lacroix's help in composing a reply straight after tea.

* * *

'Another letter, miss!' said Nora as she brought in the breakfast tray and placed it on the table. 'They're coming regular as clockwork!'

No one was more surprised about this than Dorothea. Even if letter-writing was obligatory at school, why should Roderick chose to write to her? Dorothea felt that her replies were rather devoid of interest, just a catalogue of daily life at Clifton. Roderick did not seem to mind. His letters, in any case, kept coming.

It was the letters which brought Aunt Eloise to the Nursery. She walked in unannounced like a visitation from another world and addressed Dorothea frostily. It was her understanding, she said, that Dorothea had received some letters from her son. As it appeared that Roderick would rather correspond with *her* than with his own mother, might she be permitted to look the letters over? She seemed to take it for granted that the answer would be *yes*. In fact, she got no answer at all. Dorothea was frozen in terror, couldn't move or speak. It was Nora who went running and came back with the bundle of envelopes from Dorothea's room.

Aunt Eloise took up the letters one by one, holding them in her long, exquisite fingers, her piercing blue eyes raking over them. Still frozen in position, standing like a statue in the middle of the day room, Dorothea heard voices echoing in her head: *Mrs Brannan wants you in an orphanage . . . your aunt is very cross, very cross indeed . . . Old Sourpuss, that's what I call her: she's as sour as old milk . . . it's the house she pines for; it eats her away that she'll never own it . . . Aunt Eloise despise me because I'm a cripple . . .*

Dorothea's legs were like jelly. She felt that she'd never been so deeply terrified of anyone in her life.

Aunt Eloise folded the letters precisely and placed them on the table. 'Thank you,' she said with a regal nod of her head. Then she turned and went, her long skirts rustling as she glided effortlessly from the room. Dazed as she was, Dorothea would not have been surprised just then had her aunt ascended through the ceiling in a shower of silver.

'Goodness me, miss! You're shaking like a leaf! Come and sit by the fire.' Dorothea was aware of the warmth of Nora's arm round her waist, helping her to a seat. 'Here we are. Sit in Nanny's chair, she'll never know. Well, your head feels cool, so you can't have a fever, but you must be sickening for something. I'll go and see Cook. She'll make you one of her restoratives, then you'll be right as rain.'

Leaning back in the chair with a rug over her knees, Dorothea was at a loss to explain what had come over her. But as she looked around the day room which had become so familiar, she was strangely comforted. She thought about Uncle Albert and the bicycles, about Roderick and his letters, about Nora and Richard and Mlle Lacroix. Almost she felt that there might be a place for her here at Clifton. Would the house in time come to accept her? Or, despite everything — despite her papa's best efforts — would the mean little court off Stepnall Street always be her real home?

CHAPTER FOUR

'Why, miss,' exclaimed Nora as she brushed Dorothea's hair, 'to think what a scarecrow you were on your first morning! It seems so long ago. You're a different girl now. You'll look such a picture for Master Roderick's birthday tea, with your new frock and all.'

Sat in front of the three-folded mirror in her room, Dorothea did not think of the *picture* she would look but of the scarecrow she had been. There'd been holes in her boots, and the clothes she'd stood up in had been all that she had. There were no new frocks in Stepnall Street, no maids to brush one's hair — no mirrors, either, for that matter — not in the little room she'd shared with her papa, and Mrs Browning, and Mickey and Flossie.

She lowered her eyes. She had still not got used to seeing her own reflection. She did not like it, picture or not. Would her papa even recognise her now, after so long? With it being Roderick's birthday, she was reminded that two birthdays of her own had come and gone since she first arrived at Clifton. She'd reached the dizzy heights of double figures. And she had so many clothes now that she wasn't sure there were enough days in the year to wear them all.

Nora sighed, still brushing. 'I wish I had your curls, miss. A new frock would come in handy, too. Curls and a new frock. It would be just the thing for our Jem's wedding.'

'Why not borrow my new frock, Nora? I wouldn't mind at all.'

'It's a lovely thought, miss, but I'm not sure it would fit. Never mind. There's an old frock of Mother's that'll suit me down to the ground. It only needs a few alterations.' She stepped back, admiring her handiwork. 'There, miss, that's your hair done, ribbons and all. Shall we try that frock now?'

And so Dorothea was ready for the big birthday tea. Roderick's birthday came a month-and-a-half after hers, but Roderick would only be nine this year whereas she was ten. He was not best pleased about it.

It was early yet, however. She had time to spare before tea. She wandered around the day room which was unaccountably empty, Polly the only sign of life. The big table was littered with Roderick's tin soldiers, all massacred that morning in a vast and noisy battle. Mlle Lacroix's latest book — one from the Library downstairs — lay open and face down on the chair by the window. Dorothea picked it up. The pages crackled as she turned them.

The present house (she read) *was built by Sir John Massingham on the site of the old manor early in the eighteenth century.*

Now, when was the eighteenth century? Did it have years beginning with eighteen or with seventeen? She could never remember. Mlle Lacroix would despair.

Putting the book aside, Dorothea looked out of the open window, leaning on the ledge. The sky was glossed with clouds, but deep wells of blue had opened here and there, and the lush green landscape was mottled with a patchwork of sun and shade. Here at the back of the house a clipped meadow known as The Park sloped down towards a shallow valley where the grey ribbon of a canal was all but hidden from view.

The summer afternoon looked so inviting that Dorothea decided to go outside — *to blow the cobwebs away*, as Nora would say. Now that she was as old as ten, she didn't always need the governess to hold her hand.

Out in the fresh air, Dorothea wandered through the vegetable garden, past the beans on their poles and Becket's neat rows of cabbages, onions and carrots ('Vegetables can be just as comely as flowers to my way of thinking,' Becket said, 'and there's some utility in vegetables as there ain't in flowers.'). There was no sign of Becket himself but as she rambled along a walled walkway, the sun broke through and her spirits rose. She wished she'd asked Richard to accompany her. It was just the sort of afternoon when he would be allowed out. A turn around the gardens worked wonders. Even Dr Camborne himself admitted as much. On his last visit, he'd said that he had never seen Richard looking better.

'The credit is all yours, Florence Nightingale.' The doctor had patted her head; but her glow of pleasure had been tempered only moments later when she'd overheard him talking to the governess in the corridor.

'. . . quite a remarkable transformation . . .' She'd thought at first that he was speaking of Richard. 'One would never guess at her origins if one didn't know. It just goes to show that even a child from the very lowest orders can be raised up if the effort is made. I'd never have believed it myself. Catch them early. That must be the key.'

Mlle Lacroix had spoken rather stiffly. 'I think, *monsieur docteur*, that Dorossea would be the same girl whatever her circumstances.'

'Perhaps you are right, mademoiselle, perhaps you are right. She may be the exception that proves the rule. *Naturam expellas furca, tamen usque recurret.*'

Dorothea pulled a face as she turned left, passing under an archway into a rather neglected corner of the gardens. She did not want to be an *exception*, she did not think of herself as having been *raised up*. A few posh clothes did not change who you were. Whether you had holes in your boots or not was neither here nor there. Perhaps that was what Mlle Lacroix had meant when she said *Dorossea would be the same girl whatever her circumstances.*

The sun faded. Dorothea looked round, standing in the middle of what might once have been a neat lawn but was now overgrown and strewn with weeds. There were some hives, crumbling, the paint peeling, many dead and silent, one or two still active. Watching the bees coming and going, engrossed in their own affairs, Dorothea experienced an inexplicable feeling of restlessness. Their buzzing was the only sound apart from the wind in the grass. Then, from far off, as if in answer to her mood, she heard the chimes of the church clock marking the quarter hour. Ever since the dreams of her first night, those chimes had held a mysterious significance for her. Today they were like beckoning fingers — as if the village was calling her, the village she heard so much about but so rarely saw. Sometimes she thought it the one place she might truly belong, living with her papa in a little cottage like Nora's — with her mama, too, if in some other life her mama hadn't died. Perhaps there'd have been brothers and sisters as well — real brothers and sisters, not stand-ins like Mickey and Flossie.

The village, she thought longingly. *And the wedding, Jem's wedding.* (Jem was Nora's brother.) *If only—*

Oh, but what was the use? The village might beckon, but she was netted here, confined to the house and grounds, wandering like a waif in the gardens. The bees were full of purpose, but she had nothing, just silly dreams like the one about the cottage. She didn't have a mama, never had.

Her skirts dragged through the long grass as she walked to the far wall. Ivy grew all over the crumbling brickwork and dangled in front of a doorway. The door itself had rotted away long ago leaving just the rusty hinges. Brushing aside the tendrils, she stepped through, entering the orchard, a remote and little-known outpost. It hardly seemed part of the gardens at all. There was no wall or hedge round it apart from the one she had just passed. The orchard simply faded into the big field beyond.

Her heart was beating. Suddenly she felt oddly excited, the house hidden behind her, the wide world just a few steps away on the other side of the unmarked boundary. Uncharted lands stretched ahead of her. Rookery Hill with its crown of trees was hunched against the sky. If she had possessed any courage at all, she thought — if she'd been like Roderick, fearless — she would have gone running heedless right to the top of the hill and back again. Roderick would think nothing of it, never mind if it was forbidden. But Roderick was a boy. Such mischief was expected of boys. She was a girl. A girl with a new frock and ribbons in her hair. Running anywhere would spoil how she looked. But perhaps if she put a foot — one toe, even — out into the field, she might feel as if she had achieved something.

She walked forward, ducking under the straggling branches of long-neglected apple and plum trees, but as she rounded a gnarled old trunk she suddenly realised with a shiver of alarm that she was not alone in the Orchard as she'd thought. Someone else was there.

The someone was a boy — not much older than her, she recognised on second glance — a short, wiry boy with a sun-browned face and a thin white scar on his forehead. He was wearing a grubby shirt and a tatty waistcoat. His coarse trousers were fraying at the ends. His cap, wedged on his head, was too small for him. Unruly brown hair stuck out. In one hand he held an apple that he had just picked from a tree, in his other hand was a sack in which he had obviously gathered a great many other apples. Something about him made Dorothea want to take a step back but it was too late to retreat. He had seen her.

She shrank against the gnarled tree as he approached her, glowering.

'What d'yer want?' he demanded.

'I . . . I . . . my name is Dorothea. What's yours?'

'Mind yer own business.'

'What are you doing?'

'Nothing. I ain't doing nothing. What's it to you?'

She drew herself up. 'There's no call to be rude!'

'*There's no call to be rude*,' he mimicked with a sneer.

'Those apples don't belong to you.'

'They're not yours, neither.'

'You shouldn't take them without asking.'

'There's no harm in a bit of scrumping. But don't you go telling anyone, see?'

'You can't tell me what to do! I shall tell who I like!'

'Oh, will you, now!'

He hoisted his sack on his shoulder, came nearer, menacing. Dorothea had met boys like this before, in Stepnall Street and thereabouts. But in Stepnall Street there had always been people around, there had been Mickey to look out for her. Here in the orchard she was on her own.

'My, you're an uppity one, int yer.'

'No I'm not! I'm not uppity at all!'

'Yes yer are. I've seen yer, tripping in and out of church of a Sunday with your nose in the air. You're from up the Big House, int yer, Miss La-di-da Posh Frock.'

'But I'm not posh at all, really I'm not, I'm—'

'Don't give me that! You people up at the House with your airs and graces, I hate you — we all hate you. You're against us. You've always been against us. Ask anyone in Hayton and they'll say the same.'

'But—'

'If you dare tell anyone I was here — if you dare tell a living soul—'

'I won't, I promise, I—'

'You'd better not, or it will be the worse for you!'

He dropped his sack, bunched his fists, came so close she could smell him, his eyes boring into hers.

'Leave her alone, you swine!' The unexpected voice came down from on high, making them both jump. It was as if a guardian angel had appeared to protect her. But the voice certainly wasn't the voice of an angel.

She looked up. Roderick was balanced on top of the wall, staring at them ferociously.

The boy with the apples didn't flinch. 'I int scared of you, Roderick Brannan.'

'Then you jolly well should be. I've knocked you down more than once, Nibs Carter.'

'Don't think I've forgotten, neither. I'll get you back, you just wait.'

'That's what you think, you worm!'

With that, Roderick leapt from the wall. Dorothea's heart was in her mouth, afraid he would break his neck. He seemed to hang in the air for an eternity. Landing in a heap with a resounding thump, he was up in an instant. The other boy had grabbed his sack and was off, zigzagging through the orchard, but Roderick was too quick for him, hurled himself bodily at his enemy.

The two boys crashed onto the ground, rolled over and over in the grass, pummelling each other, heaving and grunting. It was nothing that Dorothea hadn't seen a hundred times in Stepnall Street — and not just amongst the boys. But here in the peace of the neglected orchard it seemed somehow a hundred times worse, sickeningly brutal. What if they killed each other?

'Stop it! Stop it! Please . . . please . . . stop!'

But they took no notice. She wrung her hands, not knowing what to do. Once, she remembered, when Mickey had been going at it hammer-and-tongs in the court with some deadly foe, a woman had opened an upstairs window and emptied a chamber pot over them, followed by a string of terrible oaths. But Dorothea had no chamber pot to hand, and she dared not use the wicked words (though they were graven on her memory).

At that moment the boy slithered free of Roderick's grasp and staggered to his feet. Roderick leapt up, but this time the boy dodged out of reach. Snatching up his sack, he went haring through the trees, yelling over his shoulder, 'I'll get you, Roderick Brannan, you see if I don't!' And then he was away, flying across the field, a thin streak of next to nothing.

Dorothea turned her attention to Roderick who had stumbled and fallen in attempting to catch the boy. He was now sitting in the grass gulping air. The fight, though brief, had been vicious.

'Oh, Roddy! You're bleeding!'

'I bit my lip. It's nothing.' He gave a blood-drenched grin. 'I showed him what for, didn't I!'

'I don't see what's so funny! You could have been killed!'

'Killed? What rot! Nibs Carter couldn't hurt a fly! He might be two years older than me, but I always come out on top — well, nearly always.'

'Why don't you just leave him alone?' She found that she was shouting, couldn't understand why she was so furiously angry. 'What has he ever done to you?'

'What's he done? I'll tell you what he's done, the worm, the swine—'

'I don't care! I don't want to know! Fighting is silly, is stupid!'

'Well, I like that! After I saved you!'

'I don't *need* saving!'

'I suppose you'd rather have knocked him down yourself? I suppose that's what girls do, where you come from.' He looked up at her, scowling, rather pitiful with his cap missing, his black hair tousled, clothes askew, blood running down his chin. 'You're a rum sort of girl, I must say,' he added, aggrieved. 'I was only trying to *help*!'

Dorothea opened her mouth to speak but no words came out. A wave of desolation washed over her. She felt as if she was about to fly into pieces. What was wrong with her? Tears pricked her eyes. To cry in front of Roderick would be the ultimate ignominy, so instead she turned and fled.

The day room was just as she'd left it, deserted except for Polly — poor Polly who spent her whole life in a cage. But wasn't it the same for people, too? Weren't houses cages, even a house as big as Clifton? And life, life was just a series of traps and pitfalls and dead ends.

She sobbed, thinking of a dream she sometimes had: not the dream of the cottage or the portentous chimes of the church clock but a cold, clammy, smothering sort of dream in which she was walking the streets at dead of night trailing after her papa and sucking her thumb, her tummy empty, her feet sore. She had an idea that something of the sort had really happened — perhaps more than once, in the days before Mrs Browning and the room in Stepnall Street. But she couldn't be sure. London was slipping away from her, getting hazier and hazier in her memory.

She thought of the girl in her dream, the girl she'd once been. She thought of the words that the boy had used: *la-di-da . . . uppity . . . Miss Posh Frock*. Would the people in Stepnall Street — Mrs Browning, Mickey and the others — would they see her in the same light, all airs and graces, a toff? Was she too grand now even for her papa?

But she didn't fit in here, either. She was an outsider, a cuckoo in the nest, the girl who'd been *raised up*, nothing more than a guest, a lodger. 'You should think yourself lucky, my girl,' Nanny often said. 'You ought to be grateful.' And she *was* grateful, she really was. She tried her hardest to be the perfect guest. But that didn't stop her from feeling they might send her away at any moment. Uncle Albert, perhaps, wouldn't, but Aunt Eloise would have no compunction, nor Nanny or Mrs Bourne. And as for Roderick . . . *I suppose that's what girls do, where you come from . . .*

Where you come from.

She ground her teeth, stamped her foot, hating Roderick with a passion, setting himself up as a hero, so nice in his letters from school, so horrible in real life — so *contradictory*, you never knew where you stood with him.

Hardly aware of what she was doing, she began to sweep the toy soldiers off the table and stamp on them, enraged, howling. Polly watched in amazement, flexing her wings anxiously. Finally she gave a single loud squawk.

The sound of Polly's squawk was like a douche of cold water. Dorothea stood stock still. She looked down at the tin soldiers on the floor and began shaking. She had never lost control like that in her life. It made her afraid. And the soldiers, the poor soldiers!

She fetched their box and knelt to pick them up, putting them slowly away one by one. Many were broken and mangled; some were squashed quite flat. Here was one, its head skew-whiff, its legs missing. What had it ever done to deserve that?

Tears began to flow again, silent tears, sliding down her cheeks, dripping onto the little body of the disfigured soldier that she held in her hand.

* * *

'Why, Miss Dorothea, whatever's the matter?' cried Nora when she came into the day room some minutes later to begin laying the table for tea.

But Dorothea couldn't explain. It was all such a jumble in her head: the toy soldiers, the boy in the Orchard, the sense of being adrift.

'Don't you worry about those soldiers, miss. Most of them were broken already, and no wonder the way Master Roderick treats them. As for Nibs Carter — well, I'm sure he didn't mean to upset you. He's a handful, I'll grant you, but he's not a bad boy at heart. What's a few apples when all's said and done? There's no need for Master Roderick to go picking on him and pointing the finger. They've enough troubles, the Carters, what with their mother passing on and then their dad, and Arnie Carter being left to bring up his brothers and sisters all on his own — and him little more than a boy himself! I think he's done a grand job, whatever folk say, but there's always someone ready to pick holes, even when they wouldn't have coped half so well had they been in Arnie's shoes!'

Nora grew heated in her defence of Arnie Carter and Dorothea, drying her eyes, wondered who he was. Before she could ask, Nanny suddenly loomed up, catching them unawares.

'What's this? What's this? What nonsense are you filling the girl's head with now, Turner? Why isn't the table laid?'

Nanny hated to be left out of anything, so of course the whole story had to be gone through again, such as it was. But, like Nora, Nanny didn't seem to understand what Dorothea was trying to say either.

'Well! Pardon me, I'm sure, if I've got it wrong,' she said officiously, 'but it was always *my* understanding that it says in the Bible, *Thou shalt not steal*. And what's taking those apples if it's not stealing? I'm surprised at you, Turner, for suggesting otherwise. I thought you'd been brought up better than that, even if your father is only an *agricultural labourer*. Yes, yes, Miss Dorothea, I know very well that the apples aren't being used for anything, but that doesn't mean just *anyone* can take them! Where would we be if everyone got their food for free? No one would want to do any work at all! Everyone would live in idleness! And need I remind you that the devil makes work for idle hands? No. No. People must go hungry, that's what I say. People who go hungry soon find an appetite for work to match that of their bellies. Those Carters of yours, Turner, would do well to remember it. But now, that's quite enough of that. I won't hear another word about it. I want that table laid, Turner, and Baby needs feeding once you've finished. And as for you, my girl, you just go and make yourself presentable. You look a fright with your eyes all puffy and grass round your hem! Where's that governess, I'd like to know? I shall be having words, you may be sure!'

Nanny folded her arms and looked down her nose and Dorothea hung her head but Nora said nothing, merely pursed her lips and began laying the table, banging the cutlery about and rattling the crockery in a most un-Nora-like way, almost as if she didn't give a fig for Nanny at all.

* * *

Don't worry about the toy soldiers, Nora had said. All the same, Dorothea could not help but worry. She felt duty-bound to own up. 'If you give Master Roderick an inch, he'll take a mile,' Nora warned but Dorothea didn't care about inches or miles. She just wanted to do what was right.

She confessed as they sat down to the birthday tea, adding, 'Don't worry, Roddy, I shall buy you some new ones.'

He looked perplexed as he piled his plate with cakes, ignoring the sandwiches. 'There's no need for you to buy me anything. Mother will buy new soldiers if I ask. She likes to buy me things.'

'You mustn't tell Aunt Eloise about the soldiers! She will be angry! She will want to send me away!'

'No she won't! I shan't let her, anyway.'

'It's not up to you.'

'It's up to Father and he shan't let her either.'

'But I *will* buy you new soldiers.' She felt she should.

His mouth was too full of cake for him to argue anymore and she was glad to have that settled. But now there was something else to worry about. Where would she ever find the money?

She was no longer mad at Roderick. It was never possible to stay mad at him for long — especially this afternoon when he looked as ill-treated as his soldiers, with his split lip and bruises. Nanny had given him a beating, too, for it would be her head on the block (she'd said) when the mistress saw the state of him. Roderick had shrugged off Nanny's punishment as if it was nothing but he was sitting on his chair rather gingerly all the same. It would almost have been possible to feel sorry for him — if he hadn't been so infuriating.

He was eyeing the table with a disgruntled air. 'There is to be a dinner party downstairs in honour of my birthday, but all I get is this shabby tea.'

Dorothea thought it was a sumptuous tea, and said so, although secretly she thought her own birthday tea six weeks ago had been better. But then she was Cook's special friend and Roderick was not. (Was he anyone's special friend?)

Roderick helped himself to more iced buns. 'There is a chink in the dining room door. We could watch the grown-ups as they eat and listen to what they're saying. I don't see why we shouldn't. It's all in *my* honour.'

'But wouldn't that be rather . . . naughty?'

'I don't care if it's naughty or not, it's what I'm going to do. *You* can do what you like.'

'We could ask if—'

'That's no good. One doesn't get anywhere by *asking*.'

'But—'

Roderick rolled his eyes. 'We can't all be as *pure* as you, Miss Goody-Goody. I'm surprised they haven't made you a saint already.'

Dorothea was stung. 'I am *not* a goody-goody! And I *shall* look through the chink!'

Roderick broke into a grin, spoke with his mouth full. 'I knew you would.'

* * *

Dorothea's heart was thumping. What if they were caught? Oh, but it was worth the risk, she thought, putting her eye to the chink and seeing the long table draped with a white cloth and glittering with glass and silver. Candles flickered in the tall candelabra which served as a centrepiece. There were a dozen or so grown-ups seated there. They looked as if they'd been polished up just as diligently as the cutlery.

It wasn't such a lavish occasion as the party on the night Dorothea arrived. There had been no more parties of that sort. Aunt Eloise, it was reported, had considered that evening a failure. *And that is all my fault*, thought Dorothea, recalling the consternation that had greeted her unexpected arrival. Clifton's social occasions in the days of Aunt Eloise's youth had been renowned, Dorothea had learned, but after the failure of her New Year's party, Aunt Eloise had vowed never again to try to emulate the past — which was rather a shame, thought Dorothea, nursing feelings of guilt.

Roderick gave her a shove. 'It's my turn! Let me look!'

'In a minute, Roddy. I haven't finished! Stop pushing!'

Some of the guests Dorothea recognised. Colonel Harding was there — the bluff man who hated motors. His son was there too. Mrs Somersby of Brockmorton Manor was accompanied by her eldest daughter. And the Fitzwilliams were in attendance, Dorothea's especial friends. Henry, of course, had been her knight in armour that day on the Welby Road but his mother took an interest too and never failed to ask after 'Albert's little niece' whenever she called. Dorothea's allies told her this, for not all the servants were as ill-natured and terrifying as Nanny or Mrs Bourne. There was Nora, there was Cook, there was Bessie Downs and Becket, and even Tomlin would pass the time of day when he was pushing Richard in the bath chair.

Roderick gave her another shove and she surrendered her place to him, stepping back, looking up and down the dusky corridor. Light still glimmered through the glass panels of the back door, the tail end of twilight.

Roderick was giggling, his eye pressed against the gap. 'Look at the way Henry eats his soup! He *is* a goose! And Miss Somersby is making eyes at him, like this—' He rolled his eyes wildly. 'I don't suppose Henry has even noticed, the pudding-head!'

'Henry is *not* a pudding-head, nor a goose!'

'Yes he is. And so is Charles Harding. Charles Harding is a half-wit, everyone says so. And — oh, I say! Father has bits from the soup caught in his moustache! How killing!'

Roderick doubled up with laughter and Dorothea took the opportunity to push him aside and reapply her eye to the chink. Why did Roderick have to pick fault and laugh at people all the time? Why did he *exaggerate*? Miss Somersby was not making eyes at anyone. She looked far too stodgy for that, was busy with her soup, a frown of concentration on her face as she lifted the spoon to her mouth. Henry had finished his soup already. He looked very dapper and gallant in his dark jacket and waistcoat, his hair slicked back and shiny with oil. He was crumbling his roll absently as he listened to Colonel Harding going on and on as usual.

Dorothea watched as Henry narrowed his eyes, puffed out his cheeks, as if he was trying to stop himself from yawning.

'Stromberg, Magersfontein, Spion Kop: disaster after disaster!' boomed the Colonel. 'I was beginning to have my doubts, I don't mind telling you. Is this what the British Army has come to, I asked myself? Things must have changed, I said, if this is the kind of shambles that . . .'

But Colonel Harding, strident and bombastic though he was, was somehow not as imposing as Uncle Albert, sitting there silent at the head of the table. He was just as smart and polished as the others (even if he did have bits in his moustache) but there was also something blunt and rough-edged about him, his big hands resting on the table as if, at any moment, he might get to his feet and say — she could not imagine what he would say, but his words would be hard, incisive, to the point, not like Colonel Harding, blustering and bumbling.

'. . . it wouldn't have happened in my day! No! No! You can be sure! In *my* day—'

'*In my day*,' Roderick imitated, elbowing her aside.

'Stop *pushing* Roddy!' She gave him a shove, turned back to the chink.

'The Boer, the Boer,' thundered Colonel Harding, reaching a crescendo. 'The Boer is—'

But Dorothea's gaze was drawn to where, enthroned like an empress, Aunt Eloise sat at the far end of the table. Her mauve gown shimmered as she moved. Her hair was up, made her neck look slim and graceful, like a swan's. She was listening to the Colonel with a slight smile as if to say, *Yes, yes, go on, you are doing well, you are doing oh so well.* As Dorothea watched, however, Aunt Eloise glanced along the length of the table, her blue eyes questing. With an all but imperceptible movement of one finger she brushed her upper lip before turning back to the Colonel. At the other end of the table, Uncle Albert laid hold of his napkin and mopped at his moustache.

Dorothea's heart beat fast. So *that* was what it meant to be married, *that* was the secret: a flick of the finger, a dab with a napkin. She remembered Bessie Downs's words: *she only married the master because no one else would have her*. But that couldn't be right. There was more to it than that, much more.

Dorothea struggled to put this feeling into words. 'Aunt Eloise is . . . is beautiful!' she breathed.

'Mrs Somersby is beautifuller,' said Roderick at her side, mulish.

'Mrs Somersby is *not* beautifuller! She looks like a . . . like a *Christmas tree*, with all those jewels stuck on her!'

Turning her back on Roderick, she looked through the chink once more, saw Tomlin the footman clearing the plates. As he did so, a moth came fluttering in through the half-open window and began circling round and round his head.

'—those . . . those *people* . . . those Boer sympathisers, those *traitors* — Lloyd George!' Colonel Harding seemed to be running out of steam at last. 'And that Hobhouse woman . . .' He trailed to a stop, as if words failed him, as if nothing he could say would adequately describe *that Hobhouse woman*.

In the silence, Mrs Somersby said, 'For myself, I shall simply be glad when it is all over and my son . . .'

Even as she was speaking, the moth made a sudden dive towards the candelabra. There was a spark as it met the candle flame — then nothing. The moth had gone. Dorothea caught her breath. No one in the room seemed to have noticed. No one remarked on it. And yet it was horrible — ominous.

Roderick gave her a hearty push. She pushed back. They tussled in the doorway, fighting to get at the chink.

'*What* do you think you are *doing*?'

The sudden voice was like the crack of a whip. It made Dorothea jump out of her skin. The terrifying figure of Mrs Bourne was bearing down on them, eyes blazing. Even Roderick cowered.

'Should you not both be in *bed*? What *is* Nanny *thinking* of? This is bad, too bad!'

She swept them up as if they no more than moths and drove them towards the stairs. They fled up them, pursued by Mrs Bourne's voice. 'This is bad, too bad!'

But once in bed, Dorothea found it impossible to settle, tossing and turning, her head full to bursting and everything jumbled up. Her new frock. The ribbons in her hair. Jem Turner's imminent wedding like a glittering prize just out of reach. Nibs Carter in the orchard. Stepnall Street like an old fading picture. Roderick, hard, strident, disconcerting. His tin soldiers, squashed and mangled. The grown-ups sitting resplendent at dinner. Half-awake and half-asleep, muttering to herself, her mind weighed down by it all like the branches of a tree overburdened with plump ripe plums.

Plums, she muttered, grappling with the bedclothes. *Apples and plums*. Richard's apples, Richard's plums. Because everything belonged to Richard.

No! Her eyes snapped suddenly open and she sat up, staring into the dark. *Not plums. I don't mean plums. Things are not plums on a tree, just as Mrs Somersby is not a Christmas tree. Things are what they are in themselves. So why did I call Mrs Somersby a Christmas tree, how could I be so cruel when her son is in danger, fighting the wicked Boers?*

The Boer . . . the Boer . . . She lay down again, her eyes fluttering, closing. She sank slowly back into the mire of sleep, Colonel Harding's voice booming and reverberating in her head (*the Boer . . . the Boer . . .*), but seeing only the moth, the poor moth, consumed in the candle flame.

So shall it be at the end of the world! Colonel Harding's voice changed into that of the sour-faced vicar who she saw in the pulpit each Sunday. *So shall it be. The angels shall come forth and sever the wicked from the just, and shall cast them into the furnaces of fire. There shall be wailing and gnashing of teeth . . .*

God, she thought as she felt herself sinking deeper, deeper, her eyes flicking back and forth behind their lids. But which was the real God? Was it Mlle Lacroix's God who held your hand to guide you? Or was it the vicar's God, the God of the fiery furnaces, the God who let moths burn? How could you be sure? How could you be sure of anything? How . . . how . . .

Her eyes came to rest. She finally lay still. Sleep lapped over her.

* * *

'Dorossea, you are not paying attention, I think?'

'I . . . I'm sorry, mam'zelle.'

Mlle Lacroix closed her book. '*Bon*. I think we will take our walk now, yes?'

'Our walk? But it's not time!'

'Ah, but if we go now, *ma petite*, we shall be able to see the bride and groom as they leave the church.'

'Oh! May we really go? Oh, mam'zelle, thank you, thank you!'

Dorothea jumped up, astonished that the governess seemed to know the wedding was the very thing occupying her thoughts. It was the reason for Nora's absence today. Now that the harvest was over, Jem was to marry the inn-keeper's daughter. Not that Jem was involved in the harvest anymore. He'd given up his job on the farm to work in a shoe factory in Lawham, walking three miles there and three miles back every day. Nora had shaken her head at such folly — not the six miles, which she seemed to think was nothing — but the factory. Working in a factory, she said, was only one step above the workhouse, which meant it must be bad indeed, for in Stepnall Street not even the fiery furnaces had held more terror than the workhouse.

Dorothea buttoned her boots in a rush, grabbed her hat. She was to visit the village, see the wedding. She could barely contain herself!

The sun was golden. The fields, stripped of corn, were bristly and pale brown. The footpath stretched like a ribbon from stile to stile. They were taking a short cut from the house to the village, not going round by the road. Dorothea had never been this way before. She pressed ahead, her heart brimming with happiness. A crow took fright, swept into the air with ragged black wings. *Crow,* she said to herself. *La Corneille* in French.

It was quite extraordinary, the things she knew, the names of things in French and English, the names that Nora used too. And did she not read from great big books and do sums in her head at a whim? Who would ever have guessed she would become so wise! Astonishing!

She waited for Mlle Lacroix in the shade of some elms. The governess was serene, smiling, her skirts trailing, her dress plain but oh-so-elegant. She came to the stile, balanced her parasol, lifted her legs, eased herself over, effortless. When Dorothea tried to do the same, she wobbled and lost her balance, went sliding and tumbling — laughing — landing with a bump in the grass. This field — Row Meadow, Nora called it — was where the rabbits had their burrows. Yellow ragwort grew here, goatsbeard too, which Nora called Jack-go-to-bed-at-noon. The church was nearby, just the other side of the meadow, the grey crenulations of its squat tower etched against the sky. It was the only place in the village that Dorothea knew at first hand, the place where the sour-faced vicar held forth about the fiery furnaces, where the seats were hard and uncomfortable, where the daylight came dim through stained glass. It was always cold in the church, no matter what the weather outside. But Mlle Lacroix knew nothing of it, because she went to her own church in Lawham.

They were just in time. Standing on the Green, hand-in-hand, they watched the bride and groom emerge from the church and walk slowly — meekly — down the path. So that was Nora's brother, thought Dorothea — the famous Jem in his Sunday best with a smart new waistcoat, a burly-looking fellow with a plain round face all scrubbed and glowing, colour flaring in his cheeks. And the bride — her name was (had been) Pippa Cheeseman — she had a smile as bright as the sunshine. Her frock was the one her mother had been married in, exquisite, but Nora said it was out-of-date with its big bustle and all that hand-worked lace. Pippa, Nora said, had no idea when it came to clothes, had no idea about anything. All she knew was how to pour beer in her father's pub. You had to wonder, Nora said, if she was quite the girl for Jem, but — and here Nora had sighed — Jem had made his choice and there was nothing more to be said.

There was a wagon waiting in the road festooned with flowers and bits of bunting (left over from the Jubilee, according to Nora). Jem and Pippa climbed aboard. The wagon rolled away. A concourse of people followed on foot, chatting, smiling, laughing, Nora amongst them. Dorothea waved and Nora waved back, pointing her out to a woman walking at her side — a woman who could only be Nora's mother, they were so much alike. Walking with them was an old man with white whiskers and a weather-beaten face. His eyes, dark as a crow's, cast a keen glance in Dorothea's direction. Noah Lee, thought Dorothea: Nora's grandfather. She shivered, for the glance did not seem entirely friendly.

'So lovely,' murmured Mlle Lacroix as the people dwindled away down the street. '*Très beaux. Très heureux.*' She sighed. 'But now—' She stirred, closing her parasol. 'I am going to the shop, Dorossea. Will you come?'

But Dorothea said no, she would wait outside on the Green. As Mlle Lacroix walked towards the shop, Dorothea took a seat on an old bench (a plank nailed to two sawn pieces of tree trunk) under the twisted boughs of a sycamore.

So that was a wedding, she said to herself: lovely, as the governess had said. But, sitting there, Dorothea found all her excitement and happiness slipping through her fingers, dribbling away. She found herself thinking of the mother she had never known. What sort of frock had *she* worn on her wedding day? And Papa. How had he looked? Perhaps in those far-off days he too had owned a Sunday suit like Jem. If so, it was long gone. She remembered once — many, many years ago — coming across a little wooden box. Her tiny fingers had grappled with the lid. Inside there had been lots of pieces of paper which had delighted her infant mind. She realised now that those pieces of paper had been pawn tickets. What had they represented, all those tickets? What cherished possessions had been lost forever, sacrificed to a greater need? Who now was wearing Papa's Sunday suit? And the little box, what had become of that? Her papa had taken it off her, prised it out of her grasping fingers. She had never seen it again.

She had been lost in her thoughts for some time but now suddenly looked up and was startled to find that she was no longer alone. Five boys were standing in a row, staring at her. The midmost boy, the one who was scowling most ferociously, was Nibs Carter.

Her heart was thumping as she got slowly to her feet. She was outnumbered, alone.

Nibs Carter stepped forward. 'What you doing here?'

'I—'

'What you doing in *our* village?'

'I—'

'You don't belong here, a toff like you. You belong up the big house with the other toffs.'

'But . . . but I haven't done anything!' cried Dorothea desperately.

'*I haven't done anything!*' Nibs sneered. The other boys laughed. They closed in around her, jostling her, plucking at her frock the way Cook plucked a chicken. It seemed all the more terrible that it should be happening here, on the peaceful Green, beneath the leafy boughs of the sycamore.

'Putting on airs. Swaggering about as if you owned the place.' Nibs's face was up close to hers. She could see the streaks of dirt on his cheeks, smell his sour breath. 'Well, you'd best not come here again — or it'll be the worst for you!'

Dorothea felt giddy and defenceless. Just then a bell jangled. On the far side of the Green, the door of the shop opened. Mlle Lacroix came out with her parasol and a parcel in brown paper. She looked around, espied the little group by the bench.

'Dorossea!' she called. 'It is time to go now!'

The boys stepped back as the governess glided across the grass towards them. Nibs Carter turned to face her, squaring his shoulders, but Mlle Lacroix was not perturbed, her expression unchanging, her eyes as always bright with curiosity as if at any moment she expected to make some great discovery, under a stone or round the next corner or opening the pages of some old, old book.

'What friends are these, Dorossea?'

Dorothea could not speak but her terror was quickly subsiding. Soon she would be under the protection of the governess's broad-brimmed hat.

The governess advanced. Abruptly the boys broke rank, scattering like dry leaves before the breeze. As he ran, Nibs shouted over his shoulder: 'Remember what I said, posh girl! Just remember!' Then they were gone. The Green was empty and peaceful once more.

'Who were they, those boys, *ma petite*?'

'They were . . . nobody, they were nobody. Shall I carry your parcel, mam'zelle?'

'Ah, *merci*. And now we must go back, yes?'

They crossed the street, hand-in-hand, and took the little path that slipped between the vicarage and the churchyard, leading towards Row Meadow. The sun had gone in. Grey clouds were churning in the sky behind Rookery Hill. The world seemed suddenly colourless and flat.

Looking back as she climbed the stile into the meadow, Dorothea could see one corner of the Green glimmering remote behind her. There was no place for her here, she thought. There was no cottage where she might have lived with her papa and a mother who hadn't died and unknown brothers and sisters. She did not belong in the village any more than she belonged up at the house.

Where, then, did she belong?

* * *

After tea Dorothea could not settle. The day room seemed as dull and drear and confining as it had done in the old days. The day outside had turned overcast. Standing at the barred window, she suddenly remembered the flowers that she had picked on the way back from the village. She had left them on the table in the hall. Dared she go and fetch them?

She looked round. Nanny was snoozing, the governess deep in her book. Creeping quietly out of the room, Dorothea slipped past the green baize door and ran helter-skelter down the stairs with her heart in her mouth. But the house was unusually quiet and somnolent, almost as if it was deserted.

The flowers were on the little table where she'd left them. They looked small and wilted compared to the vast blooms in the tall vase next to them, and yet in the meadow they'd seemed so bright and happy! She was reluctant to touch them, hesitated, looked all around the hall, as if she wanted to find—

But she was not sure what she wanted to find. She sighed. The grandfather clock ticked ponderously, remorselessly. After a time, she noticed that the front door was ajar. She could just imagine what her uncle would say, frowning and shaking his head. 'A house full of servants and still the front door is left open!' He thought it profligate, having so many servants. 'We had none in Seton Street when I was a boy; even when we moved to Forest Road we had just one maid and a cook.' When he spoke of such things, Dorothea felt as if a curtain was being lifted giving her a glimpse into his past; she felt almost as if she was beginning to get to know him. But she also felt that she understood the house, too, whereas he did not. The house required attendants, acolytes. If it was to be placated, if it was not to be roused from its eternal sleep, the time-honoured rites had to be performed — grates must be blacked, fires lit, meals carried up in procession. But the acolytes, for all their discipline, were only human beneath their uniforms, and so the front door was left ajar — by Tomlin, perhaps, who could be slapdash, or Bessie Downs, lazy.

Dorothea went to close the door so that Uncle Albert would not huff and puff, so that Tomlin or Bessie Downs would not be taken to task, but at the last moment, instead of pushing it to, she stepped outside to stand on the doorstep. It was a still, breathless evening, on the cusp of dusk, the memory of daylight like a faint glimmer in the air. Rain was falling, coming down thinly and softly in long straight lines. There was no sound but the sigh it made in falling, and the steady *drip-drip-drip* of a leaky gutter. Everywhere was wet, apart from the doorstep under the canopy, and an island of dry beneath the cedar tree. The wall which separated off the gardens seemed almost to glow, its red bricks stained a darker red.

The profound peace soaked into her like the rain soaking into the ground. All fear, excitement, boredom, joy, despair was rubbed out and smoothed over. Not that the world itself had changed. No. Even here she could sense it, feel it, almost hear it, coming remote from over the horizon — or was it merely memories stirring in her mind? She could hear cats were howling as they fought to the death, drunks squabbling in the street, a famished child feebly grizzling. She knew without doubt that there were places — far away but all too real — where the air was not clean and washed but rank and choking, where nameless horrors lurked in the shadows, where evil eyes peered in the dark. In slimy gutters, tattered old men sat without hope, talking to themselves. People slunk along next to sooty walls, their shoulders slumped. They climbed unlit, foetid stairs. They lay down to sleep on bare boards. Rats swarmed. Fleas bit. Misery and hunger fogged people's eyes. Even here, in the village — in the house itself — there were reminders. She saw Nibs Carter's eyes, brown and brutal. She saw the moth plunge into the extinguishing flame.

No, the world had not changed. Those things were true; she had seen them all. But she no longer felt overwhelmed by them. It was as if she had been standing on a beach with a monstrous wave racing towards her threatening to wash her away. It had crashed in ruin, sending up mountains of spray, reaching out long feelers towards her — only to seethe and fade and dribble away across the sand. What did anything matter when set against the soft-falling rain, the still and quiet of the evening, the vast grey-dark sky? There was a feeling, a whisper, a presence — here, there, everywhere: in the rain, in the sky, in the dripping trees, in the air itself. Dorothea felt it vibrating inside her. It was like a steady smile at the back of everything. Was this God perhaps? Or was it something else? But maybe that was what God really was — a steady smile at the back of everything.

God — Mlle Lacroix's God — would never make a world where wickedness would flourish and horror win out. Horror and wickedness were nothing, as flimsy as dandelion seeds on the wind, mould to be scraped easily away; the fiery furnaces could be snuffed out as easily as a candle flame. All that really mattered was here and now: the doorstep, the rain, the sigh in the air and the house — the house that endured, the house with its time-honoured rites. This was not flimsy, this could never be snuffed out, and one did not have to be a goody-goody to believe in it.

Dorothea stood on the doorstep, breathing slowly, holding on to this great discovery as the rain came down and dusk deepened into night.

CHAPTER FIVE

Dorothea yawned, holding on to her new hat, the yellow ribbons flying in the wind. She watched Richard sleeping beside her with a rug over his knees; she watched fields, hedgerows and grassy verges spin past as the motor bowled along the road. They were on their way back to Clifton, taking what Henry called 'the scenic route'. Henry was driving, Uncle Albert sitting beside him. They were talking in raised voices above the noise of the engine.

'They're simply not reliable, these machines of yours, Fitzwilliam. You can ride a hundred miles one day, and not budge an inch the next.'

'Teething problems are only to be expected, sir, in something as new as an autocar, but improvements are being made all the time.'

'They're so infernally complicated!'

'No more complicated than a bicycle.'

'Oh, come, Fitzwilliam: I'm not having that! There are many more component parts in an autocar — so many more things to go wrong! And what do you do when you need to replace one of those parts, eh? Answer me that!'

'Components can be something of a headache, sir, I'll grant you. But I often find that, with a little jiggery-pokery,

I can reuse what I've already got. And if all else fails, there's Young, the blacksmith's apprentice. He's a dab hand at rustling up what I need. He's quite taken with autocars.'

'You youngsters, with your fads and fancies.' Uncle Albert shook his head as if he disapproved but Dorothea knew better. After so long at Clifton — two and a half years now — she felt as if she'd known him all her life. She smiled at the thought of it, but the smile turned into another yawn. Although she had expressed disappointment when, after the picnic, she'd discovered a puncture in her tyre, secretly she was relieved to be riding home with Richard and Henry and Uncle Albert. Three miles back to Clifton was a long way to cycle, and Roderick would have wanted to race her all the way.

Uncle Albert had dubbed their trip 'the Great Expedition'. They had ventured to far-flung Lawham, the furthest Dorothea had yet ridden. She, Roderick and Mlle Lacroix had cycled; Richard, Henry and Uncle Albert had gone in Bernadette. The governess went to Lawham every Sunday to attend her church, but Dorothea had never been there before. Lawham was where Nora's brother Jem worked in a shoe factory, he whose wedding she had caught a glimpse of last August (the happy couple would soon be celebrating their first anniversary). Lawham was also the place where many of the tradesmen who supplied Clifton had their businesses. Once it had been a thriving place. Henry had told them all about it as they ate their picnic amongst the ruins of the old priory — how Lawham had been an important stop on a busy coaching route, how there had been more inns and taverns than you could count. A few inns remained, relics of the boom times, but the horse-drawn coaches had long since disappeared. Lawham had become a backwater, so old-fashioned that the railway — which had been its ruin — had only reached the town a mere twenty years ago.

A surprise had awaited in Lawham today. They had found a crowd gathered on Market Place, waving flags and cheering. A brass band had been playing marching tunes next to a flower-bedecked water pump. Swinging along in perfect step, rank after rank of soldiers had passed by, heads held high, eyes to the front, uniforms spotless, boots and buttons gleaming.

'They are home from the war,' Mlle Lacroix had said, 'the war in *L'Afrique du Sud*.'

'Is one of them Mrs Somersby's son?' Dorothea had asked.

But Roderick had scoffed. 'Don't be such a dunce. This is an entirely different regiment.'

Mlle Lacroix had watched the scene with a sad smile on her lips. 'These people — so carefree, so patriotic — they forget all those who will never return.'

Because they are dead, Dorothea had thought with a catch in her throat. *They will never return because they are dead*. She had felt then — for a brief moment — as if a glittering surface had been scratched away. The sunshine had faded, the music seemed to falter. She had thought of Roderick's toy soldiers squashed and mangled on the Nursery floor nearly a year ago. But what did a *real* soldier look like, dead?

'Why do they forget, mam'zelle?'

'It is easy to forget what war is like, *ma petite*, when war is far away. But in France it is only thirty years since *les Prussiens* came. *Mon père*, he was a young man then. He lived in Paris. The city was besieged. There was much hardship.'

'War will never come to England!' Roderick, who hated to be left out of anything, had muscled his way into the conversation. 'England is the most powerful country in the world, with the biggest empire. Nobody will dare to attack England!'

Mlle Lacroix had smiled at him. 'France has her empire too, Monsieur Roderick. She has a long a glorious history. Think of *Le Roi Soleil*; think of Napoleon!'

'Napoleon was the biggest scoundrel who ever lived.' Roderick had dismissed France's long and glorious history with a casual curl of his lip.

Sat on the back seat of the motor holding onto her hat, Dorothea wondered if Roderick ever tried to imagine what a dead soldier looked like. She didn't believe that he did. Nor would he ever feel as she'd felt, that the glittering surface was being scratched away.

She shuddered. Someone had *walked over her grave,* as Nora would say. But then she glanced at the parcel next to her on the seat and she felt a glow of achievement, for at last she was going to right the wrong she'd done to Roderick last summer when she'd trampled on his toy soldiers. In the parcel was a set of brand new toy soldiers which she would give to him on his birthday next week. She'd been able to afford toy soldiers of the highest quality because luck had lately smiled on her and she'd been presented with a whole half-sovereign — and all because of Richard. But that was another story. All that mattered for now was that the trip to Lawham had not been without benefit despite the damage to her bicycle.

'Just a puncture, nothing to worry about,' Uncle Albert had said. 'I'll mend it in a jiffy when we get back.'

'Bernadette gets punctures too,' Henry had consoled her. 'I'm forever having to change her wheels.'

'Yet another drawback to those machines of yours,' Uncle Albert had said with a glint in his eye. It was this remark which had begun the conversation that was still in progress as Henry's motor bumped and jolted over the ruts in the Newbolt Road.

'I'll say this much, young Fitzwilliam — you make a good advocate for these horseless carriages or whatever you like to call them. Puts me in mind of a chap I met on the train the other day. He was all for these new-fangled things, too. Talked a lot of sense, as it happens. He's designed some new type or model but he can't get any backing for it. I've got his name and address here somewhere, just in case.'

'Just in case of what?' Henry gave Uncle Albert a wary glance. 'I don't want to speak out of turn, sir, and I'm all for motors as you know, but there are a lot of charlatans out there who see the motor craze as a way of making easy money.'

'I think I'd back myself to spot a charlatan, don't you?'

'Well, yes, now that you mention it, I would, sir. But why this sudden interest — if you don't mind me asking? I thought you had no time for motors.'

'I like to keep an open mind, Fitzwilliam. Move with the times. That's how I got into bicycles. I might still be making watches otherwise. Flogging a dead horse. Now these machines of yours — they might be just a fad, then again they might not. Same was said about bicycles in the beginning and look how they've taken off! All the same, they're not selling quite so well as they used to. It never hurts to look around for new ideas. I've seen some motorised bicycles at the Cycle Show in recent times. That's one avenue. Then there are these machines of yours, these autocars. But there doesn't seem to be much money in the motor trade. Companies are forever going out of business.'

'A lot of them aren't really companies at all, sir. They're just fancy catalogues and grandiose schemes which come to nothing. But even the ones that do get off the ground often struggle. They're run by engineers, you see, when a man with a head for business is what's required. You'd have no trouble making a motor company pay, sir.'

Uncle Albert laughed. 'I daresay. I daresay. But let's not get ahead of ourselves. *Look before you leap*, that's my motto.'

His words were cautious but Dorothea could tell that her uncle's interest had been aroused. She wondered with a leap of excitement if Uncle Albert would go so far as to buy an autocar of his own. She had a great interest in autocars. Henry's enthusiasm had rubbed off on her. It rubbed off on most people eventually — except the die-hards like Colonel Harding. Uncle Albert wasn't a stick-in-the-mud of that sort. He was careful, yes. Prudent, yes. But once he got the bit between the teeth, there was no knowing what might happen . . .

'There's Windmill Hill,' cried Henry, pointing ahead as Bernadette negotiated a humpbacked bridge over the canal. 'My home — Hayton Grange — is at the foot of the hill.'

Dorothea sat up, eager to see where Henry lived, but the house was invisible: tucked away in a fold of land, perhaps, or hidden by the clump of trees that Henry called Grange Holt. The hill, on the other hand, was plain to see, round and green, steep sides rising to a flattened crown. The white sails of the mill were etched against the cloudless sky.

On the other side of the road, to the left, fields sloped gently down to the shallow valley where the canal meandered, mostly out of sight. In the distance ahead, a thin grey line of smoke spiralled up into the blue.

Dorothea watched Windmill Hill slide away behind them. Bernadette coughed and chugged as they climbed a slight incline. The outlying buildings of the village came into view — *her* village, as she thought of it, Hayton. The squat tower of St Adeline's was now in sight. But rising higher than the church, billowing into the late afternoon sky, the spiral of smoke was growing rapidly to a grey-black column which was being flattened out high above into a canopy like a great grasping claw.

For some reason, the smoke struck fear into her. 'Uncle? What is it?'

'I'm not sure, child. A chimney fire, maybe.'

But he did not sound convinced and even Dorothea could see that there was far too much smoke for that.

Bernadette nosed into the village. Dorothea had never approached it from this direction before but she soon got her bearings. There was the school and the smithy and the post office, all grouped round the duck pond and the Jubilee Oak. Three roads met at this point: the road from Newbolt along which they had just come; Back Lane to the left; and School Street straight on. In School Street she could see a crowd of people milling around — women, children, the elderly (most of the men would still be at work at this time of day) — all pointing, gesticulating, calling to each other. Smoke was billowing over the rooftops, casting a shadow over the village, bringing more people at a run from near and far.

Henry reached for the break lever and brought the motor to a stop outside Brittens' Bakery. (Nora's mother often took her Sunday joint to be roasted at the bakery. The Brittens, in some complicated way, were relatives of the Turners. Dorothea knew all this and more from Nora.)

'What's happening? Where are we?' asked a sleepy voice. Richard had woken at last and sensed that something was amiss.

'Just a little blaze, I think, nothing to worry about,' said Uncle Albert. 'All the same, I'll have a quick word, see if there's anything I can do. If you'll take the children home, Fitzwilliam?'

'Of course, sir. Then I'll come straight back.'

'Good lad, good lad. Well, off you go.'

Uncle Albert swung out of his seat, jumped down from the motor, went striding up the street. Fearless, thought Dorothea, but sensible, too. He would set things to rights.

Inspired by a feeling she could not quite put her finger on, Dorothea found herself scrambling out of the motor and making a leap for the ground even as Henry was manoeuvring to turn round. She stumbled, regained her balance, hesitated. Would Uncle Albert be angry if she followed him? And what about Nibs Carter? *You'd better not come round here again, or it'll be the worst for you!* Did his threat still hold after nearly a year? But this was the village — *her* village — and what harm could come to her with Uncle Albert at hand?

Standing tall, shrugging off the protests of Henry and Richard, she marched up the street. There were allotments on her right; on the left was a row of tiny sandstone cottages. Ahead of her, a knot of people had gathered in the middle of the street round the tall and imposing figure of Uncle Albert. Dorothea joined the edge of the group, hanging back lest her uncle see her. A beady-eyed old man was talking. Dorothea recognised him as Noah Lee, Nora's grandfather, whom she'd seen last year at the wedding. She remembered that she had not liked the way he stared at her.

'It's one of the hayricks, Master Brannan, in Wilmot's yard. That's where it started. And with this breeze fanning it, it's spread to the stables. Most of the horses are in the fields, but there's two that are lame — they're trying to get them out. They'll need to hurry. The fire will take hold in no time, in this wind.'

Dorothea knew that Wilmot's was a small farmhouse right in the centre of the village. People were pointing to a narrow entry, a gap in the row of little cottages, and she guessed that the farmhouse must be down there, set back from the street. Circling the group of people — who were all talking loudly now, eager to have their say — Dorothea moved to a position where she could look into the entry. She saw the farmyard beyond with a curtain of flame which must be the remains of the hayrick. To the right, wooden stables were smouldering; some of the timbers were actually glowing. Figures were darting back and forth across the yard, silhouetted against the blaze.

As she watched, a great cart horse suddenly appeared in the entry. A man in shirt sleeves was leading it by the mane, talking to it softly; but the horse's eyes were rolling and it was snorting and stamping its feet, foaming. People backed away as it came cavorting into the street but Uncle Albert stood his ground, nodding encouragement to the man leading it.

Noah Lee had stayed put, too. 'The farmhouse is out of harm's way, I should say, master. The wind's in the other direction. It's these cottage on the right that will be next, once the stables go up.'

'Water,' said Uncle Albert: 'we need water.'

'Here comes the fire engine now, master.'

Dorothea looked up the street, saw a burly man in a leather apron pushing along a box on wheels, helped by a younger man. A hose trailed away behind them. Dorothea recognised the burly man as the blacksmith, he came on occasion to the stables up at Clifton to shoe the horses. The other man was Young, his apprentice — the one who, according to Henry, was more interested in motors than horses.

As the cart horse was led away, the fire engine drew near. Uncle Albert strode forward, clearing a path for it, his booming voice rising above the tumult, taking charge. Order was quickly imposed on the chaos. The fire engine was set to work, Young busy with the pumping handle while the blacksmith took hold of the hose. Uncle Albert told him to direct the flow of water towards the stables. The hayrick, he said, was beyond saving now.

Next Uncle Albert gathered some of the villagers and sent them round to the back of the cottages where there were many ramshackle sheds and huts leaning one against the other and also against the stable wall, making a handy path for the fire. An effort was begun to try and demolish them. Out in the street, meanwhile, Dorothea found there was work even for her. She joined a long line of women and children passing buckets, basins and cans from hand to hand, bringing water up from the duck pond. It was precious little to set against the raging fire but Dorothea realised that the feverish activity served a second purpose. It gave everyone something to do. There were no longer people milling uselessly in the street. Panic was being kept at bay.

The village was now under a pall, the very air thick and brown. The wind seemed to be strengthening. In the heat of the day, the gentle breeze had been welcome as they ate their picnic amongst the ruins of Lawham priory; here in the village it seemed entirely sinister, driving the flames before it, scattering sparks, whipping up the last bits of glowing hay from the rick. A fiery rain began to float down into the street and beyond.

Busy passing buckets along, Dorothea suddenly felt a heavy hand on her shoulder. She turned to find Uncle Albert there. She quailed, felt sure he would be angry that she had disobeyed him but he merely drew her out of the line and pointed to the flying sparks. Could she organise some of the youngsters, get them to chase the sparks and stamp them out? Could she do that?

She nodded vigorously and when he said, 'Good girl!' and patted her on the head, she felt herself grow in stature. Uncle Albert had singled her out, was relying on her. She mustn't let him down.

It seemed to her only a few minutes later when she paused to catch her breath. She was tired, hot and sweaty, and she had a raging thirst. Her frock was streaked with dirt and ash; her new hat with the yellow ribbons (how proud of it she'd been that morning!) was limp and heavy on her head. She took the hat off, hung it on a fence post by the allotments. Mopping her brow, she looked round. A grey gloom had descended. Dusk was at hand, she realised; but she had lost all sense of time, could not say if one hour had passed or many since they had driven into the village in Henry's motor.

The hayrick was now a smouldering ruin but the stables were burning fiercely. Sheaves of red and orange flame were leaping high, bright in the twilight. The wind was gusting strongly, blowing the flames almost horizontal at times. They licked greedily at the thatched roofs of the cottages. The cottages themselves were being hurriedly evacuated, people scurrying in and out with items of furniture, pots and pans, rugs and carpets. As she watched, to her surprise she saw Nibs Carter emerge from the middle of the three cottages on the right of the farm entry, staggering under the weight of a battered old chest. He was pale, dark rings round his eyes. Not fierce or threatening now, just a scrawny, rather frightened boy. Two wailing toddlers trailed after him, grabbing at his legs and getting under his feet.

Dorothea didn't stop to think. She ran to help, taking the hands of the two little children and drawing them to one side. If Nibs recognised her in all the confusion he made no sign, merely threw the chest down in the street then dashed back inside the cottage. Kneeling, Dorothea tried to comfort the squalling children but she kept half an eye on the cottage door. Smoke was pouring out of the upper windows; wisps of smoke curled out from the doorway. When Nibs reappeared at last with a heap of crockery in his arms, Dorothea found that she had been holding her breath the whole time. It was hard to believe that she was so concerned for Nibs's safety — Nibs, of all people! But everything was topsy-turvy, and there was no time to reason things out.

'Miss! Oh, miss!' A woman appeared from nowhere and grabbed her arm. 'Pardon me, miss, but look!'

After a second, Dorothea recognised the woman as Pippa Turner, Nora's sister-in-law. A year ago she had been pink-cheeked and smiling as she walked down the church path in the frock that Nora had said was old-fashioned. Today she looked whey-faced, was dressed plainly, an old shawl thrown over her shoulders. She was twisting the ends of it in her fist as she pointed through the dusk towards the cottages.

'It's Mother Franklin, miss. She won't come out of her cottage. I've begged her but she won't.'

The cottage that Pippa Turner was pointing at was next door to Nibs's. Great flames like gluttonous tongues were flicking over the roof. The thatch was smouldering. Smoke was gushing from under the eaves and out of the upstairs windows. The front door, however, was shut. Dorothea saw a glimmer of movement in the downstairs window. An old wrinkled face appeared briefly, looked out; then it was gone.

Something stirred in Dorothea's memory. It had been two and a half years ago, the day of her abortive escape. As she had passed the Green, an old woman had come out of the shop and stared at her, making her feel ill at ease. This was the very same woman: Mother Franklin, as Pippa called her.

'I'm sorry, miss, for being so familiar and all,' said Pippa, 'but I do feel in a way that I know you. Nora talks so much about you. But, oh, miss! I don't know what to do! Mother Franklin says she'd rather burn than lose all her bits and pieces. Someone ought to help her, someone really ought to.'

But there was no one at hand. Everyone was busy. Even as Pippa was speaking, flames began to shoot up from the thatched roofs of the cottages. Pippa caught her breath, ran stumbling to Mother Franklin's door, began banging desperately, calling for the old lady to come out before it was too late.

Dorothea looked down at the two little children whose hands she was holding — Nibs's brother and sister, she presumed. Summoning a smile from somewhere, she quickly told them to be good, to stay where they were, to guard the pile of belongings that Nibs had brought out from their cottage. The children nodded solemnly, pouting.

Dorothea ran to join Pippa. But as she came to the door of the cottage she found Pippa being dragged away by a man who had loomed up out of the murk.

'What in heaven's name do you think you're doing, Pippa? Come away! Come away at once!'

It was Jem Turner, Nora's brother — Pippa's husband — his plain round face grim and sweaty and streaked with dust.

'Oh, Jem, it's Mother Franklin—'

'Never mind Mother Franklin! What are you doing here, Pippa? You should be at home! Have you no thought for the baby?'

Pippa's hands strayed down to her belly which was, Dorothea now realised, rather distended. It explained Pippa's rather wobbling gait. It explained, too, why Jem was so cross. Dorothea had completely forgotten that Pippa was expecting — even though Nora had been full of it for months.

'Just come away, Pippa! Come away, for Christ's sake!'

'But Jem—'

Jem brooked no argument, steering his wife away from the cottage with a brawny arm. As she was led away, Pippa looked round and caught Dorothea's eye.

'Please, miss! Don't forget Mother Franklin! Please!'

'Don't worry! I'll help her, I promise!'

But what could she do, a girl on her own? She trembled, looking round in desperation. The place was swarming now, as busy as Stepnall Street on a Saturday night. The men were back from work and people had come flocking from miles around, or so it seemed. But still there were not enough hands to do everything that needed to be done. She watched, wide-eyed, as a group of men — Uncle Albert amongst them — came staggering out form the entry to the farmyard, coughing and spluttering, faces blackened with soot. They had at last abandoned their attempts to demolish the sheds and huts. Meanwhile, the fire swept remorselessly on. Even as Dorothea stood in an agony of indecision, there was a terrible sound of rending and splintering, and a huge explosion of sparks. Giant flames shot up into the evening sky. The stables had collapsed. And now the cottages were burning. They would be the next to succumb, there could be no doubt about that anymore.

Dorothea gritted her teeth. It would take far too long to fetch help, to find someone and explain what was needed. She had only herself to rely on.

She began banging on the door, kicking and punching it. It seemed to be barricaded from inside. She couldn't move it. Heaving and shoving, sobbing with the effort, she was beginning to despair when Nibs Carter suddenly erupted out of the next doorway followed by a tail of smoke. He had two Windsor chairs in his hands, another balanced upside down on his head. He threw them into the street, turned to go back — then saw her.

'Miss, what you doing? It's not safe!' He tried to push her away from the cottages but a fit of coughing seized him.

Dorothea grabbed hold of his grubby hand. 'It's Mother Franklin! She won't leave her cottage without her things. There's no one to help and I can't get in!'

Without another word, Nibs squared his shoulder, preparing to ram the door, but at that moment it finally opened. Old Mother Franklin stood there, dithering in the hall, her toothless gums chewing. But no matter how they pleaded, she wouldn't come out. 'Not without me bits and pieces,' she said.

'Alright, Mother!' said Nibs grimly. 'If that's what yer want, I'll get yer things, don't you fret. You go with Miss Dorothea and let me get in.'

The wizened old woman, grumbling under her breath, allowed herself to be led hobbling into the street. Soon she was settled in her own battered old arm chair which Dorothea helped Nibs to carry out of the cottage. Back they went into the gloom and the drifting smoke, Dorothea laying hold of anything that came to hand. Gradually, Mother Franklin's meagre belongings began to pile up around her. She sat there, licking her gums, watching the leaping flames slowly devouring her home.

Dorothea was choking, fighting for breath. The cottage was full of smoke. She had to feel her way towards the exit. Nibs caught her by the elbow on the doorstep. 'Don't go back after this, miss.'

'But Nibs—'

'There's not much more to fetch. One more trip and I'll—'

He ducked inside, disappeared.

Dorothea felt giddy as she tottered into the street. Her legs gave way. She sank down onto the battered chest that Nibs had rescued form his own cottage earlier. Her eyes swam. Everything looked hazy, distant, blurred. The smoke seemed to have gotten inside her head so that she couldn't put her thoughts in order. The hurly-burly all around her made her head spin.

It was fully dark now. The flames were horribly bright, dancing along the cottage roofs. Sparks twirled and twisted in the gusting wind. On the opposite side of the street, the butcher's was all in darkness, but next door the gates of the carpenter's yard were open and men were busy moving piles of wood and throwing water on the shavings and chippings that littered the ground. Where in all this mayhem was Uncle Albert? And Henry, had he come back as he'd promised? If either of them had ordered her home now, she would have gone without a murmur. There was nothing more she could do — nothing anyone could do. The fire raged on and on. The whole village would be burned — her lovely village. It would be destroyed before she'd had a chance to get to know it.

There was a loud crunching and cracking. She looked round in time to see the roof of Mother Franklin's cottage give way with a thunderous roar and a storm of flames. Sparks exploded into the night sky.

Dorothea jumped up in horror. '*Nibs . . .*!'

But there he was in the doorway, hugging to his chest an old pillow and some ragged sheets, his other hand hanging loose, the skin raw with burns.

Dorothea ran to help. 'Nibs, your hand!'

'I w-went up-upstairs,' he spluttered. 'The ceiling was coming down. A piece of it fell on my hand. I . . . I swallowed a lot of smoke.'

He fell to his knees, swayed, his face pinched and pale, eyes rolling. Dorothea helped him up, half-carried him, leading him away from the burning cottage. She settled him on the chest where she'd been sitting a moment before. He sagged, eyelids drooping, coughing feebly. Dorothea gathered herself. One last effort — and for her enemy Nibs! But who would have guessed he was so brave?

Finding water, she made him drink, then she ripped a strip from the hem of her petticoat (goodness only knew what Nanny would say) and bound up Nibs's burnt hand with it. He seemed all but oblivious.

She had just finished tying the makeshift bandage when a familiar voice exclaimed, 'Miss Dorothea! So this is where you've got to!'

'Oh, Nora! Thank goodness!' Dorothea had never been so glad to see anyone. Help was here at last. Nora would soothe, cure, reassure, protect — just as she always did.

'I didn't know what to think, miss, when you didn't come back for tea, and then I heard that the village was all ablaze and I could see the smoke for myself. I couldn't stay up at the big house, I don't care what Mrs Bourne says or anyone—'

There was nothing soothing about Nora just now. Her face was creased with worry.

'I've just seen our Jem. He told me he'd sent Pippa home but when I went down their cottage she wasn't there and she's not up at ours either and I can't find her anywhere. Oh, miss, what about the baby! What if something's happened?'

Dorothea's heart shrank within her. Here was another emergency when it was all she could manage to stay on her feet. She felt that she could have lain in the road and gone to sleep right there and then. Why was Nora so concerned for Pippa, when she'd always said that Pippa wasn't right for Jem and had no idea about anything?

Dorothea rubbed her eyes. It must be the smoke in her head, making her so ill-tempered. Now was not the time to fall short, not when Nora needed her, Pippa too — Pippa, who'd shown such concern for Mother Franklin.

With a great effort, Dorothea got to her feet.

'I knew I could rely on you, Miss Dorothea! Now, if you go round by the Green, I'll go the other way, and we'll . . .'

Nora's words were lost in the hustle and bustle of the street as she sped away. Dorothea hesitated a moment, loathe to leave Nibs in the state he was in, not to mention poor Mother Franklin with the tears rolling down her cheeks. There were only the children to fall back on, Nibs's little brother and sister. She impressed on them that they must look after their brother and the old lady. We will, they said. She was not sure they really understood, but it was the best she could do.

She set off, hurrying up School Street, following the fire engine's hose pipe towards the village green where it disappeared down the well. Deep night closed round her. Pausing to look back, she saw the fire as a lurid orange stain in the sky.

'Pippa! Pippa!'

She stumbled onwards, calling repeatedly. There was no reply. The village was still and silent, for all the world as if it was deserted. Even the wind had dropped now. Not a leaf stirred.

'Pippa!'

She went along the High Street as far as Tumbledown Cottage where the houses came to an end. Turning left, she hurried down Back Lane. She had never been this way before, but — dazed as she was — she still felt a burning curiosity to see where Nora lived. The Turners' cottage, she knew, was first on the left. It was smaller than she'd imagined, what she could see of it in the gloom, squat and lifeless, the windows blank. And the garden — full of wonderful flowers, Nora said, all the colours of the rainbow — looked grey and desolate in the moonless dark. An unexpected feeling of disappointment swept over her; the whole world seemed dreary and diminished just now. The empty night was all around her, and she was alone. She longed for the safety and comfort of the nursery. That was her place, if anywhere was. She did not belong here in the village. Nibs had been right.

She shook herself. This was no time for moping. Trying to decide what to do next, she guessed that Nora would be coming up Back Lane from the other direction, so there would be no point in going that way herself. Wasn't there a footpath to the left of the Turners' cottage? It ran across a meadow. Seed Meadow, Nora called it, where she had played as a little girl: 'The grass was taller than me, miss . . .'

With a little searching, Dorothea found a gap in the hedge. There was the path, like a thin dark ribbon across the grey meadow. She began walking. The sound of her skirts brushing through the grass was like a sinister hissing voice. All else was quiet, except for the thumping of her heart. She pressed on, not calling out now — she wouldn't have dared, in that dark silence — but stopping every so often to listen. All was still. The air was heavy and breathless.

Half way across the meadow a feeling of fear seized her. She forced it back. It was not as if she was lost — not really. She knew these places so well from listening to Nora's talk that it was as if she had lived here all her life. Just ahead now was a hedgerow and beyond it a patch of tangled trees and shrubs known as the Wilderness. She could just make it out in the gloom — but it looked very dark in there. Did she dare to go in?

Her steps slowed, stopped. She could see above the leaf-laden boughs of the trees an orange glow in the sky, the fire raging on and on like a ravenous beast. Very faintly she could hear the din coming from School Street.

Without warning, something or someone touched her nose. She jumped a foot in the air but was too terrified even to scream. Her chest heaving, she reached up with one finger and felt the place on her nose where she'd been touched. Her finger came away wet. Water. How odd! Where could it have come from?

She looked up — and a second drop of water hit her right in the eye. It was followed by a third, a fourth . . . More and more drops were falling, faster and faster. She could hear them pattering on the grass all around.

It took her dazed brain some time to work out what was happening.

It was raining.

Rain! Her heart leapt. Now surely they stood a chance! The village might not burn after all! She wanted to get back as quickly as possible to see what was happening. The shortest way was straight on, the path through the Wilderness. She ran towards the hedgerow, Pippa for the moment forgotten.

The rain was falling harder and harder. It was torrenting down as she squeezed through a gap in the hedge. Leaves brushed against her face. Brambles snatched at her. For a moment she was trapped — then she was through. She plunged into the Wilderness.

The darkness was as thick as cobwebs. The wind had come back, too, and was gusting in the tree tops. Rain hammered. Dorothea moved forward, one step, then another, eyes searching the blackness. Suddenly, in the distance, a clap of thunder rolled across the sky. Nearer at hand, and mixed with the sound of the thunder, came a blood-curdling scream. Dorothea stopped dead, frozen in terror.

The thunder died away. The scream too was cut off. Dorothea breathed again, listening to the wind and the rain and the rustling leaves.

Then the scream came again. Not the evil howl of some terrible lurking monster, she realised. It sounded more like a desperate cry of pain and fear. If there was somebody nearby who needed help, she couldn't just run away and leave them.

'Hello? Is there somebody there?' She didn't allow herself time to ask if her courage was up to the task, but all the same her voice sounded terribly thin and feeble, and was quickly swallowed up by the dark. She listened.

A faint reply, away to her left. 'Help! Please help me!'

It was no monster or ghost. It wasn't even a stranger. It was a voice she recognised. In a rush she remembered her quest and realised she had completed it. She had found Pippa Turner.

She felt her way in the dark, inching towards the place where Pippa's voice had come from. Every so often, a single rain drop, working its way through the tangled canopy above, landed on her with a splat.

After a time, the darkness drew aside a little. She had come to a clearing. On the far side, splayed on the ground between the roots of an old, gnarled tree, was the washed-out figure of a woman, glimmering like a ghost.

'Who is it? Who's there?' Pippa's voice was thin and brittle. 'Oh miss! Oh miss, it's you! Thank goodness! I thought no one would ever come! I tripped in the dark — tripped over these old roots. I've hurt my ankle. I can't walk on it. I should never have come this way, but I got frightened waiting at home and when I couldn't find Jem or— Oh miss! Miss!'

'What is it, Pippa? What's wrong?'

'It's the baby, miss. The baby's coming.'

Dorothea backed away. 'I'll . . . I'll fetch someone. Nora. Jem.'

'Please don't go, miss! Please don't leave me on my own again! I couldn't bear it!' Pippa stretched out a hand and Dorothea let herself be drawn closer, kneeling as Pippa reached up to grip her arm. 'It's too late, anyhow, miss. I think . . . I think . . . oh miss, it hurts! It hurts! It's — oh, ah, oh . . .'

Pippa's voice swooped up into the same howl of pain that had curdled Dorothea's blood in the dark just now. Up close, the sound made her dizzy and she swayed on her knees. She'd felt like this before, long ago. She'd felt faint and dizzy, walking the streets with her papa, walking with an empty tummy in the cold and the dark.

The memory was so unexpected and yet so vivid that it was like a dose of salts. The mist in her head cleared. Her eyes focused on Pippa writhing between the tree roots. Pippa's skirt had rucked up, one leg was stretched out, the swollen ankle clearly visible inside her stockings. Her screams faded, subsided to a low moan. Her eyes fluttered and closed. She looked done in, as if she had run out of energy and was now fading away — as if, thought Dorothea with a sudden chill of fear — as if the baby inside was slowly killing her, just as Dorothea's own mother had been killed all those years ago. Bessie Downs, who never shied away from anything, had once explained exactly what it meant to die in childbirth. Dorothea, knowing that you had to take Bessie Downs with a pinch of salt, had not believed the half of it. Out here in the Wilderness — with Pippa's groans fading to nothing, Pippa's grip on her arm loosening, Pippa's hand slipping to the ground — out here it seemed to Dorothea that Bessie Downs had not been half macabre enough.

Dorothea knew about babies. In Stepnall Street it had been impossible not to know. There were no nurseries and no nannies standing guard in Stepnall Street. The grown-ups didn't watch their words when the children were around; they hardly noticed if children were there at all. It seemed sensible, therefore — wise as she was — to loosen some of Pippa's clothes. With shaking hands, Dorothea groped and fumbled, pushing up Pippa's skirt, pulling down her drawers. All the time the deluge continued, more and more drips sliding off the leaves as the wind tossed the branches. Far off, thunder growled like an angry giant.

When she got a peek of the baby's head, half in and half out, the shock nearly bowled her over. She gripped Pippa's hand. 'It's here, Pippa! It's here! I can see it!'

Pippa stirred, mumbling; but she wasn't making any sense, and she didn't squeeze Dorothea's hand in return.

Without warning, and in a way which turned Dorothea's stomach, the baby came slithering and squelching out onto last year's leaves, a scrap of flesh, just skin and bone, sticky, slimy, messy. Pippa groaned then was silent. The baby was silent too, half dead by the look of it — perhaps completely dead. Dorothea wished she could feel sorry for it but she couldn't. She couldn't feel anything. The darkness seemed to be closing in on her — washing over her, blotting everything out, the wind, the rain, the baby, Pippa, everything. She felt as if she was falling — or was it that she was floating, floating away . . . ?

As if in a dream, she suddenly heard voices all round her, saw a swinging lantern. Women were giving orders, speaking soothingly to Pippa, questioning each other anxiously. And then came a most peculiar noise: a sort of grizzling and whining rising rapidly to a high, angry wail. How odd, thought Dorothea vaguely, it sounded almost like a baby . . .

But of course! It *was* a baby! It was Pippa's baby! Was it alive after all? And Pippa?

Dorothea tried to scramble to her feet but couldn't quite manage it. She swayed, felt herself falling again, but before that could happen, a strong arm encircled her waist, a big jacket was thrown round her shoulders.

'Don't worry, Dorothea. I've got you. You're quite safe now.'

It was Henry. Henry had come. He was beside her, holding her. He had come to her rescue again.

She was only half aware of walking through the pouring rain back to School Street (she wouldn't let him carry her, she still had enough about her to remember the prestige and responsibility of being eleven). Uncle Albert was waiting in Bernadette, red-faced and wheezing, holding the umbrella that Nora had packed with the picnic that morning, 'just in case'. Only that morning!

'Home, I think, Fitzwilliam,' said Uncle Albert once Dorothea was safely aboard.

'Right away, sir.'

Henry, in sodden shirt sleeves, hatless, his hair plastered on his head, started the engine. As they drove away, Dorothea had a confused impression of the gaunt, roofless shells of the cottages looming up in the dark, of people laden with goods and chattels trudging through burnt straw and puddles of water, of low murmuring voices and the sobbing of children. Then the village fell away and they were whirling through the night. It felt like flying on the back of an eagle.

It was only when Bernadette had come to a stop and the big house was suddenly there, waiting, lights in all the windows and the front door wide open; it was only as Dorothea was being helped out of the motor and went stumbling up the steps; it was only then that she remembered she had forgotten to pick up her hat.

CHAPTER SIX

Dorothea woke up coughing.

Once the fit had passed, she lay back, exhausted. Her room was calm and peaceful after the dreams of flames and darkness from which she had just surfaced.

After a while, she got out of bed, crossed to the window, pulled back the curtains, opened the sash. She breathed in, tentative. The air was cool and fresh with no smell of burning, no hint of soot. She breathed in more deeply. She didn't know what the time was, but it had to be very early. The morning was bright and golden, the sky a deep, clean blue. A thin white mist lay on the fields. Spider's webs glistened like strands of silver.

Resting her elbows on the sill, she listened to the distant church bell striking the half-hour and, remote, the *chuff-chuff* of a locomotive, hardly more than a ripple in the air. The sound of crunching gravel was loud in comparison. Down below, the governess came walking out from the stable yard. She must have let herself out of the side door and was crossing now to the entrance in the red-brick wall that led to the gardens. She was hatless, with her hair up. Her hips swayed. Her skirt trailed. Serene, solitary, she passed out of sight.

Dorothea took a last breath, then drew back, shutting the window quietly. The dregs of her fiery dreams had been tipped away and she got back into bed, pulled the covers up, and slipped into peaceful sleep.

* * *

A most unexpected visitor arrived just before luncheon.

'I've brought your hat, miss, which you left behind, seemingly.'

Nibs Carter hesitated before taking a step forward. He placed the hat on the nursery table. Her poor hat! She had been so proud of it yesterday when getting ready for the Great Expedition. Now it was a sorry looking thing, smudged with soot, stained by the rain, ruined. Nibs too looked different: smaller, somehow, even more scrawny than usual. He cradled his bandaged hand. His clothes hung off him like rags. He was not cocksure today: Dorothea wondered that she'd ever been afraid of him.

Nora had been full of news that morning. The fire had been terrible, the worst disaster ever to be visited on the village but — mercifully — no one had been seriously hurt. Pippa and her newborn son were both doing well. Mother Franklin — together with her 'bits and pieces' — had been taken in by her married daughter who had room to spare down Back Lane now so many of her children had left home. The Carters, Nora had added with a sorry shake of her head, had not been so lucky. Their little cottage had been gutted and they had been split up, taking refuge where they could round the village.

'What will you all do now?' Dorothea asked Nibs.

'I don't know, miss. Our Arnie says we'll end up in the workhouse but he always looks on the black side, our Arnie.'

Poor Nibs! He looked so trampled down — so much so, that she almost regretted that the old Nibs had gone, nasty though he'd been. But who was the *real* Nibs Carter? She didn't even know his proper name.

'My name's Robin, miss. But I hate Robin. I'd sooner be called Nibs — even if it is a joke at my expense. It's what me dad used to call me — *his nibs* — on account of my getting above myself when I was a kid.'

The dad who was dead, thought Dorothea, trying to remember everything that she had learned from Nora about the Carters. Their mother was dead too, and now their home was gone. The fire had left behind such a wretched muddle, as tawdry as her hat.

'Don't you worry about us, miss,' said Nibs, scowling at her as if he could read her mind. 'We'll be alright. But I just wanted to . . . well, to thank you for all you did, and for helping out and that, and for binding my hand. It was . . . was good of you.'

'You're very welcome—' Dorothea began fervently, but she had barely got the first words out before Nibs had gone.

A moment later Roderick came nosing into the day room, suspicious. 'Who was here? I heard voices.'

'No one,' said Dorothea. And it felt almost like the truth, for Nibs had looked — and sounded — like a ghost of his former self. Or had there been, perhaps, a hint, a spark, something of his old touchiness? It seemed almost appealing now.

'You're lying,' Roderick accused her. 'It wasn't no one. It was Nibs Carter. I'd know his stupid voice anywhere. What do you want with Nibs Carter?'

'Nothing. It's none of your business.'

'You shouldn't talk to him. He's a rat.'

'Why don't you leave him alone? What's he ever done to you?'

'What's he done? I'll tell you what he's done! He spooked my pony, for a start, so that I fell off and cracked my head open. And then, after I'd caught him by the canal and knocked him down for the swine that he is, he got his ratty friends together and they ambushed me in the Spinney and beat me black and blue. So after that I—'

'You're as bad as each other!' cried Dorothea. 'You want your heads knocking together!'

'Well, I like that! *Me*, as bad as Nibs Carter! Of all the cheek! You've changed your tune, I must say. You used to say he was—'

'Oh, stop it, Roddy, just stop it!' She couldn't explain why her feelings had changed towards Nibs — why her feelings had changed altogether since yesterday; nor would Roderick have listened if she tried. 'You're *worse* than Nibs, Roderick Brannan, because you ought to know better, only you don't!'

She ran out of the day room and into her own room, slamming the door. As she threw herself onto the bed she found she was sobbing. All of the peace she had discovered earlier that morning was gone. All the horrors of her dreams were back. But it was even worse, because her dreams weren't as bad as the real thing, the raging fire, the suffocating smoke — not to mention Pippa's unearthly screams as she writhed in agony in the dirt and the dark and the wet. There was the baby, too — that slimy little bundle. Dorothea felt sorry for it and repelled by it at the same time — the way it had been disgorged onto the rotting leaves as casually as one would empty the lees from a tea pot. A baby was nothing, tipped out into the world to live or die as chance decreed. And at any moment its parents might be snatched away or its house might burn down or it might be left — abandoned — at some stranger's home, unwanted, alone.

'Now then, miss: what's all this?' Nora was suddenly there, gathering her up, and Dorothea put her arms round her and sobbed into her pinafore, and never mind the responsibility and prestige of being eleven. 'There, there! Don't take on so! It can't be as bad as all that, surely? Master Roderick said as I should come and find you, he said you might be upset, but I never expected to find you in this state! Come on now. Dry your eyes. The doctor's here to see you — to look you over after yesterday. I'll just put the brush through your hair and straighten your frock, and then we'll let him in, shall we?'

Dorothea nodded glumly. Nothing seemed to matter just then, not even a visit from Dr Camborne. But as

Nora made her presentable before going to fetch the doctor, Dorothea suddenly thought of Nibs Carter coming all the way from the village to bring her hat. And fancy Roderick noticing that she was upset, let alone sending Nora to look for her! How strange, she thought. How odd. Could it be that Nora was right? Could it be that things weren't quite as black as she'd imagined?

* * *

Uncle Albert came to see her once the doctor had gone.

'Ah, here you are child. In bed, I see.'

'Dr Camborne said I should rest.'

'Quite right, quite right. He had the same prescription for me. We had quite an experience yesterday, didn't we, eh?' The mattress sagged as Uncle Albert sat down. 'I'm to stay home for a week, no work allowed. Lot of nonsense, if you ask me, but Ellie insists I do as I'm told. Anyone would think I was on my last legs! I was a bit short of breath, that's all! Ah well. You know what doctors are like. They know best. They *think* they know best.' He gave a snort, as if he didn't hold a high opinion of doctors. 'I'm sure I'll find lots to keep me occupied while I'm on leave. Thought I might write to that chap on the train, the one who's designed a new sort of autocar. Chaps like that — the go-getters — should be given every encouragement. It's good to have ambition. It was the making of me. Where'd I be now if I'd simply stuck with my father's watch-making business? When I took up bicycles they said I'd never make a go of it, said I was barking up the wrong tree. Proved them wrong there, didn't I, eh? It's all bicycles in Coventry now. Watches have gone by the board. But times change, and I like to change with them.' He glanced down at her, smoothing his moustache. 'You're very quiet today, child. That fire took the wind out of both our sails, eh? But you showed a lot of pluck, a lot of pluck. Take after your mother, I daresay. But tell me . . . what are you worrying about in that pretty little head of yours, eh, eh?'

Greatly daring, Dorothea reached out and took his hand as it lay on the coverlet. Her fingers seemed very small and thin compared to his but he squeezed her hand and smiled at her from behind his moustache, and she felt at that moment that she could tell him anything.

'Uncle . . . ?'

'Yes child? What is it?'

But there was too much in her head to tell him even half of it. All she could find words for was the fate of the Carters, who'd lost their home and were scattered across the village.

Uncle Albert didn't hum and haw as she might have expected. He didn't change the subject or say that the Carters ought to pull themselves up by their bootstraps. The fire had changed Uncle Albert too, it seemed.

'Don't go upsetting yourself, child. These things have a habit of working out for the best. You'll see.'

'But I *won't* see, Uncle, because I never go to the village, *never*, and I'd so like to! Nora said I can go to tea with her anytime, but Nanny says—'

'Oh, well, Nanny.' Uncle Albert snorted again as if he had a similar opinion of Nanny to that he had of doctors. 'Nanny is not your keeper, child. You go to the village if you want. I don't hold with all this mollycoddling and wrapping in cotton wool. I used to play in the street all the time when I was your age.' He stood up, stretched, caught sight of her hat as he did so. 'What's this? Not much good for anything now, is it, eh? We'll have to see about getting you a new one. Oh, and before I forget, you left this in Fitzwilliam's motor contraption yesterday.' He handed her a box, smiled, nodded — nodded as if, unlike Nanny and doctors, she was someone of whom he *did* approve.

When he'd gone she looked at the box he had given her and realised it was the toy soldiers she'd bought in Lawham yesterday. It seemed an age ago now. She thought of the money she'd spent on them and the money she had left and wished she could give it all to the Carters who needed it — who deserved it. But would Nibs have taken it if she'd offered? Or would he have turned up his nose and called it *charity*, the way some people did? She rather thought that he would have.

She sighed, remembering how she'd come by her riches, her half-sovereign. It had been entirely out of the blue. She'd been on her way back from her afternoon walk with the governess. An ancient man, wrinkled and bent over, had been descending the front steps shadowed by two tall attendants in splendid livery. The old man's watery eyes had fixed on her, he had beckoned her over.

'You must be the girl my grandson was speaking of.' He'd laid a wasted hand on her head, then clicked his fingers. One of the attendants had jumped to it, handing the old man a little bag. 'Here. A small token. On behalf of my grandson. For your kindness.' He had taken something from the bag, passed it to her.

She had only remembered her manners at the last moment, stammering a *thank you* as the old man was helped into his magnificent carriage. She had realised who he must be: Richard's grandfather — his mother's father, the earl whom Becket had told her about. To meet a real live earl had made her head swim. She could not have been more in awe if an angel had come down from heaven.

But Richard had not been in the best of moods when she rushed up to tell of her remarkable encounter. His grandfather's visit had made him peevish and irritable. 'All he ever talks about is the weather and if his horse will win the Derby. He cares more about horses than he does about people. He doesn't care about me at all. He only comes because he thinks he owns me, and he likes to inspect all his possessions.'

Sitting now in bed with the box of soldiers on her lap, Dorothea thought of the shiny half-sovereign the earl had given her and wished that she hadn't accepted it. *For your kindness*, he'd said. But she wasn't kind to Richard out of duty or in hope of some reward (unlike Nurse, according to Nanny). She was kind to Richard because she liked him — *loved* him.

Was Richard's grandfather really as bad as all that, liking horses better than people? Or was it just Richard being Richard? She did feel that the earl was not someone one could *love*, unlike Uncle Albert, for instance, who— Well, it seemed odd now that she had ever been afraid of him and that, as recently as three years ago, she hadn't even known he existed. She felt now as if she'd known him forever. To have him sit on her bed and hold her hand buoyed her up, as if nothing could touch her, as if no harm would ever come to her again. How glad she was to have an uncle like that!

* * *

'Are you ready, Miss Dorothea? It's time!'

'Coming, Nora. Coming.' Dorothea took one last look out of the window. She'd been watching Uncle Albert and Henry in their shirt sleeves tinkering with Bernadette on the gravel below. If, by ordering Uncle Albert to stay at home, Dr Camborne had expected his patient to rest, then he ought to have known better. Uncle Albert had been busy all week — not just in writing to the mysterious man on the train, but in repairing Dorothea's puncture, replacing the brake pads on Mlle Lacroix's bicycle, and embarking on a thorough overhaul of Roderick' rather battered machine. 'Don't know what the boy does to it. Look at the state it's in!' Today Henry had called to see how they all were after the drama of the fire and Uncle Albert had decided to examine Bernadette. Henry was beaming with pleasure, of course.

Dorothea very much wondered where her uncle's newfound interest in motors would take him.

'Miss Dorothea!'

'Ready, Nora! On my way!'

It was Nora's half day. She was off home. And — such excitement, such a treat! — Dorothea was to go with her, to take tea at the Turners'!

'Dad and Billy will be at work, of course,' said Nora, taking Dorothea's hand as they walked down the long drive, leaving the motor enthusiasts to their own devices. 'And our Daisy will likely be out in the fields helping to look after the youngsters. So it will be just you and me and Mother.'

But it did not turn out that way. When they reached the little cottage in Back Lane, old Noah Lee was there too, sitting at the gate-leg table with his white whiskers and beady eyes.

'Hello, Grandpa! This is a surprise! What are you doing here?'

'Come to see your mother, of course. Is there a law against it?'

Nora laughed. 'Come to inspect our guest, more like.'

'And why not? 'Tis not often someone from the big house comes calling.'

Dorothea was not at all sure that she wanted to be inspected by Noah Lee but she was determined that nothing would spoil her afternoon. The Turners' cottage was clean and tidy but rather small — small, that is, when compared to what Noah Lee called *the big house*. Next to the crowded rooms in the courts off Stepnall Street, the cottage was the lap of luxury. The gate-leg table was set by the front window. Geraniums grew in a pot on the sill. There were windsor chairs either side of the hearth and a wooden staircase leading to the upper rooms. There were two rooms upstairs, Dorothea knew — one for Mr and Mrs Turner, and one that Nora shared with her little sister Daisy. Nora's brother Billy mostly slept up at the big house, above the stables where he worked. 'I could have had a bed at Clifton, too, miss. I think Mrs Bourne would prefer it, to keep an eye on me. But I knew I'd miss home too much. Our Billy doesn't bother about things like that, he's a boy. Not that he isn't always in and out at home, and he still gives his wages to Mother.'

The back door of the cottage was open, giving a glimpse of the garden bathed in sunshine and of Seed Meadow beyond. It had been dark and terrifying on the night of the fire, now it was entirely green and peaceful.

Mrs Turner was all smiles, a plump woman with rosy cheeks and a clean apron. 'Now sit yourself down, miss. Tea will be ready in two shakes of a lamb's tail. I'm so glad you've come,' she continued, taking Dorothea's hat, nudging a stool towards her with her knee, setting the kettle to boil, laying the table. 'We wanted the chance to thank you for all you did on the night of the Great Fire.'

'It was her uncle who did all the work,' Noah Lee put in. 'I've never had much to do with Master Brannan afore. He's not from round these parts. But I speak as I find, and he stopped to help when he could easily have passed on by. That's what I call neighbourly. That's what I call being a good Samaritan. There's others I could mention who wouldn't so much as give you the drippings off their nose.'

'It wasn't all Mr Brannan,' said Mrs Turner, placing bowls of lettuce and radishes on the table, and a jar of homemade raspberry jam. 'Heaven knows what would have happened to our Jem's Pippa if Miss Dorothea hadn't been there! But all's well that ends well, and the baby's thriving now. They're going to call him Richard, miss, as you suggested. They liked the name. But I'm sure Nora's told you. You'll be coming to the christening, too, I hope?'

'I shall call the lad Dick, like Dick Turpin,' said Noah Lee, reaching for some bread and butter. 'My second great-grandson, he is. And I've three grandsons. But I never had a son of my own. Two daughters, I had, but no sons. Famous beauties they were, my daughters — though you wouldn't think it to look on her now.'

Mrs Turner laughed as she poured tea. 'I've no need of beauty at my time of life! Now, miss, here's your tea. And have some lettuce and a radish or two. It's all from our own garden.'

'Moll here is my younger daughter,' Noah Lee continued, biting into his bread. 'Meg was the elder. She's at peace now, God rest her. She married a Cardwell. Used to be a lot of Cardwells in the village at one time. Bred like rabbits, they did.'

'Grandpa, really! That's no way to talk in front of Miss Dorothea!'

'Get on with you. The girl's not stupid. Not stupid, are you? No. No. I thought not.' Noah Lee turned his back on Nora, addressed Dorothea. 'Now I never did take to them Cardwells. Thought themselves a cut above, they did. But they weren't, most on 'em. And they's all but extinct now. There's just my Meg's widower — he's the shopkeeper, if you know who I mean — and his son David: my grandson, that is to say. There's a few of the womenfolk left. The blacksmith's wife, she's a Cardwell, and the mistress at the Barley Mow, and them two old maids at the Post Office. And then there's that girl what lives with 'em. Mercy Bates, they call her. Came by the light of the moon, so they say. But she's a Cardwell or I'm a Dutchman. Her father was Ted Cardwell, like as not. A black sheep, was Ted Cardwell. Went off to Broadstone, if you can believe it, went and lived in Broadstone.'

He spoke of Broadstone as if it was the ends of the earth, but Dorothea remembered there'd been talk of cycling there one day so it couldn't be that far. Roderick, in fact, claimed to have cycled there already on more than one occasion, but what Roderick hadn't done wasn't worth knowing about.

'Now this Ted Cardwell,' said Noah Lee, tapping the table to get her attention. 'There's some right old stories I could tell you about him — things that would make you hair curl!'

'That's enough, Dad!' Mrs Turner interrupted. 'You'll talk poor Miss Dorothea to death. And why should she be interested in the Cardwells? She don't know them from Adam. Well, now, miss, will you have another cup of tea? And how about some more bread and jam?'

But Noah Lee wasn't to be silenced so easily, even if he did steer clear of Ted Cardwell. Dorothea didn't really mind. She liked hearing about the village and its inhabitants, although she soon got lost amongst all the different names. After a time, however, Noah Lee turned his attention to 'the goings-on up at the big house'. He hadn't been up there for a good while, he said: not since the days of that 'old villain' Mr

Rycroft. Could this *old villain*, Dorothea wondered, really be the same Mr Rycroft who Becket had told her about, the one who had been Aunt Eloise's father and had kept the gardens spic and span? *A proper gentleman*, Becket had called him. But he'd been by way of a tyrant, according to Noah Lee, putting the rents up, persecuting the poachers, 'and carrying on like he owned the place'.

'That's because he did own the place,' Mrs Turner put in. 'Or most of it, leastways.'

'Stole it, you mean. What about that there common land? Belonged to everybody, that did, but he just took it and cut it up into fields.'

'Get away with you, Dad! That weren't old Mr Rycroft! That happened long since!'

Noah Lee cast a sour look at his daughter. He obviously did not care to be contradicted. But Mrs Turner seemed immune to his ire, gathering up the plates and bowls, singing under her breath.

'You don't say much, do you?' Noah Lee poked Dorothea's arm. 'What's *your* news, then? What have you got to tell us? What about that boy up there at the big house, the cripple? Is he living still? They say he's the heir and all that, but I heard as he's kept locked up in the attic.'

Nora laughed. 'Where do you get such ideas, Grandpa? Master Richard isn't locked up anywhere. You ask Miss Dorothea if you don't believe me!'

All too soon it was time to go. Dorothea thanked Mrs Turner for having her, and Mrs Turner said she was most welcome and must come again any time.

'Don't take no notice of Grandpa,' Nora said as she led the way down the garden path and into the street. 'He likes the sound of his own voice, that's all. And he thinks he knows everything — as I'm sure you worked out for yourself.'

But Dorothea was, in a way, rather taken with Noah Lee, although she was still a little afraid of him. He treated her as if she was just anyone, made no allowances either for her age or because she came from the big house. She liked that.

Nora was pointing across the street. 'Look, miss, that's the cottage where the Carters are living now. They were lucky it was empty — though, of course, they wouldn't have been able to afford it before. It's all thanks to Mr Brannan that they can afford it now.'

This was something else Uncle Albert had been busy with over the last week. Not charity, he'd said, merely a helping hand. There was nothing wrong, he'd insisted, in helping those who wanted to help themselves. And so he had helped the Carters into their new home and taken Nibs on as gardeners' boy (help, at long last, for Becket), and one of Nibs's sisters was to work in the kitchens. As for Arnie Carter, the eldest brother, he had been given a position in Uncle Albert's bicycle factory. The only drawback was that Arnie would now have to spend most of his time in Coventry. This had come as a bitter blow to Nora. Though she now had the Carters living opposite, the one Carter she most wanted to see was the one least at home. Not, of course, that Nora would ever have admitted to having a soft spot for Arnie Carter.

Nora said her farewell on the Lawham Road and Dorothea walked the last lap on her own. She felt very grown-up, proud of herself too, as she turned up the driveway between the tall evergreens swaying in the breeze. Denizen of Clifton Park, habitué of the village, she had the whole world at her feet — all of the world that mattered, anyway.

* * *

Much was made of the ruined hat. Nibs had brought it all the way up from the village, Uncle Albert had promised a replacement, and now Henry was taking her to Lawham especially to choose the new one.

'Such a to-do,' said Dorothea, 'over a hat.'

Mlle Lacroix had smiled. 'The hat is of no consequence, *ma petite*. People wish to oblige you. Monsieur Henri wishes to oblige you. That is what is important, rather than the hat.'

Bernadette was swooping now bright and early along the Lawham Road. Gleaners were at work in the fields. The canal glittered like silver under the morning sun. Secret shadows nestled under the beech trees of Ingleby Wood. Watching the world swing by, Dorothea mulled over the governess's words and wondered why people should wish to *oblige* her. She could only think that everyone was much nicer than you have imagined. Roderick would pooh-pooh such an idea — but even he had *obliged* her after a fashion by making peace with Nibs. The two boys had shaken hands, albeit reluctantly. But she had brooked no argument. She had wanted it settled once and for all. It was important, now that Nibs was coming to work at Clifton.

'I will shake hands if I must,' Roderick had said sulkily, 'but you can't expect *everyone* to be friends *all* the time.'

But what did he know? Precious little, she felt. She wondered what on earth they taught him at that school of his. Nothing of consequence, obviously. Nothing about the significance of hats and all that hats stood for.

Henry was his usual garrulous self this morning. He was still cock-a-hoop about the recent visit to Clifton of a Mr Stanley Smith — none other than the man Uncle Albert had met on the train. Mr Smith had brought with him his design for a new type of autocar — a *light car*, Henry called it. The design had yet to get off the drawing board.

'That's because Mr Smith is a humbug,' Roderick had said with a superior sneer.

'Mr Smith is *not* a humbug! Uncle Albert would never invite a *humbug*! Why must you always think the worst of people?'

'And why must you be so gullible?' (*Gullible* was Roderick's new word, brought home with him from school. By now — the end of August — Dorothea was heartily sick of it.)

Mr Smith hadn't *looked* like a humbug, whatever Roderick might say, but then he hadn't looked like anything much — certainly not like a thwarted genius. With his greying hair and greying moustache, he was rather like a watered-down version of Uncle Albert himself. He had come to tea, along with Henry and Henry's friend Mr Giles Milton (another motor enthusiast). Together with Uncle Albert, they had sat round and discussed Mr Smith's design.

Dorothea had longed to be a fly on the wall. She had not been able to think about anything else, sitting in the day room wondering how things were progressing downstairs. 'Egg sandwiches, pate sandwiches,' she had murmured. 'Cucumber sandwiches, toast, brioches . . .'

Roderick had looked at her as if she was mad. 'What on earth are you talking about?'

'It's all the things that Cook has prepared for tea. I know, because I helped her. There's chocolate cake, coffee cake, scones—'

Roderick had mocked her. 'You oughtn't to be so gullible as to do Cook's job for her. Servants are there to work.'

'Did Aunt Eloise teach you to say that?' It was the sort of thing Dorothea imagined Aunt Eloise *would* say.

'I *can* think for myself, you know, and I never take any notice of Mother, in any case. I am not a *mummy's boy* like your precious Henry.'

'Henry is not a mummy's boy!' She had felt like stamping her foot. Roderick was so infuriating. 'Why must you be so *horrible*? I shall be glad when you've gone back to school!'

He had turned away then, hiding his face, and she'd been afraid that she'd hurt his feelings.

'I didn't mean it, Roddy. I'm sorry. I wish you *didn't* have to go to school, I really do.'

But he had turned back to face her, grinning from ear to ear in the most maddening way. 'It would take more to upset me than *you*. Your trouble is, you are just too, too *gullible*!'

Listening now to Henry talking about Mr Smith and his design as Bernadette dived under the railway bridge and then up, up, so that the distant spire of Lawham church swung into view, Dorothea could not help but wonder if Roderick was so totally wrong. Others beside him might have called

Henry a *mummy's boy*. And what if Mr Smith actually was a humbug? But mummy's boy or not, Henry was worth a dozen Rodericks and although Henry might get carried away in his enthusiasm for motor cars, Uncle Albert was not someone who would get taken in by a humbug. By all accounts, Uncle Albert had been impressed by Mr Smith's matter-of-fact attitude to his work.

'All we need now,' Henry said, 'is to persuade your uncle that autocars really are worth investing in. The prototype will help us there.'

'What's a prototype, Henry?'

'Something that's the first of its kind.'

'Like Adam and Eve?'

'Well, yes, I suppose so. Apparently, your uncle has spare capacity in his factory just now, so that's where we're going to build the prototype. I say, *Eve* would be rather a good name for it. What do you think?'

Dorothea thought it perfect. Now she had a hand in the prototype, even if it was just giving it a name. But next to her Mlle Lacroix was leaning forward in some concern as the motor swung round a brace of empty wagons heading back towards the harvest fields.

'Oh, Monsieur Henri, you must take care!'

'Don't you worry, mademoiselle!' cried Henry, manhandling the steering wheel, sending the motor veering from one side of the road to the other. 'You're quite safe with me!'

And Dorothea laughed, because she did feel safe with Henry — for no one knew more about motor cars then he did.

* * *

Dorothea, balanced on her bicycle, stopped to catch her breath, looking back along the Lawham Road towards the village. It was a bright October afternoon, the air still, the blue sky mottled with high white clouds. Mlle Lacroix was some way behind, labouring up the gentle slope on her bicycle, pedals going slowly round, round. But they needed to hurry, or they would miss all the excitement back at Clifton.

'Why, hello, Miss Dorothea! Fancy meeting you here!'

Dorothea swivelled on her saddle and found herself face-to-face with Mrs Turner, Nora's mother, plump and rosy-cheeked and smiling as ever, puffing a little after walking up from the canal. She had a covered basket on her arm.

'I've just been to Lawham, miss. There were one or two things I needed that couldn't wait for the carrier.'

'You walked all the way to Lawham, Mrs Turner? But it's so far!'

'Bless you, miss, but it's no more than three mile.'

'You should get a bicycle like mine. It would be ever so much quicker than walking.'

'Oh, I couldn't do that, miss!' exclaimed Mrs Turner as she mopped her face with a spotted handkerchief. 'I'm too long in the tooth to be learning new tricks. Our Jem, though: he's taken to cycling. He cycles to work every day now. But I'll stick to Shanks's pony, if it's all the same to you.'

'Whose pony?'

'Shanks's. My own two feet.' Mrs Turner laughed. 'You may be sure I've never owned a *real* pony. Not like your aunt. She was a great one for riding when she was a girl. Out in all weathers, she was. Fearless, too. But then they always said she could ride before she could walk.'

Aunt Eloise, out in all weathers, a fearless rider? It was impossible, somehow, to imagine. It was impossible even to picture her as a girl, she seemed so impermeable and unchanging. Yet she must have been young once — as must Mrs Turner. They were perhaps of a similar age, Nora's mother and Aunt Eloise, but they were chalk and cheese in everything else.

Mlle Lacroix came toiling up just then. 'Ah, Dorossea, you wait for me, *merci*. And Mrs Turner. How do you do? *Bonjour*.'

'Bon journey, mam'zelle.' Mrs Turner's smile grew even broader. 'Hark at me, speaking French! Who'd have thought it? But that's our Nora for you. She's always teaching us something new, things she's picked up at the big house. So you've both been in the village, have you?'

'Dorossea is always anxious to meet her friends.'

'Well, of course. She has so many friends in the village now.'

'Today, Madam Turner, we also chase a— how do you say? *Un cochon.*'

'A pig,' said Dorothea.

'A pig?' exclaimed Mrs Turner. 'Not the Hobson's beast again? If it's escaped once, it's escaped a dozen times! I don't know. Those Hobsons.' She shook her head, as if she doubted whether there was anything to be done about the Hobsons.

Dorothea set her foot on the pedal. 'I'm sorry, Mrs Turner, but we must go. Eve is coming today!'

'Who might she be, when she's at home?'

'I'll tell you another day!' cried Dorothea, setting her bicycle in motion. 'Goodbye Mrs Turner! Goodbye!'

Quite a crowd had gathered in front of the house. Interest in the new autocar had grown apace in the two months since Mr Smith's visit. The prototype had been built at Uncle Albert's factory in Coventry. It was being driven today by Henry down to Clifton on its first test run. Mr Smith himself was a passenger. Uncle Albert headed the welcoming committee. Aunt Eloise was there too, along with Henry's mother and Henry's friend Mr Giles. Mrs Somersby was also present. She had just happened to call by. As Dorothea propped her bicycle against the garden wall, she could hear Mrs Somersby giving Uncle Albert the benefit of her wisdom. She had an opinion on everything. Motors were something of a novelty, she was saying, though mainly only of interest to men. They might have more of an appeal for women if the clothes could be improved on. Motoring attire was mostly frightful. She herself would not be seen dead in such clothes. It was her decided opinion that motors would never really take off until these important matters were addressed. It was high time someone took note. Uncle Albert nodded and muttered that she was right, quite right, and Mrs Somersby smiled, for she liked people to agree with her. As if to test Uncle Albert's metal on this point she added that it was rather warm for October, didn't he think so? Luckily he did.

Aunt Eloise and Lady Fitzwilliam were sitting on the bench under the cedar tree, looking up at the house with its glinting windows and grey pilasters. Such a pleasing facade, said Lady Fitzwilliam, so neat and well-ordered — she had always thought so.

'That's all very well, Alice, but what about the crumbling brickwork, the broken slates, the leaning chimney?' Aunt Eloise lamented. 'Not to mention the leaks, the dry rot and the piles of mouse droppings in the attics.'

'My dear! You make it sound positively decrepit!'

'But it *is* decrepit. It has been frightfully neglected.'

'It wouldn't take much to put it right, a few repairs, a lick of paint.'

'It's the cost, Alice, the cost! That's the nuisance of it. One really can't expect Albert to pay when it isn't his house; one really can't expect it. But the trustees are so niggardly, the house could go to wrack and ruin before they ever lifted a finger!'

Taking a fresh look at the house, Dorothea wondered if things really were so bad, or if Aunt Eloise was exaggerating. She remembered Bessie Downs's words from ages ago: *the house is all she's ever cared about.* Watching it crumble away would break anyone's heart — if it was really possible to feel that way about a mere building, and if that building really was crumbling away.

There was no more time to consider these questions for at that moment there came a shout from Mr Giles who was on lookout at the top of the drive. Everyone was swept up in the excitement of Eve's imminent arrival.

Sleek, compact, hood down, bodywork gleaming, wire wheels spinning, Eve crunched across the gravel and came to halt outside the house. An admiring crowd gathered round as Henry jumped down, tearing off his goggles. The machine was a triumph, he cried. Lightweight but strong as steel, it ran smoothly, handled easily, and the fuel consumption was nothing short of miraculous. Mr Smith was a genius! Would anyone like a ride?

Of course, everyone did — even Mrs Somersby. 'So much less *noisy* than the usual run of motors,' she declared. 'So elegant, too. One feels like a queen. One might be tempted to purchase such a vehicle oneself — if only one could find the right clothes!'

'I am pleased to announce, Viola, that such a purchase will indeed soon be possible,' said Uncle Albert. He stepped up onto the running board to make a little speech. He was proud and delighted, he said, to proclaim this very afternoon the founding of a new concern: the *BFS Motor Manufacturing Company*. The initials stood for the three investors: himself, 'young Fitzwilliam there' and 'that very talented and forward-looking engineer, Mr Stanley Smith'. The order book would open immediately. 'But don't all rush at once,' he added, drawing a general laugh.

So, thought Dorothea, Uncle Albert had once again moved with the times and was taking up the challenge of autocars. No wonder Henry was beaming from ear to ear, no wonder Mr Smith looked bowled over. As she ran her hand over Eve's paintwork, traced with one finger the rim of the spare tyre, caressed the shiny brass lamps and felt the heat coming through the radiator slats, Dorothea wondered what would happen to all the copies of Eve that were to come. Uncle Albert had gambled. Would it pay off? Only time would tell.

* * *

The prototype took its leave next morning. Henry was to drive it back to Coventry accompanied by Uncle Albert along with Mr Smith who had stayed overnight at Clifton. The BFS Motor Manufacturing Company was to begin in earnest.

After the feverish excitement yesterday, Dorothea found herself feeling rather flat. She wished she could have gone off with Eve too, to join in the adventure. What was Uncle Albert's factory like? What was Coventry like? Uncle Albert had lived there for years and years until moving to Clifton to become Richard's guardian — and to please Aunt Eloise, no doubt.

Going down to the library that afternoon to choose a book, Dorothea's head was still full of thoughts of Coventry. Uncle Albert had been born somewhere called Seton Street, in a little court that sounded very much like the place where latterly she had lived with her papa in London. Later, Uncle Albert's family had moved to a bigger house in Forest Road and that was where Dorothea's mama had been born. Sitting at the desk in the Library, absent-mindedly turning the pages of an old book she had picked at random, Dorothea wondered what her mama had been like as a girl and how she had spent her days up until the time of the fateful elopement. And what then? Where had they run to, her papa and mama? Where had they lived? How had they ended up in London? She dared not ask Uncle Albert.

Looking down at the book, she became aware of the small, intricate and highly-coloured illustrations. The text was all about fabulous creatures said to inhabit the far corners of the earth: birds as big as houses, sea serpents that swallowed ships, men with faces in their chests. It was faintly disturbing, somehow, to read about such things. The world was so big it made her head ache to think about it. Her curiosity about Coventry withered. She pushed her unknown mama to the back of her mind. Clifton, the village, an occasional trip to Lawham — that was quite enough for anyone. She had no desire to meet the fabulous creatures from the pictures.

At that moment she heard the faint sound of a door opening — the Drawing Room door at a guess. A bell tinkled in a distant part of the house. She stood up, her heart thumping. Although she had permission to be in the Library, it was still something of an ordeal to run into Aunt Eloise or

Mrs Bourne. But the footsteps she heard in the hallway were heavy and slow-paced, a man's footsteps.

Moving to stand by the ajar door, Dorothea saw Bessie Downs come dashing past, running to answer the bell, presumably, behindhand as ever. Despite the dangers of loitering, Dorothea edged out into the passage and made her way slowly towards the front hall. She heard Bessie say, 'M'lord?' And then a stranger's voice snapped, 'My hat! My stick!' The words were curt, clipped, short-tempered.

Holding her breath, Dorothea peered around the corner. There in the hall was a man tapping his foot on the black-and-white tiles, side-on to her. Tall and thin, he had a pale, gaunt face, like the face of an effigy in church. His dark hair was streaked with grey. There was a hauteur about him — a supreme indifference to his surroundings — that made Dorothea uneasy. Though he wasn't as big as a house, though he didn't have a face in his chest, it was almost as if one of the fabulous creatures had stepped out of the pages of that old leather-bound book — a man from another world.

Bessie came hurrying with his things. Of course, being Bessie, she dropped the hat, fumbled with the stick, almost tripped over her own feet. The man snatched his hat and stick then pushed past her as if she wasn't even there. Bessie had to dodge round him to open the door. The tall man went down the steps and out of view. Dorothea caught a glimpse of a waiting carriage before Bessie shut the door with a resounding crash. She sniffed, wiping her hands on her apron.

Dorothea emerged into the hall, daring to breathe again. 'Bessie, who was that?'

'Humph! Hoity-toity, that's who he was. Lord Snooty. *The Viscount Lynford*, to give him his right name. I'll give him *viscount* if he speaks to me like that again. Huh! Humph!'

'But who *is* he? Why was he here?'

'I don't know and I don't care. Why don't you ask Master Richard? That's who he came to see, supposedly — though he spent as much time in the drawing room with the mistress as he did upstairs. It's hardly surprising. Him and the mistress make a right pair — two crabby old miseries together. Well, he's gone, and good riddance!'

It was most unlike Bessie Downs to let anyone put her nose so seriously out of joint. She didn't stop to chat. That wasn't like her either.

Richard was also out of sorts. The man who'd called was his uncle, he reported. He'd heard his grandfather occasionally speak of an Uncle Jonathan but there had been no sightings of him until today. 'I don't like him,' Richard said. 'He made me feel unwell. I don't want to see him again.'

Richard, of course, never liked anyone — to begin with, at any rate. But this time Dorothea could not help feeling that he had a point. One glimpse of Viscount Lynford had been enough for her. His lordship had now gone back to the unknown places from which he'd come. She hoped he would stay there.

CHAPTER SEVEN

When Uncle Albert made an abrupt and unexpected appearance in the nursery, some six months later — not long after Easter — Dorothea was bursting with questions about Eve and the BFS Motor Company, now a fact of life if not yet firmly established. But Uncle Albert was not his usual self this evening. He answered vaguely, leaving his sentences hanging as he paced around the room, picking things up, putting them down, lost in thought. His behaviour was odd — unnerving, even. Going back to her place at the big table, Dorothea pulled a book towards her — one of the big, stuffy ones from the Library that the governess seemed to enjoy — and opened it at random. *Roger Massingham*, she read, *acquired a sizeable estate*— But which Roger Massingham was this? There had been several, all distant ancestors of Aunt Eloise (and of Richard). One was apt to get them confused.

'Mam'zelle!' Uncle Albert spoke abruptly, making Dorothea jump. 'A word, if I may.'

'But of course, Monsieur.' Mlle Lacroix laid aside her sewing and her spectacles and got up.

They talked in the vestibule. Hanging over her book, Dorothea could not help cocking her ear at the door. Uncle Albert's deep growl was unintelligible. The governess's high sing-song voice carried better. One could make out some of the words.

'. . . ah, you talk of *Monsieur le vicomte*, poor Richard's uncle, no . . . ?'

Growl, growl, growl.

'. . . every week, sometimes twice in one week. He talk to Richard and . . .'

Growl, growl.

'*Mais, oui*! *Le vicomte* — the viscount, I should say — he takes tea with Madam Brannan, sometimes they walk in the gardens. They are old friends, is it not so?'

A very deep growl.

'Monsieur, if there is anything I can—'

A final brief growl followed by the sound of the baize door slamming. Silence.

Dorothea returned to her book, her heart thumping. *Roger Massingham acquired a sizeable estate* . . .

Mlle Lacroix reappeared. She took up her sewing and her spectacles, resumed her seat, a picture of calm. Dorothea was burning with curiosity, but knew that the governess would never entertain any thought of speaking out of turn.

Le vicomte . . . They had been talking about Lord Lynford, Richard's mysterious and unsettling uncle. Any hopes that his visit last October would be both his first *and* his last had been short-lived. He had returned many times since — including that very afternoon. Dorothea had only found out after he'd gone. Returning from her walk in the gardens, running ahead of the governess, she had overheard Bessie Downs and Tomlin *tittle-tattling* (as Nora called it) in the morning room.

'And has his high-and-mighty lordship gone yet?' Bessie's voice had carried loud and clear out into the hallway, making Dorothea wince when she thought who else might be able to hear — Mrs Bourne, for instance.

'He's been gone a good while,' Tomlin had replied. 'He didn't stay so long today.'

'Good riddance. I can't abide him, with his nose in the air.'

'The mistress likes him well enough.'

'And what do you mean by that, Mr Tomlin?' Bessie had asked archly. 'Have you been eavesdropping again, you naughty boy?'

'What if I have? You're as bad yourself, Bessie Downs. At my last situation, the missus used to h'entertain gentlemen regular in the afternoon, and was not to be disturbed in the drawing room. She forgot about the keyhole, though!'

The sound of giggling had come from the morning room but at that moment Mlle Lacroix had caught up with her and Dorothea had not been able to linger to hear more.

She looked down now at her book. It really was the dullest thing she had ever read. Her eyes kept going over and over the same words without taking them in. Was it her imagination, or was there an *atmosphere* in the nursery this evening? Not just the nursery, either. It seemed to be seeping through the whole house.

Polly could feel it too. Without warning she broke out with, 'Hello! Hello! Hello! Hello!'

As if on cue, Nanny burst into the day room, back from one of her *quick words* with Cook.

'Well! What do you think? You'll never *guess*!' Her eyes were popping out of her head as she looked from Dorothea to the governess and back again. 'There's such mayhem downstairs, I've never known the like! The Master's gone off, not five minutes ago, and all out of the blue. Cook says it's because of the glove and—'

'*Excusez-moi*.' Mlle Lacroix broke in rather stiffly. 'What is zis glove?'

'Why, his lordship's glove, of course. The glove that he left behind this afternoon. That girl Downs found it and — what do you think! — the silly thing only went and took it to the Master and asked what she should do with it. And that's how it all came out — about his lordship's visits and everything!'

'But Monsieur Brannan, he know all about the visits, no?'

'No. I mean yes. I mean, he didn't until just now. And Cook says he was so angry you could hear him from down in the kitchen. And it's no wonder he was angry when—' Here Nanny paused, glancing briefly at Dorothea before enunciating her words slowly and clearly as if by doing so she would render them meaningless to anyone except the governess. '—when at one time his lordship wanted to marry the mistress! Well then! What do you think of that!'

'It is none of our concern—'

'Cook knows all about it, you may be sure. Mr Brannan just took off, then and there, she says; and Mrs Brannan was on the doorstep begging him to stay, and Mr Brannan more or less accused her of carrying on with—'

'*S'il vous plaît! L'enfant!*' Mlle Lacroix's razor-sharp voice made Dorothea jump. Nanny stared, open-mouthed. Her face showed first shock, then incredulity, then anger. Her mouth snapped shut. Blotchy red marks appeared on her cheeks, matching the red of her nose. Finally she drew herself up.

'Well! There's no need to use *that* sort of language, I'm sure!'

The governess did not reply, carrying on with her sewing as if nothing had happened.

Nanny sniffed, stuck her nose in the air. She said, to no one in particular, 'Pardon me for breathing. I don't know nothing about nothing.'

'Hello! Hello! Hello!' shrieked Polly as Nanny took her seat by the fire with injured dignity. Dorothea stared down at her book, burying herself in it as the day room lapsed into silence. *Roger Massingham acquired a sizeable estate in the mid-sixteenth century following the dissolution of Lawham Priory* . . . She had read the same sentence at least eight times without understanding a word. Her head was in a spin. Had Uncle Albert really gone away? Why? When would he come back? What did Nanny mean when she said that Aunt Eloise had been 'carrying on' with his lordship? Was it the same as *h'entertaining* (spoken in the sly tone that Tomlin had used)? Was it really true that the Viscount had once wanted to *marry* Aunt Eloise?

Questions, questions: and no answers. There was no one to ask.

Roger Massingham acquired a sizeable estate, she read. The clock ticked. Polly bit the bars of her cage. Mlle Lacroix's needle bit into the cloth.

Outside, the May evening faded into twilight.

* * *

There was an unsettling, breathless mood in the house. The usual routines seemed to fall into abeyance. People spoke in whispers. Dorothea took the risk of following Nanny down to the Kitchen, which she would never normally have dreamed of doing. Cook was there, and the scullery maid, and Milly Carter the kitchen maid. Bessie Downs was lounging against the range. Dorothea lingered in the doorway, listening.

'Come to hear the latest?' said Bessie Downs to Nanny.

Nanny was affronted. 'Me? Listen to gossip? I've never heard the like!'

'Nor me, neither,' said Cook. 'The very idea!'

They nodded and winked at each other, looking superior.

'Well, I say what I think and I don't care who hears,' said Bessie Downs. 'And what I say is that his lordship came looking for money, and the Mistress let him have it and all!'

Nanny and Cook tutted and shook their heads. What a saucy wench, they said to each other, talking out of turn like that! Who did Downs think she was? You'd never catch *them* tittle-tattling, oh no! In any case, Downs had it all wrong. Why would his lordship come looking for money when he was one of the richest men in the country (he was a viscount, it stood to reason)? His father was richer still. No, the truth of it was — and far be it from them to tell tales, but really! Downs needed to put straight! — the truth of it was, his lordship had never ceased to pine after the woman he'd wanted to marry all those years ago and now he'd come to win her back. But (Nanny and Cook dropped hints in meticulous detail), although the mistress was torn in two, her agonies impossible to describe (Cook did her best), she had remembered her wedding vows just in time and would stay with her lawful wedded husband — and no wonder, when you considered that the viscount, though fabulously rich, was also unbearably snooty.

'Then the Mistress is a fool,' said Bessie Downs. 'I'd marry the viscount at the drop of a hat, if he's as rich as you say.'

Nanny and Cook threw up their hands in horror. Of all the brass-necked cheek! It was shocking, the way young girls talked nowadays. In any case, it was Downs who was the fool, for the Mistress could not possibly marry the viscount, not unless she got a *divorce*.

Divorce! The word sent a shudder through the whole kitchen. It was unthinkable, said Cook; the scandal would be impossible to live down. She herself would never stoop to working in the home of a divorcee. The shame would kill her.

But it seemed very likely that someone else would kill her first, because at that moment Mrs Bourne appeared as if from nowhere. There was considerable carnage in the kitchen from which Dorothea barely escaped with her life.

* * *

'Oh, Dorossea! I am so forgetful! I have left the letter from *Maman* in the garden!'

'I'll fetch it, Mam'zelle!' Dorothea jumped up from her chair. It was a welcome relief, the way things were, to run errands rather than sit at her lessons.

More than usually wary of Mrs Bourne after the massacre in the kitchen the other day, she edged her way down the back stairs and out of the side door. In the stable yard, she was surprised to find Henry tinkering with the engine of Uncle Albert's own copy of Eve.

'It's not running smoothly. I promised your uncle that I would take a look at it. I rather expected him to be here today, but when I asked after him I got some very shifty looks. Your aunt,' he added with a wounded air, 'seems very out of sorts, I must say.'

Dorothea could not stop herself. She had been bursting to talk to someone about the goings-on and this was too good an opportunity to miss. One could say almost anything to Henry, he took it all in his stride — although she thought it wise to leave out some of Bessie Downs's more lurid details.

'Ah. So that's it,' said Henry. 'Viscount Lynford.'

'Henry, who is Viscount Lynford?'

'He's the son and heir of Lord Denecote.'

But she knew that. What she itched to know was different, less tangible. She gave him a questioning look.

Henry rubbed his chin, looking round the yard uneasily, but there was no one about, only a horse tethered over by the stable door while the stable boy, out of sight, mucked out its stall within. The horse regarded them with some interest as Henry said hesitantly, 'Look, Doro, I really can't tell you much, I'm afraid, only what Mother has let slip, and some things that Milton has told me. You know Milton — my chum Giles Milton? He's got about a hundred brothers and sisters, and one of them, Philip, was great friends with Lord Lynford once upon a time. Philip was something of a black sheep, by all accounts. His father turned him out of the house in the end — got fed up of paying off his debts, so Giles said.'

What had this got to do with Uncle Albert and Aunt Eloise? Dorothea was used to Henry's penchant for going off at a tangent and decided to let him run on for a while in the hope of learning something useful.

Lord Lynford and the black sheep Philip Milton, she gathered, had also been friends with Frederick Rycroft.

'Richard's father?'

'And your aunt's brother: that's the chap,' said Henry. 'They met at university and lived something of a wild life, or so one is given to understand. *The Three Musketeers*, Mother called them. Her idea of a joke, I suppose. Drinking, gambling, wom — er, yes, gambling, gambling and so on. All manner of dissolute behaviour. Young rakes, they were. But nobody took much notice. It's expected of young men of their sort when they're at a certain age.'

Dorothea hesitated to interrupt again in case Henry clammed up (he looked like he might do so at any moment). What, she wondered, did it mean to be *dissolute*? Had Henry also been *dissolute* when *he* was at university? Doubtful, she thought. She remembered Becket once saying that Frederick Rycroft had been a *rapscallion* in his youth. Was this the same as being a *rake*? Or different?

The three friends, Henry continued, had often stayed in one other's houses and had got to know one another's people — which was how Frederick Rycroft had come to marry Lady Emerald Huntley. She was Lord Lynford's sister.

Lady Emerald, said Dorothea to herself, slotting the names into place. Lady Emerald was Richard's mother, of course. Becket had said of her long ago that she'd had *no sense* and had *not fitted in*. Henry now added that she'd been something of a hedonist (which meant what?) as well as a headstrong sort of woman; while Frederick, after his marriage, had been notoriously *uxorious*. (Was this equivalent to *rake* and *rapscallion* or did it have an entirely different connotation?)

'Lady Emerald was five years older than Frederick,' Henry added tangentially. 'Mother seems to think that was the root of all their problems. But I . . . I don't think age matters when two people are . . . are fond of each other — do you?'

'No, Henry, of course not,' said Dorothea patiently. (What had this got to do with *anything*? She had been out of the nursery for *ages and ages*. Someone would come looking for her if Henry didn't get to the point.)

Henry resumed. Frederick Rycroft and Lady Emerald — Richard's parents — had got married in 1880. Henry knew the date off pat because it was the same year that his father had lost his seat in the election. (Lost his *seat*? In what way?) 'My father took up Fred as a sort of protégé.' (A *what*?) 'Of course, he would have liked to win his seat back himself but — reading between the lines — I think he knew that he didn't have it in him. He had realised by then that he was ill, hadn't much time left. So he pinned all his hopes on Fred.'

This, in a way, was interesting. Dorothea had often wondered about Henry's father. But if (she thought) she had been writing an essay on Viscount Lynford and had included all these superfluous details, Mlle Lacroix would have crossed it all out and written *not relevant* in the margin. Time was getting on, and even the horse had now grown bored and turned its withers on them.

Sifting Henry's words, she understood him to be saying that after the wedding Frederick Rycroft had stopped being a rake and/or rapscallion, and had become sensible and respectable instead. Partly this was due to his wife, who stood no nonsense ('unless it was her own nonsense,' Henry added), partly it was because he saw less of his dubious friends, Lynford and Milton. Mainly it was due to his newfound interest in politics. Politics was to have been Frederick Rycroft's glittering career (did Richard know about this?) but unfortunately everything had come crashing down round his ears when he lost in the election of 1885. And that, said Henry, had been that.

'Father was terribly disappointed, I remember,' he went on, toying with a spanner, a distant look in his eyes. 'Our house was rather under a cloud for weeks. It put me off politics for good. Put Fred off, too. He was not a sticker, Fred. He got easily discouraged. After the election he went travelling with his wife all over the continent — leaving, if Mother is to be believed, a trail of unpaid bills.'

But now — at last — Henry was getting to the interesting bit. It had been in that same year of the lost election, 1885, that Lord Lynford had asked Aunt Eloise to marry him. This, it turned out, had *really* happened. It wasn't just a figment of Nanny's and Cook's imaginations. Lynford and Aunt Eloise had known one another for years, with Lynford and Fred being such friends and Fred later marrying Lynford's sister. Aunt Eloise had formed what Henry called *an attachment*, by which he meant *love*, thought Dorothea.

But 1885! It was nearly twenty years ago, ancient history! One did not really think of Aunt Eloise as being that old. Then again, one never thought of her as being any age at all. She was timeless, like the Snow Queen. But if Henry could remember these events, then he must be getting on a bit, too — he must be a quarter of a century old *at least*!

She looked at Henry with new esteem as he explained that the expected marriage had never taken place and that no one could say for certain why. Everyone had their own theory. His mother was of the firm opinion that Old Harry (as she called Mr Rycroft, Aunt Eloise's father) had been against the match from the start, especially so since he had seen how Fred's marriage had turned out. Aunt Eloise had been devoted to her father, it was well known. She would never have gone against him. And so Lord Lynford had slunk away with his tail between his legs and had disappeared from view. The next anyone had heard of him, he had sailed to America and married an heiress.

'Mother says that this proves Lord Lynford had been up to no good all along — he only wanted to marry your aunt for money, to pay off his debts. But that doesn't ring true to me. Your aunt wasn't an heiress. She had no money to speak of. So I think, in his own muddled way, Lynford did have a . . . a soft spot for her.'

Dorothea wrinkled her nose, remembering the viscount's cadaverous appearance and haughty manner — the way he unsettled Richard and ruffled Bessie Downs's feathers. She doubted that he'd ever had a soft spot for anyone except himself. Perhaps Lord Lynford — unlike Frederick Rycroft — had never given up his wild ways, was a rake/rapscallion even now.

But this didn't help in trying to guess what might happen next. She could understand why Uncle Albert might be vexed by Lord Lynford's visits, but surely he couldn't imagine that Aunt Eloise was still *attached* to the viscount — could he?

When she asked Henry about this, he went red and began stammering. 'I don't . . . it's not my place to — oh lord! Mother's always saying I should learn to think before I open my mouth! I really shouldn't have told you any of this! It's not . . . not suitable. I've been horribly indiscreet. The problem is, I always think of you as being older than you are.'

'But I *am* older, Henry; I quite grown up, nearly twelve. And you are the only one who talks to me properly, who tells me things. Even the mam'zelle won't talk about this sort of thing.'

'She's obviously got a deal more sense than me.' A grin stole onto Henry's face which — with his red cheeks — made him look rather sheepish. 'You mustn't worry, you know, about your aunt and uncle. Grown-ups are forever having disagreements. It never amounts to anything.'

'You told me that once before.' She smiled at Henry, who really was the best sort of friend one could have. But there was no time for any more talk. 'I have to fetch the mam'zelle's letter, and then—' She was already running towards the gardens. 'Goodbye, Henry! Goodbye! And thank you!'

He waved, his spanner still in his hand. 'Don't mention it! Any time!' He sounded pleased as punch, but she couldn't for the life of her think what she'd done to make him so happy.

* * *

Nora came into the day room in a fluster.

'Mrs Brannan has asked for you, without delay,' she said, bundling Dorothea into her hat and coat.

Dorothea went cold. 'Aunt Eloise *never* wants to see me!'

'Well, she wants to see you today. Oh, these dratted buttons! I'm all fingers and thumbs!' Aunt Eloise had that effect on people.

As they hurried downstairs, all manner of thoughts chased through Dorothea's mind. Perhaps Aunt Eloise was taking the opportunity — with Uncle Albert away — of sending her unwanted niece to the orphanage, as she'd suggested from the start. *Or maybe*, thought Dorothea, *I will be turned out and made to work for my living*. Girls of her age from the village were in service by now. But would Aunt Eloise *really* do any of these things? Dorothea could not decide. The thought that she might be leaving the house forever clouded everything else.

Aunt Eloise was waiting in the hall, dressed to go out. 'Come along.' She led the way, sweeping past Mr Ordish who was holding the door open, unobtrusive as always (Mr Ordish was so unobtrusive as to be almost invisible). The carriage was waiting at the foot of the steps — the carriage, not the motor. Had Henry not fixed it? Or was Aunt Eloise rejecting everything that spoke of Uncle Albert?

'Quickly, or we shall miss the train!'

Dorothea looked out from the carriage as it jerked into motion, the horses treading the gravel. Nora was standing on the steps, a tight little smile on her face. Dorothea was too shy to wave, with Aunt Eloise sitting beside her, and already the house was slipping away, quickly lost behind the trees.

They reached Welby station in no time. Aunt Eloise hastened up to the platform. Dorothea ran to keep up.

Almost at once, a train came in. They got on. The train pulled away, hissing and clunking. It trundled over the Hayton Road on the grey brick bridge and quickly gathered speed. Facing backwards, Dorothea saw Welby dwindling into the distance. Goodbye to Welby — to Hayton, to Clifton too. Goodbye forever?

The door to the corridor opened. A man in a dark suit and a bowler hat stood there. He was carrying a rolled-up newspaper. His eyes took in the spare seats, then swivelled round to look with obvious approval at Aunt Eloise. Aunt Eloise met his gaze. Her cold, blue stare raked over him. The man stepped back, seemed suddenly overcome with embarrassment, as if he'd been caught out in some unseemly act. The door slid shut. He was gone.

They were alone together. Dorothea had never been alone with Aunt Eloise before. She did not dare to look at her, looked out of the window instead. The train was bowling along, swaying and rocking, the clackety-clack of the wheels loud in her ears.

Without warning, they plunged into a tunnel. The darkness outside roared and seethed. The lamps in their compartment gave out a pale yellow glow.

'Duncan's Hill Tunnel,' said Aunt Eloise: the first words she had spoken since leaving Clifton. 'My father remembered it being built. Navvies from Ireland worked on it. They were hard-bitten men. When they went on the rampage in Welby village, the militia had to be called in. But even their games were perilous. They dared each other to leap across the top of the air shafts. One slip equalled death.'

Aunt Eloise spoke almost as if she approved of the rough-and-ready navvies. For a split second, Dorothea had a glimpse of a different Aunt Eloise, the young girl Mrs Turner had spoken of, riding wild and free on her pony or horse, her hair flying in the wind.

But then the train poured out from the tunnel into the daylight again and the brief vision shattered like glass. The navvies, too, who'd loomed up real and threatening in the dark, were now swept away, lost in the whirling hedgerows. With a sharp, precise movement, Aunt Eloise straightened her skirt. Dorothea thought of Nanny and Cook and Bessie Downs, and all the talk of Aunt Eloise *carrying on*. It seemed monstrous, meaningless. It couldn't possibly be true. Perhaps once, long ago, that wild girl on her pony might have been dazzled by Lord Lynford — he'd been older, glamorous, titled — but not now. Now, sitting poised on the seat, her back perfectly straight, her face set, Aunt Eloise was a pillar of virtue. Her very blood ran with it.

'Rugby! This is Rugby!'

They had come to a station. Dorothea looked out of the window, watched people milling on the platform, saw them pointing, gesticulating, their mouths opening and closing soundlessly on the other side of the glass. Uniformed porters pushed trolleys, carried bags. The black minute hand of the station clock moved forward one notch. Immediately, a whistle blew.

The train jerked into life, eased away from the platform, quickly got up a head of steam, went streaking into the green spring countryside. Overhead, grey clouds swirled and began to thicken. Despite her apprehension, Dorothea was aware of an irrepressible excitement building up inside her. The speeding train, the ever-changing view from the window — it was buoying her up, sending her spirits soaring like a bird on the wing. And she knew now where they were going. This must be the very journey Uncle Albert made each morning on his way to the factory. They must be going to Coventry.

* * *

They took a cab from the station. Dorothea was glued to the window. After Hayton — after Lawham — Coventry seemed like the centre of the world. Crowds of people surged along the pavements. Traffic clogged the streets. Carts and carriages rattled over the cobbles. Horses were plodding here, prancing there, their hooves clip-clopping, their eyes hidden by blinkers. Motor cars buzzed like angry bees. A stately tram glided past.

There was a sudden gust of wind. Shop awnings flapped, hands clutched at hats. People went scurrying for shelter as rain began to fall, a sudden downpour, an April shower. Umbrellas popped up. Raindrops bounced high off the road. The cobbles glistened. Water streamed in the gutters. Puddles formed and spread.

The outside world grew remote as the window fogged up. Dorothea saw rows of shops, caught a glimpse of a lowering grey sky. A tall spire pierced the clouds like the point of a knife but was quickly obscured by the fat raindrops which spattered on the window and ran down the glass in streaks of wet. All the while, Aunt Eloise sat still and silent.

The rain ceased as abruptly as it had begun. They had left the city centre behind, turned into a long avenue lined with trees. Rows of well-appointed villas were set back from the street. Through the misty glass Dorothea made out a sign: *Forest Road*.

The cab came to a halt outside one of the villas, a solid brick-built house with a large bay window. Angry clouds churned overhead as they stepped down onto the pavement. Dorothea looked along the empty street. The trees swayed in the gusting wind. Smoke trailed from the chimneys. Water dripped from the branches, pooled in the gutters, glistened on the paving stones. It seemed very quiet and tranquil after the noise of the train, the bustle of the city.

Dorothea followed Aunt Eloise up the short path to the front door, jumping over the puddles. A woman in cap and apron came hurrying to answer the bell. She was middle-aged and capable-looking. She gave a start of surprise at seeing Aunt Eloise.

'Mrs Brannan! We didn't know — we didn't expect—'

'Good afternoon, Mrs Reade. I believe my husband is in residence.' (Did Aunt Eloise know this for sure? Or was it merely a guess? There was no sign of doubt at all.)

The woman was apologetic. 'Mr Brannan is at the works just now, ma'am. Mr Simcox too.'

'Then we shall wait.'

Aunt Eloise swept into the house, handing her hat and gloves to Mrs Reade. Dorothea followed meekly.

They sat together on a wide settee in the room with the bay window. There was a decorated screen in front of the fireplace and a large mirror over the mantelpiece. The woman called Mrs Reade brought them tea and sandwiches. Mrs Reade was the housekeeper, Dorothea assumed — a very different personage to the forbidding Mrs Bourne. They ate and drank in silence. A carriage clock on the mantelpiece ticked away the slow minutes. Why had they come?

After a time, Aunt Eloise got up, taking her empty cup and saucer and placing it on the side table. She held out her hand for Dorothea's. Now that she was standing, she was reflected in the big mirror over the mantelpiece. It was as if there were suddenly two Aunt Eloises in the room.

'This is where Mr Simcox lives.' Aunt Eloise put Dorothea's cup aside, looked slowly round the room as if reacquainting herself. 'Mr Simcox has worked for your uncle for many years. The house itself belongs to your Uncle Albert. For a time — after we were first married — your uncle and I lived here. Four years . . .' The words trailed away, making four years sound like an eternity. She crossed to the mantelpiece, her back to Dorothea.

It was impossible, somehow, for Dorothea to imagine Aunt Eloise established in these surroundings, even thought she knew it had really happened. Over the years, she had pieced together the story, how Aunt Eloise had been visiting her cousin in Coventry, how she had met Uncle Albert at some sort of gathering and gone on to marry him, how they set up home in the city. It was in Coventry — perhaps in this very house, incredible though it seemed — that Roderick had been born. Dorothea wondered what sort of a boy he would be if he lived here still. He claimed to have no memory of Coventry.

The second Aunt Eloise stepped forward in the mirror, like a ghost out of the past. The ghost's eyes stared into the room, cold and blue, deep too — and sad, thought Dorothea suddenly, so terribly sad.

'I—' Dorothea bit her lip, not having meant to speak.

Aunt Eloise turned towards her. 'What is it?'

'I'm . . . sorry — sorry that you were unhappy here.'

Aunt Eloise looked at her in a way that made her shiver, as if the cold eyes could see right through her. Yet it also seemed to Dorothea that this was the first time in the three and a half years they had lived together that her aunt had really *noticed* her.

Aunt Eloise's expression changed — softened perhaps. Her eyes grew distant as if a mist had descended. 'I used, when I lived here, to dream often of home — of Clifton . . .'

Like me, thought Dorothea, *dreaming of Stepnall Street* . . .

At that moment they heard the sound of the front door being opened followed by voices in the hall. Aunt Eloise stepped away from the mantelpiece, her eyes straying towards the door. The ghost in the mirror receded, vanished.

It was not Uncle Albert who came into the room but another man, short, slight, with a straggly moustache and a balding head.

'Mr Simcox.' Aunt Eloise bowed her head ever so slightly. 'Forgive the intrusion. I have come to see my husband.'

'Of course. I . . . I . . . we . . .'

'And if he won't see me, he can hardly refuse to see his own niece!' Aunt Eloise wrenched Dorothea up from the settee, pushed her forward. Dorothea could almost feel the strength of her aunt's iron will, transmitted through the long, elegant fingers that gripped her wrist, but she tore herself away, suddenly angry. Aunt Eloise had tricked her, cared nothing for her; she was just a pawn in a game, a decoy.

She stood between the two of them, her cool, calm and collected aunt, and timid Mr Simcox, her chest heaving. They both looked at her. She grew afraid. What would happen next? And whatever would become of her?

* * *

Dorothea sat on the stairs in her borrowed nightdress with her hands in her lap, pressing her fingers together, listening to the muffled voices coming from the room with the bay window and the mirror over the mantelpiece. She could not hear much of what Uncle Albert and Aunt Eloise were saying. She felt guilty about listening at all. If only Roderick had been with her! He often said that grow-ups told you nothing, that eavesdropping was the only way to find anything out. In this situation, he would be neither intimidated nor conscience-stricken. But he was miles distant, out of harm's way at school. He knew nothing of what had been happening.

Last night, Dorothea had eaten her dinner with Mr Simcox and his daughter, a quiet girl of fifteen who wore spectacles and whose name was Peggy. Arnie Carter had been there too. Dorothea had forgotten until she saw him — pasty-faced and famished-looking as always: a worrier, Nora said — that this was now where he lived, ever since the great fire last summer. She thought how jealous Nora would be — sitting to dinner with Arnie Carter! But when would she ever see Nora again?

There had been no sign of her uncle and aunt last night. At bed time, Mrs Reade had taken her up to a little room at the front of the house. 'I hope this will suit, miss.' The housekeeper had sounded put out, reproachful. Dorothea had wanted to shout at her: *It's not my fault; I didn't ask to come here!* She had stopped herself just in time, had got undressed like a lamb, put on the nightdress borrowed off Peggy Simcox. Lying awake, lonely and miserable, she had wondered what Nora was doing, and the mam'zelle and Richard — Baby, too. 'But we must,' she had said out loud, her voice sounding small and flat in the darkness, 'we must stop calling her Baby. She is growing up. She has a name of her own.' But for some reason, this thought — that Baby was growing up, was a baby no longer — had brought tears to her eyes.

She had slept at last — though fitfully — to be awoken by Mrs Reade with a breakfast tray. Dorothea had picked at her food as Mrs Reade lingered in the room, opening the curtains, tidying round, taking clothes out of the wardrobe. *Spying on me*, Dorothea had said to herself. But having such uncharitable thoughts made her feel contrite.

'I will come back for your tray by-and-by,' Mrs Reade had said at last, heading for the door. 'I must just take this clean shirt to Arnie — to Mr Carter, I should say. This is his room, of course.' She had hesitated a moment longer, adding, 'When you are up and dressed you might like to come to the shops with me. It will do you good to get out of the house.'

But Dorothea had not wanted to go anywhere with Mrs Reade and when the housekeeper returned she had pretended to be asleep. Mrs Reade had gone away. Dorothea had lain with her eyes shut, listening to doors opening and shutting, footsteps on the stairs, muted voices, water gurgling in the pipes. Finally the front door had banged shut one last time. The house had creaked, settled, lapsed into silence. Had they all gone away and left her? She had opened her eyes, staring up at the cracks in the ceiling. An occasional cart or carriage had passed by outside, wheels rattling, hooves clopping, fading into the distance. She had thought of poor Arnie Carter whose room she had taken. Where had he spent the night?

After a while, she had got out of bed and crossed to the window. Trees were swaying in the breeze. The sky was overcast. On the lawn below, a blackbird had been prodding the grass with its sharp yellow beak. It had run a few steps, prodded again, then, with a sudden cackle, it had flown away over the trees in a flurry of wings.

That had been when the voices started, the muffled voices downstairs. Unable to stop herself, she had crept out onto the landing and half way down the stairs. Here her courage had failed her and she had sat down. Here she was still.

Drawing her knees up to her chin, she listened, recognising the deep bass rumble of Uncle Albert, the cold, clipped tones of Aunt Eloise. The words were all but indecipherable, like writing blotted by rain.

'. . . nothing *improper*; then there *was* something . . .'

'. . . and if I am not to be permitted . . . an old friend of the family . . .'

'. . . behind my back! Behind my . . .'

'. . . never, I would *never* . . .'

'. . . taken you for a fool, Ellie . . .'

'. . . a mistake, lending him . . . my head, in such a muddle . . .'

The disconnected words swirled around, made Dorothea's heart pound. It seemed, too, that she could hear other voices, voices in her head, voices from the dim past, voices she had listened to as she lay half-asleep in the room off Stepnall Street, her papa and Mrs Browning stumbling around on the other side of the pinned-up sheet.

. . . I never, I never did, you take that back, you're a blinking liar . . .

. . . damn you woman, damn you . . .

. . . and don't you damn me; take that, *you old sod . . . and* that . . .

. . . bloody hell, bloody nora, just you wait . . .

Dorothea put her hands over her ears, trying to block out the voices — the voices from below and the voices in her head. But they wouldn't go away and she couldn't stand it anymore. She scrambled to her feet and ran up the stairs, tripping over the skirt of her nightdress, her feet thudding. She didn't care if they heard or not, she didn't care that they'd realise she'd been listening. She just wanted to get away.

She slammed the door of her cupboard-like room , flung herself face down on the bed, stuck her fists in her ears, buried her face in the bedclothes, lay silent and still, eyes closed, her own laboured breathing the only sound she could hear.

* * *

There was a knock on the door. Uncle Albert came in. Dorothea sat tensed-up on the bed, dressed now, wary. Her uncle's big frame seemed to fill the little room.

'Well, child. How do you like Forest Road? Not quite as grand as Clifton Park, eh?' To her surprise he sounded almost jolly — or as jolly as so serious a man could ever get. 'I thought this place a mansion when we first moved here. I was still a boy then, a child; your mother wasn't even born. My father's watch business was booming in those days. He had money. We started to live well.' He crossed to the window, looked out, jingling some coins in his pocket. 'The trees have grown since my day.' He peered upwards. 'Looks like rain again.' Turning, his eyes came to rest on her. Frowning slightly, he said, 'How would you like to see my factory? We've time, I think, before lunch. Then afterwards we have to catch the train.'

'Catch the train?'

'The train to Welby, of course. There's one around half past four, if my memory serves. That will give us plenty of time.'

'But, uncle—'

'Your aunt, of course, won't want to come to the factory. It's not in her line at all.'

Dorothea jumped up, threw her arms round him, because suddenly she knew it was going to be alright. They would all be going back together. In the inexplicable way of grown-ups, everything had been settled.

'What's all this, eh?' Uncle Albert sounded amused — rather taken aback, too. He patted her head, stroked her hair. 'Such a fuss, child. I'd have taken you to the factory long ago if I'd known you felt like this about it! Sometimes you're a mystery to me, you really are. I never know what to expect. But your mother would have been proud, no two ways about it. She was no fool, your mother. She'd have been proud as punch.'

* * *

The bicycle factory was in Crown Street, a stone's throw from the city centre. There was a signboard with big bold letters: BRANNAN BICYCLE COMPANY.

It had started out as a simple workshop, Uncle Albert told her, little more than a lean-to propped against one of the last fragments of the old city wall. Over the years the place had grown in an ad hoc way so that now there was a forge shop and a turnery, workshops for wheel and gear making, departments for finishing and packing, store rooms, mess facilities, offices — not to mention the corner that was now given over to the BFS Motor Manufacturing Company. This factory was where all the Eves were made, as well as bicycles.

They walked in through the gateway and across an untidy yard, damp from the rain. He held her hand and she gripped his fingers tightly as they entered one of the buildings — a vast place, it seemed to her, with long grimy windows and a high wooden ceiling held up by iron girders. There were long trestle tables with bicycles in various stages of completion, and lots of men in caps and aprons who were busy about their work — but not too busy to smile and wink at her as she passed. She blushed and hung her head.

The noise and the dust and the dirt, the smell of oil and metal and sweat made her head swim — made her feel out of place. But Uncle Albert seemed entirely at home here, relaxed and uncommonly garrulous as he pointed here and there, explaining what was going on in various parts of the big room, giving her snippets of history too, the long story of the works, how he'd built it all from nothing.

'My father — your grandfather, that is — his business was watches, as you probably know. He made his fortune, such as it was, from watches, him and his two partners. But by the time he passed on and I stepped into his shoes, the market for British-made watches was falling away. People had started buying foreign watches, Swiss and American. It was cheapness that counted, not craftsmanship. I wanted to modernise, branch out. Sewing machines might have worked as a side line. But old George Taylor — he was the last of the original partners — he wouldn't hear of it. He was a watchmaker, he said, and watches were all he knew. *Stick at it*, was his motto. And he stuck at it until the business nearly died under him. When I came to sell it, after he'd gone, it was worth only a fraction of what it had been. But by then I had this place, something I worked on as a hobby to start with, but which became a business in its own right.'

He'd started alone, he said, but had soon poached Simcox from the watch business, his first employee. Ever since then, Simcox had been his right-hand man. They had worked together through thick and thin. Now, nearly twenty years later, there was a workforce of over a hundred. Dorothea could well believe it. There were men everywhere she looked. It seemed amazing to her that out of such apparent chaos, something as intricate and functional as a bicycle was produced.

In the relative quiet of Uncle Albert's office — merely a partitioned-off corner of the big workshop — Dorothea sat on a chair by the door. This, she thought, watching as her uncle sorted through a jumble of papers on his desk, was where he belonged. Here you could see all of him, every facet, not like at Clifton where he was merely an adjunct, an interloper: *Mr Brannan, not from round these parts.*

On the face of it, said Dorothea to herself, Uncle Albert and Aunt Eloise were worlds apart, had nothing at all in common, yet they seemed to fit together in the same mysterious way as the parts of a bicycle. They worked well together. And the bond was strong, had brought Aunt Eloise all the way to Coventry, the place where she'd been so unhappy. She was willing to employ any strategy whatsoever to bring Uncle Albert back to Clifton. She was even willing to use her own niece as a bargaining chip — that was how it felt. As for Uncle Albert, he must know in his heart — Dorothea was sure of it — that Aunt Eloise was a pillar of virtue. How could anyone think otherwise, unless you were Nanny or Cook, picking over old bones, or Bessie Downs, telling taller and taller tales?

But where in all this do I fit in, Dorothea asked. *Where is my place?*

She wasn't Roderick, the beloved son. She wasn't Richard, the heir-in-waiting. Who, then, was she? What part did she have to play?

She couldn't even begin to guess.

CHAPTER EIGHT

Dorothea, back at Clifton, soon felt as if she'd never been away. She slipped back into what she now realized had become an established routine: lessons in the day room, a walk each afternoon round the gardens, the occasional foray further afield by bicycle, church every Sunday. Time never dragged now. Her days were full. Even Sundays had a certain lazy contentment. And so the weeks went by, spring gave way to summer, summer turned to autumn, autumn faded into winter. Roderick came and went as school terms dictated.

Roderick came and went as term followed term. Richard, on the other hand, was always around. Nanny too seemed a fixture but the nursery these days was no longer the invidious place it had been before the advent of Mlle Lacroix. Uncle Albert was far from stranger even if work took up a great deal of his time. Aunt Eloise remained more remote but even she had a human face now. To all appearances, the trouble over Lord Lynford was completely forgotten.

It was summer again, Dorothea's fifth at Clifton. Uncle Albert made an announcement, surprising them all: he'd acquired a house in town. By 'acquired' he meant bought and by 'town' he meant London. London! Dorothea's yearning to go back there had never quite withered even after her failed escape. Now they were all to go London, said Uncle Albert, the whole family — of which it seemed to be accepted that Dorothea was now a part. London, of course, was an adventure in itself, but to Dorothea it was something more. If she was ever to learn of her papa's fate, then surely it was in London she would learn it. And perhaps — just perhaps — she might even be reunited with him at long last.

It wasn't too much of a dream, was it?

* * *

'Why did you all stay away so long?' asked Richard petulantly. 'What were you *doing* in London all that time? You were gone for weeks and weeks.'

If there was one thing she had missed in those weeks, thought Dorothea, it was Richard. Hearing his complaints, listening to him feeling sorry for himself, was like putting on a favourite frock. It felt comfortable, it felt good, she was glad.

'I wanted to go to London too!' Richard complained. 'I wanted to see the new house!'

'You had to stay here. You were too ill to travel.'

'I was not ill. I've been perfectly well for months and months.'

He never *looked* entirely well, that was for certain, being so pale and thin, but finding him today dressed and out of bed, sitting in a big arm chair by the fire, she was struck by the change in him, as if she'd been away for years instead of weeks.

'I have not been ill,' Richard added, 'since *he* stopped coming: Uncle Jon.' He whispered the name as if it was some terrible secret. '*He* was the one who made me ill. Sometimes he frightened me too. He was so queer. I am glad that Uncle Albert told him not to come anymore.'

He spoke of Viscount Lynford as if he was a figure from the distant past and it was true that his lordship had not been seen at Clifton Park for over a year now. But Dorothea could still remember every single detail of a terrible clash she'd witnessed between Lynford and Uncle Albert a year ago last June. She had never mentioned it to Richard.

She shivered and changed the subject, telling Richard about London, about the house that Uncle Albert had bought and the new BFS showroom on the Edgeware Road with its huge windows and display of shiny new motors.

'Did you—' Richard leant forward, lowering his voice again although there was no one to hear — not even Nurse. 'Did you see your papa as you hoped?'

'No. No, I didn't. I—' How could she explain? The wild idea, the hidden hope she'd nurtured before the trip, now seemed like a silly child's fantasy. The London from which she had just returned had not been *her* London; it had been a different city altogether, a city of wide streets and swept pavements, of majestic omnibuses travelling in procession, of hansom cabs swooping past. Uncle Albert's new house in Essex Square was as far removed from Stepnall Street as one could imagine. It was tall and pristine white with black railings, set in a serene square where grass grew, and trees too, and where the gutters were speckless. Seeing the house for the first time, looking along the imposing terrace, she had wondered if, after all this time, *her* London perhaps no longer existed.

'Such extravagance, Albert!' Aunt Eloise had said as she stepped over the threshold but she had looked on the new house with favour, and Uncle Albert had preened himself, as if he'd built it with his own hands. 'It's so very long since last I was in town,' she'd added. 'One forgets quite how . . .' She'd waved her arm, as if there were no adequate words to describe all that London was.

'Why did you stay away so long?' Richard repeated, interrupting Dorothea's stories of the capital. 'I expected you back by the end of September at the latest. It's October now.'

'We couldn't come back until the repairs were finished.'

'There was no need for any repairs.'

'Yes there was. The house was falling to bits. Aunt Eloise couldn't bear it.'

'But *I* liked it the way it was. It is *my* house, and it shall fall to bits if I say so. Aunt Eloise did it to vex me. That is why she stopped me going to London, too. She hates me!'

But that couldn't be true. Aunt Eloise would have no truck with something as unseemly as *hatred*. Richard was too touchy. He took Aunt Eloise's aloof manner as a personal slight. But Aunt Eloise was the same with everyone — even Uncle Albert. As for the repairs, it was silly to say they hadn't needed doing and Richard should be thankful that Uncle Albert had covered the expense himself. It hadn't cost the miserly trustees — and therefore Richard — a penny piece.

'But the workmen made such a noise!' Richard grumbled. 'Every day, hammering and banging for hours on end. It made my head ache!' He frowned, his eyes sulky, but then, unexpectedly, he brightened. 'I didn't mind it so much when Henry was here. I liked it when Henry came.'

Henry had been installing electric wires while they were away, another up-to-the-minute novelty that Uncle Albert had been persuaded to try. Henry had wired up his own home, Hayton Grange, months ago — much to his mother's disquiet. 'I have no faith in this electricity. We shall all be killed in our beds by it one of these days!' Aunt Eloise had been equally dubious, but Uncle Albert had come to trust Henry, especially after the success of the BFS motors. It came as somewhat more of a surprise that Richard should be interested in electricity too.

'Henry explained it to me, he explained about the wires and the switches. And I had a good idea — well, we had the idea together, really. We used the stable boy's ferrets to run the wires under the floorboards. Isn't that clever? And when everything was ready, I filled the generator with oil, and I was the first person to switch it on, and— Do you know, Doro? A person who does electricity and makes generators is called an *engineer*. That's what I'm going to be when I'm older: an engineer. Henry said he could see no reason why I shouldn't.' He stopped, bit his lip, looked at Dorothea almost shyly. 'You . . . you don't mind, do you?'

'About you being an engineer?'

'No. About me being friends with Henry. He was your friend first, and—'

'Silly! Of course I don't mind! I can think of nothing better than that you and Henry should be friends.'

'Good. I'm glad.' Richard's rare smile seemed to brighten the whole room. 'I *do* like Henry. He took such trouble. He carried me downstairs himself.'

'But Tomlin always carries you!'

'Tomlin has gone. He has been sent away.'

'Why? Whatever for?'

But Richard knew nothing of the circumstances and was, in any case, more interested in his plans to become an engineer. A withered leg was no hindrance, he said. Henry had assured him on this point. And maybe, just maybe . . . He would always need a stick, of course — two sticks, probably — but (he looked at Dorothea shyly again) imagine if he could learn to walk! They'd always said he was too weak, but if he did his exercises, if he grew stronger . . .

Dorothea smiled, covering her doubts. 'You need Bovril. Bovril makes muscle. I read it on the side of an omnibus.'

Richard laughed at this, as if he hadn't a care in the world, and she wondered if her first instincts had been right, if he really had changed. The change was masked when he was being peevish and petulant, sulking about being left behind at Clifton. He'd seemed like a child still. But now, smiling, laughing, getting animated about the idea of becoming an engineer, confiding his secret hope of one day being able to walk, he suddenly seemed a lot older. He was fourteen, she reminded herself, not such a boy anymore. There was a year's difference between them. She had never really felt it before.

She tried to work out what was different about him. It was as if there was suddenly more to him than met the eye: new depths, a sense of gravity, a seriousness. Outwardly he did not look much different. He hadn't grown markedly taller, he hadn't filled out. He was still thin and pale, his clothes still hung off him. But he did look very smart in his button-up jacket and tie. His black hair — rather long, rather raffish — curled over the collar of his shirt. His sunken eyes, round and dark, were like splinters of coal. He was, she thought, rather handsome in many ways.

Why not marry him?

The voice in her head, coming out of nowhere, almost set her laughing. It was absurd! An absurd idea! And yet . . . and yet . . . why not? What was there to stop her? Had she not missed him terribly while she was away? And there was no one she could think of who she'd rather marry. Her mind galloped ahead. If she *did* marry him — one day, in the future, when they both of an age — then she would never have to leave Clifton, she could stay here forever, she would *belong* here. She could make herself useful, too. She could help shoulder the burden when the house became his for real at the age of twenty-one. They could send Nurse away — Nurse who was only in it for herself — and find somebody more suitable.

Or I could look after him myself, thought Dorothea, swept up by her plans, everything seeming to slot into place. They would need a replacement for Tomlin, of course, to carry Richard about the place. Or — maybe he *would* learn to walk when he got older. Maybe he wouldn't even need a stick if he had her to lean on.

Anything seemed possible. A whole new world had opened up. She wanted to hug Richard on the spot, tell him that she had found the answer to everything. But she kept her peace. She would get used to the idea first. She was afraid, too, that Richard might scoff. Roderick would, and Richard was a boy too. He did indeed look like a boy today, sitting in his chair, and not like an invalid. Smiling secretly, Dorothea thought of all the months and the years ahead — plenty of time to bring him round.

'Oh Richard! I am so glad to be back! I *did* miss you so!'

He blushed, the colour bold and startling in his pale skin, and she thought, *yes, yes, I certainly shall marry him*. For what nicer boy had ever existed?

* * *

There was something unsettling about change, all the same — even change for the better. The house was subtly different, now that it had been spruced up. And Tomlin was not the only missing face. Bessie Downs had gone too, Dorothea discovered. But Nora couldn't or wouldn't say why either had left.

Dorothea took her walk on her own that afternoon. Mlle Lacroix had tripped up a kerb in London and was resting her ankle. It was a grey and blustery day, rain in the air, so Dorothea took refuge in the old summerhouse, a draughty, leaky place festooned with cobwebs, the floor thick with dust. Sitting in an old cane chair, she looked out of the grubby windows, watching dead leaves being blown across the lawn. Nibs Carter would have some choice things to say, no doubt, when he came to rake them up. The house looked smudged and blotted from this distance, separated off by the garden wall, half-obscured by the spreading cedar tree. Where exactly were the new slates, Dorothea wondered, and which of the chimney stacks had been rebuilt? Would the once leaky gutter really drip no more? Spiralling smoke, ragged and tattered, was blown hither and thither by the wind, grey against the darker grey of the heavy clouds.

It had been a wet day, too, the last time Viscount Lynford came to Clifton — a wet June day over a year ago, several weeks after she returned from Coventry with her aunt and her uncle. Aunt Eloise had been out that afternoon, but Uncle Albert had been at home, taking a day off as he sometimes did now, ever since the time of the great fire. Rain had started falling, Dorothea remembered, as she was walking back to the house with the governess. They had run for shelter but, coming to the doorway in the garden wall, they had seen before them the viscount's carriage standing on the gravel. The viscount himself had been half way up the steps in his tall hat and long coat, his stick firmly planted. Uncle Albert in his shirt sleeves had loomed above him on the doorstep. Their voices had carried clearly in the rain-sodden air.

'Come away, Dorossea! Come away!' The governess had tugged at her arm, but Dorothea had stood frozen. Even now, over a year later, she could still taste her fear, afraid that the two men would come to blows. They had looked so ferocious, so angry. Roderick and Nibs in the orchard had been bad enough, but Uncle Albert and Lord Lynford — it would have been like trains colliding, the very ground would have trembled.

But Lynford had been in no mood for a fight, she had realised, listening to him, his wheedling voice. He had been talking of money, a debt he owed to Aunt Eloise. So Bessie Downs had been right, Aunt Eloise *had* lent him money. He couldn't pay it back just yet, he had said. There were debt collectors stalking him and his father wouldn't lift a finger. His father, indeed, had turned against him, had taken everything he had, his home, his son . . .

Lord Lynford had sounded like Richard at his worst, thought Dorothea as she sat in the cane chair. He had felt hard done by, he had assumed people were out to get him. But Richard, a child, a cripple, had an excuse for his behaviour. What excuse did Lord Lynford have?

Uncle Albert, it seemed, had been of the same mind. 'If you are looking for sympathy, sir, you will not find it here! You have had every advantage in life, every advantage, but — from what I understand — you have squandered it all.'

'How dare you! How dare you speak to *me* like that!' Lord Lynford's voice had been shrill in the rain. 'Who are you, anyway? My family can trace its line back to the Conquest, whereas you — you should count yourself lucky you even know the name of your own father! You think you are something, with your money earned from trade, squatting in the houses of your betters, but you will never amount to anything, however rich you become. Your place will always be in the gutter!'

Dorothea had cringed at these words but to her surprise her uncle had stayed calm. There had been no anger in evidence at all as he stood there in the doorway, belying the viscount's words by looking in his element, just as he had in his factory. One's eye had been drawn to him, a figure if authority and strength.

'I must ask you, sir, to leave now.' Uncle Albert's voice had been deeper even than usual, the word *sir* spoken almost as an insult. 'Go, and don't come back. I will not have you pestering my wife. I will not have you taking advantage of the regard she once had for you.'

'Your wife!' Lynford had sneered as water dripped from the brim of his hat. 'Your wife! Ha! You are welcome to her! I may have asked her to marry me once upon a time, when I was young and foolish, but I can't be sure. I believe I was drunk at the time. At least she was passably handsome in those days. I pity you now, shackled to such a cold, heartless—'

'Oh, Dorossea, you must not listen! Come away!' The governess had clamped her hands over Dorothea's ears, but Dorothea had shaken her off, had watched Uncle Albert give his lordship such a look that it must have shaken him to the marrow. Drenched though he was, his shirt sticking to him, his hair plastered down, Uncle Albert had still cut an imposing figure. Stepping to one side, he had beckoned to someone in the house. The footman Tomlin had come sidling out, grimacing — whether because of the rain or because he was nervous, Dorothea had not been able to guess: perhaps both.

'Ah, Tomlin, there you are. This is Lord Lynford. He is leaving now. See him off, will you? And if he tries to enter this house again, I would ask you to send him on his way as swiftly as you can — with a kick up the backside, if necessary.'

'Yes, sir. Of course, sir.' Tomlin had fought back a grin, nervous no longer. 'It will be my pleasure, sir.'

And so Viscount Lynford had departed. He had not been seen since. Sitting in the summerhouse, Dorothea wondered what it had all been about. It was impossible to believe that Uncle Albert had been jealous of such a man. Maybe he'd resented being kept in the dark — as he saw it — over Lynford's visits. As for Aunt Eloise, she would have extended the same courtesy towards Lord Lynford as she did to all callers — perhaps more, as he'd been her beloved brother's friend and the man who had once wanted to marry her. Perhaps that was why she'd lent him money, for old time's sake. But certainly, comparing the two, Uncle Albert and Lynford — as Dorothea had done that wet afternoon — Aunt Eloise could not possibly doubt that she'd married the better man.

Dorothea wondered if all grown-ups got into such a muddle. If she and Richard married, would they have disagreements and misunderstandings and fall out with each other? Perhaps it would be better, in that case, to marry no one at all.

Getting to her feet, stamping on the dirty floor to get her circulation going, Dorothea found herself shivering, as much because of her gloomy thoughts as because of the cold. As she slipped out into the blustery afternoon, closing the door behind her, she caught sight of the house again and remembered Bessie Downs's words from years ago, that the house was all Aunt Eloise cared about. In which case Uncle Albert could have done nothing more likely to recommend himself to her than to effect the repairs. Maybe he knew that. Maybe that was why he had spent so much of his money on a place that was not his own. At the same time, he had treated himself to a new house in London that would be his and his alone.

Grown-ups, thought Dorothea as she battled against the wind. You might have said they could be worse than children, if you hadn't respected them so much. Well, most of them, anyway.

In the vegetable garden, she came across Nibs Carter, busy with a spade, turning the miry earth, shovelling it effortlessly, his face puckered against the wind, the scar on his forehead showing up white. He was fourteen too, she thought, the same age as Richard. But they might have been different breeds, they had so little in common.

Nibs paused in his work, tilting his cap. 'You're back then, miss.'

'Yes. Last night.' Looking at Nibs, she asked herself what it would be like to marry him. Horrible, she thought. He could be so difficult, so unpredictable. He was so clumsy and dour. But at least you could talk to him. Whether he deigned to answer was another matter.

She ventured to ask him about Tomlin and Bessie Downs.

'They got the sack, miss. Bossy Bourne sent 'em away.'

'But why? They've always been here. They've been here longer than I have. And Bessie was—' Bessie hadn't exactly been a best friend but there was something likeable about her, something irrepressible. A talk with Bessie had always been a tonic.

'Bessie got herself in trouble,' said Nibs.

'Bessie was always in trouble!'

'Not this kind of trouble.'

'What kind?'

'Nothing you need worry about.'

He stood leaning on his spade, more or less telling her to mind her own business. It was insufferable!

Something about the look she gave him must have struck home. He said hurriedly, 'Sometimes, miss, a girl has a . . . a baby . . . even if she int married.'

'Well, of *course*. I do *know* that.' She quickly put the pieces together in her mind. A baby. Tomlin's baby? Was that why he had been dismissed too? So Bessie and Tomlin had been sweethearts. That was a piece of gossip Bessie had kept to herself. But Dorothea thought it ridiculous of Nibs to carry on as if all this was beyond her. 'I am not *stupid*, Nibs. I lived in Stepnall Street. I saw it all.'

'Very good, miss,' said Nibs stiffly and touched his cap, for all the world as if she was a princess driving by in a golden carriage.

She all but stamped her foot with rage. 'Robin Carter, how dare you! Treating me like the Queen of Sheba when we've always been the best of friends!'

'Not always.' She gave him another look and he burst out, 'How else am I meant to treat yer, you with yer fine silk and me with holes in me boots!'

'I had holes in my boots too, once upon a time.'

'You've no holes now. Yer different now.'

'What rubbish! I'm exactly the same! Clothes don't *change* people. It's not clothes that matter.'

'That's how I used to think, when I was a kid. But now—' He shrugged. 'We're different, you and me. No getting round it. I gotta earn me living for a start.'

'Is that my fault? Is it? For goodness' sake, Nibs, have I ever lorded it over you, have I ever been all high-and-mighty?'

'No, miss, you've not, but . . .' He rubbed the handle of his spade, looked shifty. 'Yer needn't think I'm not grateful and that, after everything yer done, getting me this job—'

'That was Uncle Albert, not me.'

'Ah, well, if that were true, things might be easier. I done care nothing for yer Uncle Albert, we've never hardly spoke. But you and me, that's different.'

'*Different, different*, that's all you keep saying. I don't *understand*!'

'If . . . if yer must know, I, er, I hate being obliged to folk. I hate it. It's like being put in yer place.'

Pride, she realized with exasperation. Stupid pride. Roderick was exactly the same. He didn't believe in give-and-take either. He liked to stand on his dignity no matter how lonely it got. Perhaps that was how all boys were — all men, too. Hadn't it been pride which had driven Uncle Albert to Coventry before he knew all the facts? It had taken Aunt Eloise — a woman — to bring him back. Aunt Elise hadn't minded humbling herself, not if it made things right again.

Taking a leaf out of her aunt's book, Dorothea did her best to squash her exasperation. She said calmly, 'You are being silly, Nibs. If we are friends, being obliged doesn't come into it. Nor does it matter if I've got holes in my boots or not. You're as bad as Roddy, taking umbrage all the time.'

Nibs scowled fiercely at this mention of his old enemy and Dorothea held her breath. Then, most unexpectedly, he broke into a grin — that rare, lopsided grin of his, up one side, down the other, impossible to resist.

'Now, now, miss. Mention me and *him* in the same breath, and I really will fall out with yer.'

Dorothea was reminded that Roderick had once said much the same thing. *Me, as bad as Nibs! Of all the cheek!* She sighed. 'All I want is for everyone to get on. That's all I want.'

'We don't often get what we want, miss, nor what we deserve — specially the likes of me, my lot. It's all scrimping and saving for us, and our Arnie off at Coventry so we hardly see him from one month to the next. Nothing's gone right for us since the great fire. No. Tell a lie. It's been longer than that. Since Dad died. That's when it started. Nothing's gone right since Dad.'

He was not grinning now. He looked rather forlorn, in fact, standing there in the mud, his patched-up clothes offering scant protection against the gusting wind. There were spots of rain in the air now, too. But it got you nowhere, offering any sympathy to Nibs Carter. He didn't respect you for it.

'It's not as bad as all that,' she said firmly. 'You just like to grumble.'

'Huh! You're no better than our Becky. That's what she says and all. She'll be glad when she can wash her hands of me, she says. Me, her own brother! But she's glad enough of me wages each week. That's girls for yer.'

He went back to his digging and Dorothea made her way to the house, breaking into a run as the rain began to fall in earnest.

* * *

'In France we have *le kilomètre*. There are one point six *kilomètres* to your English mile. Each *kilomètre* is equal to one hundred—'

Mlle Lacroix broke off, peering at Dorothea across the table. It was a grey November afternoon. The lights were already on in the day room. There was a glowing fire, too; but despite that Dorothea was shivering with cold.

'Dorossea, what is wrong? You are very *agité* today.'

'I don't know what it is, Mam'zelle. I feel funny. I have a sore throat.'

'You feel *under the weather*, no?' Mlle Lacroix felt Dorothea's brow. 'You are hot, I think.'

Nanny stirred, dragging herself out of her chair. 'What's this, what's this? Not feeling well? Then it's bed for you, my girl!'

'But Nanny—'

'But nothing! Come along now, no arguments. Save your breath to cool your porridge. Nanny knows best.'

Dorothea did not have the strength to argue. Nanny bundled her into bed where she lay shivering under the bed-clothes. Her throat felt swollen. She was afraid that it would soon close up altogether. How would she eat? How would she breathe? What was wrong with her?

Nanny brought something called *beef tea*. 'My own particular recipe. Never known to fail. You'll soon be right as nine pence.'

It tasted vile, but it was easier to obey than to resist. She felt so weak it was rather frightening. Nora put more coals on the bedroom fire. Mlle Lacroix offered to read to her.

'We'll have none of that,' said Nanny firmly. 'A sick-room is *my* business, thank you very much. Now, out, out, all of you! Let the child rest in peace.'

Dorothea managed to sleep for a while. When she woke, Uncle Albert was bending over her. He smiled but there was an anxiety in his eyes which made her uneasy.

'How are you feeling, child?'

'Much . . . much better.' But really she didn't feel better at all, and her voice sounded strange: hoarse and croaky.

'She'll be right as rain, Mr Brannan, you can depend on that,' said Nanny, officious. 'My beef tea has never been known to fail.'

'All the same,' said Uncle Albert, 'I think we should send for Camborne.'

Nanny sniffed. 'Well, you know best, Mr Brannan, of course, but I can't see there's any need. My beef tea, it never fails.'

Uncle Albert went away. Nanny fussed around, straightening the bed clothes, plumping the pillows, poking the fire, tut-tutting all the while, muttering, 'My beef tea. Never fails.' It was exhausting having to watch her. Dorothea closed her eyes.

Dr Camborne arrived. He was not his usual self. His hands, poking and prodding, were as cold as ever, but his leathery old face looked tired and drawn, the oily smile absent for once. Something was wrong, thought Dorothea. But what? Fear like a looming claw reached towards her. Its touch made her shiver.

'Lie back now, there's a good girl.' The doctor patted her hand absently, put his stethoscope away. 'Nothing to worry about, my dear. We'll soon have you up and about.'

But he did not sound entirely convincing, and Dorothea knew there was more to it than he was letting on. It took all her strength simply to move her head. To sit up was impossible, to get out of bed unthinkable.

She closed her eyes again. The voice of the doctor seemed to come from a vast distance as he talked to her uncle. '. . . several cases so far in the village . . . it's very contagious . . . rather hopeless, I think . . .'

Hopeless! Fear now had Dorothea entirely in its cold embrace. The word reverberated inside her head: *hopeless, hopeless.* It was as if a black pit had opened up. She was falling, falling, falling and there was nothing she could do to save herself.

The darkness swallowed her.

* * *

She opened her eyes. Had one minute passed, or many? Her uncle and the doctor had gone. The fire was burning low.

A shawl had been draped over the electric lamp to mute its glow. She felt infinitely weary. There was hollow, churning feeling in her stomach.

She tried to put her thoughts in order. An hour or two had passed at the very least, perhaps many hours. It might be days and months, for all she knew. All sense of time had left her. There were many disjointed memories in her head. She was not sure which were dreams and which were real. She had not been able to stop coughing. She had struggled to breathe. Her heart had been pounding as if it was trying to beat its way out of her chest. She remembered whispered voices, stomping footsteps, rain dashing against the window, thunder rumbling in the distance. And there had been a train rocking and rolling, clanking and chugging — but no, that must have been a dream. She hadn't gone in a train. She hadn't gone anywhere. She was still in her own bed, in her own room. All the same, she *felt* as if she'd been on a long, long journey.

Hopeless, Dr Camborne had said. So she must be dying. This must be what it felt like to die — as if she was slowly draining away drip by drip.

There was a creak, a rustle. Dorothea moved her head, saw Mlle Lacroix rising from an armchair that had been placed by the bed, a book in her hand, one finger marking her place.

'*Ma petite*. How do you feel?'

'When will it be over, Mam'zelle, when will I be dead?'

'What is this? Why this talk of dying?'

'The doctor said . . . he said it was hopeless.'

'Oh, Dorossea! He was not talking about you!' The governess's hand was cool on Dorothea's brow, stroking gently, brushing the curls aside. 'There was a little girl in the village. Her name, I think, was Maggie Hobson.'

'And is she . . . is she the one who's dead?'

Mlle Lacroix nodded. 'So sad. So young. *Douze ans*.'

Maggie Hobson.

Oh, those Hobsons! Mrs Turner had shaken her head over the Hobsons that day on the Lawham Road, the day over a year ago when Dorothea and the governess had chased the Hobsons' pig through the village. *If it's escaped once, it's escaped a dozen times.*

There were six Hobson children, Dorothea remembered. Nora often said of them that they all looked like they'd been dragged through a hedge backwards. Which one was Maggie? Dorothea could not picture her. Nor could she muster any feelings of pity. It wasn't right, to feel nothing, when someone had died. One should feel *something*, for a girl of twelve.

'I can't . . . Mam'zelle, I can't . . .' She choked. Her throat closed up.

'Hush now. You must rest, Dorossea.'

She gripped the governess's hand. 'What is it, Mam'zelle? What's wrong with me?'

'*La diphtérie*. Diphtheria.'

'Will I . . . will I be like Maggie Hobson?'

'Of course not, *ma chérie*. You will be well again, by-and-by, I promise.'

Dorothea didn't believe it. She felt so weak, and the churning feeling in her stomach was getting worse and worse.

'Oh, Mam'zelle, Mam'zelle, I'm going to be sick!'

But the governess remained calm, merely nodded and reached for a basin.

* * *

Dorothea passed from dream to dream, like walking through the rooms of some vast house, unable to find her way out. Waking suddenly with a start, she lay there, exhausted. The horror of her dream slowly faded. Her room was quiet, just the crackling of the fire and rain pattering lightly against the window. The peace was bliss, after the endless, echoing dream. The pain in her throat had gone, the pain in her chest had gone too. There was no longer a sick taste in her mouth. But she was so tired. Trying to stay awake was like struggling to keep one's head above water.

Slowly she sank under once more. She was back in the interminable house, wandering from room to room as the long, long centuries wore slowly away.

* * *

As if a mist was rolling back, the real world came into focus again. She found the strength to sit up in bed. Food began to tempt her. In the past when she had been ill — when she'd had the sniffles or an upset stomach — Nanny had been on hand with beef tea and some revolting mixture called a *linctus*. But this time Nanny had gone away. She had taken Baby — little Elizabeth — out of the reach of the diphtheria. Roderick, of course, was safe at school.

'Monsieur Brannan wished me to go also,' said the governess, 'but I say no, I will stay, I will look after Dorossea. It is better than to have a stranger.'

'Has Uncle Albert gone away too?'

'No, indeed! He has come to see you every day, Madame also.'

'What! Aunt Eloise has been here?'

'Why, yes. Every day she come and sit by your bed and talk to you. Do you not remember?'

Dorothea shook her head.

'Ah, well, it is no matter. Now, *ma petite*, drink this milk. Cook has warmed it especially, and she has put honey in it!'

* * *

The next day — she knew it was the next day, for the days were running in sequence again — Dorothea woke from a blessedly dream-free sleep to feel for the first time that she was really on the mend. She was still not well enough to get out of bed, but she could at least now foresee a time when she would be. There was no hurry. She was content to luxuriate under the warm covers, watching the flames dance in the grate, the winter cold tapping impotently at the window.

She was just finishing her luncheon of steamed fish when Uncle Albert appeared in the room.

'How are you feeling today, child? Enjoying your food again, I see. All finished?' He took the tray, placed it on the bedside table.

'I feel as if I've been ill for ages and ages. I suppose it is nearly Christmas now?'

'Not quite, child. Not quite.' Uncle Albert smiled down at her; but then, quite unexpectedly, the smile flickered and went out. He became deeply absorbed with the tray, nudging it with his thick fingers so that it lined up with the table edge.

Abruptly he turned away, went and stood by the window. 'What a bleak day,' he muttered. 'A grey, bleak day.'

The coals shifted in the grate, sending up a shower of sparks and an eager lick of flame. The silence in the room became immense — became ominous.

'Ahhh . . .' Uncle Albert turned to look at her, framed in the window, edged round by the cold afternoon light. He had something to tell her, she was sure. Something unpleasant. She felt a tightening across her chest. Her mind, after resting all morning, was suddenly galloping, galloping, spurred on by her fear. She knew about Maggie Hobson, it couldn't be that. Nanny and Elizabeth were safe. Roderick was oblivious at school. Mlle Lacroix had not been ill, Nora had brought the tray less than half an hour ago. Then who? Who?

'I'm sorry, child, it's Richard—'

Richard! Her galloping mind jumped at the name even as Uncle Albert spoke. So Richard had been ill, he had suffered too. Poor Richard! Would it have been too much to hope that he could be spared just this once? But—

She looked up at her uncle's face and cowered, beginning to understand. 'No—'

'I'm so sorry, child, I'm so—'

He was wrong. It wasn't true. It couldn't be. Not Richard.

Her eyes swam. The room seemed to pitch and toss like the deck of a ship. She clung to the side of her bed, clung on for dear life. A hysterical voice was shouting, 'No, no, no,' over and over. The room was full of it, sobbing and wailing, 'Richard, Richard, no, no, not Richard!'

Suddenly the voice was muffled, cut off, and she realised that it must have been *her* voice. It was smothered now because Uncle Albert had put his arms round her, was holding her close. She clutched at his waistcoat, pawed at his jacket, held on to his big, strong arms, kicking her legs under the bed clothes, fighting it, fighting it, the terrible truth. It was like teetering on a cliff edge. She felt dizzy, off balance, about to tumble and fall, about to be dashed on jagged rocks far below.

She was still weak from her illness, however, and soon exhausted herself. Uncle Albert stroked her hair with his big, strong fingers as she lay spent on the bed. It seemed to her that an icy calm took hold of her. Her very heart was frozen. She felt nothing — nothing at all.

* * *

He had been dead for days. They had not told her before because they did not think her well enough. He had died on Tuesday the thirteenth of December, just before five in the morning.

'I killed him. I killed him. I gave him the diphtheria.'

'It could have been anybody, child: any of the servants, anyone who came up from the village. We have no way of knowing.'

'But I was going to marry him. I was going to . . . I . . .'

'Hush, child. Hush now. You're upset, you don't know what you're saying. He's at peace. At peace.'

There was to be a funeral. She was not allowed to go. Dr Camborne forbade it. When the time came — as near as she could judge — she got out of bed and crossed to the window. A wintry sun hung low in the pale sky. She could just make out the crenulations on top of the squat grey tower of St Adeline's. Richard would be there, lying in his coffin.

The old vicar would take the service, his voice as cold and cheerless as his church.

She stood there watching as the brief winter day decayed towards dusk.

* * *

Mlle Lacroix came straight from the funeral, her cheeks rosy, her hands cold. She described it all. Uncle Albert and Aunt Eloise had been there, sitting in the front pew. The old earl had come too, but not the earl's son. The governess had sat half way, leaving some empty rows out of respect for the family. At the very back of the church a few curious villagers had gathered. The service had been short. Richard had been buried in the churchyard.

In describing the funeral, Mlle Lacroix pronounced his name as she'd always done, *Rishar*. This made Dorothea cry all over again. Tears rolled unchecked across her cheeks, soaked into the sheets. Tears, tears, tears: an endless stream of them.

'Why, Mam'zelle, why?'

'It was God's will, *ma petite*.'

'Then I hate God, I *hate* him.'

'But it is now that we must have faith, Dorossea — now most of all. It is easy to believe in Him when things are good. It is when He tests us that we must find courage. All that He does is for a purpose. It is for our good. Richard has gone to a better place. He suffer no more.'

'I don't want him in a better place! I want him here! Oh Mam'zelle, I want him!'

Tears, tears, tears.

* * *

By the time Roderick came home for the Christmas holidays, Dorothea was up and about again, although she was still not allowed outside, on Dr Camborne's orders.

Roderick said, 'Now that Richard is dead, this house will one day be mine. Imagine that!'

'Master Roderick!' Nora scolded. 'That's not a nice thing to say, with poor Master Richard not cold in his grave.'

'It might not be nice, but it is the truth. I am only telling the truth. And you'd jolly well better be nice to me, Turner, or I shall give you the sack when I'm in charge. And I shall cut *her* off without a penny—' He jerked his head towards Dorothea. '—unless she stops sulking and talks to me.'

'Now, now, Master Roderick—'

Dorothea interrupted, said to Roderick in a cold flat voice, 'I hope you get diphtheria too. I hope you die.'

'Oh, Miss Dorothea! Master Roderick!' Nora threw up her hands. 'The pair of you! It's Christmas, for goodness' sake!'

Dorothea turned her back on both of them, looked out of the window.

There was silence in the day room. Even Polly had nothing to say.

* * *

Step by step, she made her way along the corridor and slowly opened Richard's door. She looked inside the room. The bed had been stripped, the mattress folded over. The curtains were thrust wide open, the fire grate empty. In one corner was Nurse's chair. Nurse would need it no more. She had been sent away.

Here, just two months ago, they had sat by the fire together, talking. Richard had decided that he was going to be an engineer. She had made up her mind, secretly, that she would marry him. He had looked so handsome and grown-up. But when she tried to remember all this, she found it hazy and unclear in her mind.

He was slipping away from her.

She found that she was crying again, but this was so normal now she barely noticed.

She shut the door.

* * *

'It's all rather disappointing, child. The BFS motors have not been selling quite as well as we'd hoped. Smith is of the opinion that it's all due to the new regulations — number plates and so on. But I'm not so sure.'

Uncle Albert came to see her every day, took time to talk to her. This afternoon — a wintry afternoon in early January — he was telling her all the latest news about the BFS Motor Manufacturing Company. Once upon a time, it had seemed so important. Nothing was important now.

'There's too much competition, that's what it is. Our vehicles do not stand out in the crowd. And then there's all the trouble we have getting hold of components. Order from abroad, young Fitzwilliam says: it's quicker and cheaper. But we shouldn't be giving all our custom to Johnny Foreigner! We should be supporting home-grown industry! That chap Chamberlain has the right idea. Protection is what's needed! Protection for English business!'

The words washed over her. Why could he not see how hollow she was, an empty shell?

He smiled and patted her hand. 'Don't you worry about the BFS, child. I've a few tricks up my sleeve. There's life in the old dog yet, you'll see.'

He got to his feet, huffing and puffing. She hardly noticed him go.

* * *

She wanted to see Richard's grave. That was where he'd be, if he was anywhere. She knew they wouldn't let, if she asked, so she didn't ask. It was like turning back the clock, running away as she'd done all those years ago with a piece of toast and not a farthing to her name — the day she'd first met Richard.

She took the short cut to the village. The air was still and cold, the ploughed brown earth of Horselands hard as iron. All was quiet except for the *tchek, tchek* of jackdaws. She felt giddy as she stumbled over the frozen ground.

Pausing to catch her breath, she looked back. There was the house, half-hidden by the naked branches of the trees in the Pheasantry. Richard's house. Now Aunt Eloise's.

. . . the house is all she cares about, the house and nothing else . . .

. . . what about that boy, the cripple? Is he still living? I heard as he's kept locked in the attic . . .

. . . Aunt Eloise despises me, she hates me . . .

It seemed to Dorothea that she could see through the mist in her eyes a vast figure take shape in the sky, a cold cruel woman, eyes filled with black fire, a dagger in her hand. 'Come you spirits that tend on mortal thoughts, unsex me here and fill me from the crown to the toe top-full of direst cruelty.' Lady Macbeth — or Aunt Eloise? The malice in the words, in the eyes, made Dorothea cower. 'Stop up the access and passage to remorse, that no compunctious visitings of nature shake my fell purpose . . .'

Had Aunt Eloise arranged it all, hiding Richard away, neglecting him, exposing him to diphtheria — all because she wanted the house for herself?

But I am as bad, Dorothea said, *wishing Roderick dead and feeling no remorse.* Was this what everyone was like deep down: cold, cruel, brutal?

But now Dorothea heard a different voice, soft, gentle, the governess. *Why, yes, Madame also, every day she come and sit by your bed and talk to you . . . every day . . .*

Dorothea shook her head. The vision in the sky dissolved in tatters, faded, vanished. The field was brown and empty. There was no looming presence. The black eyes were merely rooks flying high. The dagger was a wisp of cloud. She shook her head again, then turned and carried on her way.

In the churchyard there was a mound of fresh earth, white with frost, and some flowers, killed by the cold. Nothing else. No marker, no memorial. *Put to bed with a shovel* — one of Nora's phrases. Richard had been put to bed with a shovel and then forgotten. Dorothea sank to her knees, heedless of the chill that struck up into her. After a while she laid her head down on the mound of earth as if it was a pillow — or as if she was listening for something.

Time passed. She did not stir.

When the lych-gate clicked, the sound did not sink in; it was the voice which roused her.

'Miss Dorothea! So it *is* you! I caught a glimpse from the street, and it's lucky I did. You look half-perished!'

It was Mrs Turner. Her rosy face, usually so cheerful, was creased with concern.

'Is Richard here?'

'Master Richard's gone, dearie. He's gone up to heaven. But, now, come you with me. We need to get you in front of a fire, take the chill off you.'

Mrs Turner held out her hand and Dorothea took it, allowed herself to be drawn to her feet.

'See who's with me today, miss? It's little Dicky, that's who it is.'

A small boy looked at her with solemn eyes but Dorothea shrank from him, inexplicably afraid.

Mrs Turner led them down the path and out through the lych-gate. A little way along the street they turned off and took the footpath to Back Lane, the one that led through the Wilderness, the very place where little Dick had made his precipitous first appearance two and a half years ago. Dorothea's mind stirred. She thought about the sliver of slimy skin lying motionless on the dead leaves and she began to shiver. She was shuddering violently as they made their way across Seed Meadow and Dick was stumbling on his little legs, but Mrs Turner's leathery hand was warm in hers and after a time, as they walked, the warmth began to seep into Dorothea's chilled fingers and then slowly up her arm.

The fire had burned low in the Turners' cottage. Mrs Turner put more wood on, drew up a windsor chair, eased Dorothea into it, spread a rug over her knees.

'Now then, miss, how about a nice cup of tea? Hot, sweet tea, just the thing.'

Mrs Turner put the kettle over the fire, fetched out the tea pot, brought in cups, saucers, spoons, sugar, a tea caddy. But Dorothea was conscious of only two things: the flickering flames in the grate and the sound of Mrs Turner's voice which seemed to come from a great distance.

'It's lovely to have you visit, miss, I must say. We don't see nearly enough of you — do we, Dicky-boy? But I don't know what they're thinking of up at the big house, sending you out in this weather with no coat nor hat. You've come to pay your respects, I daresay, but he wouldn't have wanted you to catch your death, now, would he? Master Richard wouldn't have wanted that! You were such friends, the pair of you. Thick as thieves, our Nora always said. She was so upset when Master Richard passed on, you can't imagine. And you were ill, of course, and we were all ever so worried. Everyone was asking after you, you may be sure. It's a blessing to see you up and about again. But such a shame about poor Master Richard. There's Maggie Hobson, too, poor thing. Like a haystack done up ugly, she was, but always smiling, never stopped smiling. I do feel for her poor mother. She's not the easiest woman in the world to get along with, Mrs Hobson; and she will go round borrowing things — tea and sugar and the like — and always replaces it with less than you gave her. But I don't like to complain. We have to live together in the same village when all's said and done. There's her husband, too, always out of a job. So, no, I don't like to complain.

'Now then, miss, here's your tea. Drink it down. That's the way. And I'll take the weight of my feet for a moment. Oh, what bliss to sit down! I've been on the go all morning. He runs me ragged, little Dicky-boy. But if I have him for a morning it gives our Pippa a chance to get on. She's doing some dressmaking, you see, to make ends meet, so I like to lend a hand where I can. But he does run me ragged, little Dicky-boy. That's why I took him for a breath of air, to tire him out a bit. And a good job I did, otherwise I'd never have found you lying there and goodness' knows what might have happened!

'But listen to me, going on! I'll talk you to death at this rate, I'm sure! It comes natural, though, talking to you, miss. Our Pippa was only saying as much this morning. "You have to watch your Ps and Qs with most of 'em up the big house," she said, "but with Miss Dorothea it's different. She's like one of our own, is Miss Dorothea." So there you have it, miss. You'll always be sure of a welcome here. You're welcome any time.

'Well, now. Have you finished your tea? I'll take your cup, then, miss, shall I? And how would you like to have little Dicky sat on your lap for a bit? He won't be no trouble now. Ready to drop, he is. Here, up you come, Dicky-boy. You'll like sitting in Miss Dorothea's lap, won't you? Of course you will! There! That's the way. Oh, but don't you look a picture, the two of you! A real picture!'

Dorothea drew her eyes away from the flames, looked down at the boy on her knees, resisting the urge to shy away. But he was nothing like the slimy bundle she had been picturing in her mind's eye. Two years had passed since then. He was heavy and warm and alive in her arms — and his name was Richard. His name was Richard.

So there would always be reminders, she thought. There would always be pieces to cling to.

Tears pricked her eyes, but she didn't cry. It seemed an age now since she'd last cried, an age since she'd felt anything. A lifetime had passed since she left the house that morning. She looked down at little Dick, snuggled in her arms, half-asleep, sucking his thumb, and she felt her mouth twitch in an odd way, a way she had almost forgotten. The muscles in her face were rusty from long disuse, but nonetheless the smile slowly came. Dick was watching her from under half-closed lids. After a moment, he smiled too, still sucking his thumb.

The fire was hot on her legs, Dick like toast in her lap. She felt as if she was slowly defrosting. She felt sleepy, too. But most of all, she felt that she would like to go on sitting there just as she was forever and ever.

CHAPTER NINE

'Hello! Hello! May we come in?'

Dorothea was been sitting at the table with her supper of cocoa and bread and butter, the newspaper spread out in front of her. All was quiet. It was past Eliza's bed time. Nanny had gone downstairs to 'help' Cook. Mlle Lacroix was in bed with *la grippe*. Dorothea had been all alone. But suddenly—

'Henry! What are you doing here?'

He looked very smart in his dinner jacket and dickey bow, his hair brilliantined, his smile as broad as ever.

'Mrs Brannan said it would quite in order for me to come up and see you. In fact, she insisted. And look! I've brought my chum Giles with me.'

'What ho!' Mr Giles advanced, raising his hand in greeting. He spoke with a lisp. 'What a jolly nursery! Rather empty, though. When I was a kid at Darvell Hall, we couldn't move for falling over one another.'

But the Nursery did not feel empty — not now. The two gentlemen were larger than life, filling the day room with their high spirits and gusts of laughter.

'Who's a pretty girl!' Mr Giles tapped the bars of Polly's cage.

'That's no way to talk to a young lady, Milton!'

'I wasn't talking to the young lady, as well you know, Fitzy. I was, in actual fact, addressing the parrot.'

Dorothea found herself laughing as the two friends quipped and joked. It was impossible not to laugh. And to think that, less than six months ago, she had felt that she would never laugh again, grieving for Richard in the mournful month of January. Now it was June.

She was a little shy of Mr Giles. Henry seemed to sense it. He smiled at her and winked, putting her at her ease. He was very gallant, very chivalrous, always so thoughtful.

'We are here for the pre-race dinner,' he said. 'You know about the race, I suppose?'

That went without saying. There had been talk of little else for weeks. Originally Henry's idea, it had been taken up with gusto by Uncle Albert. 'Not a race as such, child,' he'd told her. 'Not an event for those Grand Prix cars with their monster engines. This will be more of a reliability trial. The perfect opportunity to show what BFS motors can really do!'

'But only if you win, Uncle.'

He had rubbed his hands together. 'That's what makes it all the more interesting!'

'We have come to Clifton to settle our plans,' said Henry, straddling a chair. 'Mother, of course, has been dreading it, all the shop talk, but it can't be helped. Then tomorrow we're off — off to Darvell Hall for the final preparations. You . . . you'll be coming on race day, I hope?'

'I wouldn't miss it for the world!'

'I'm glad!' A smile quivered on his lips, but his eyes were hesitant. He looked at her sidelong. 'I say, Doro, you're looking very . . . very pretty this evening.'

Mr Giles, astride the rocking horse, guffawed. 'You're making her blush, Fitzy, you fool!'

But it was Henry who was blushing. At least, that was how it looked. But probably it was running up the stairs too quickly that had brought the colour to his cheeks.

He grabbed hold of the newspaper. 'What have you got here? *The Times*, is it?'

'Reading the newspaper is one of my chores. Mam'zelle says it's important to keep abreast with the world.'

'Very wise of her,' said Mr Giles. 'I never find the time myself.'

Henry was peering at the print. '*The Battle of Tsu Shima*,' he read out. '*Admiral Togo's strategy*. Where's Tsu Shima, Milton? Any ideas?'

'Somewhere near China, I think. The Russkies got rather a pasting, one hears.' Mr Giles swung off the rocking horse. 'We should get going, Fitzy. Don't want to show ourselves up by being late for dinner, what?'

'Talking of which,' said Henry, tossing the newspaper aside and jumping to his feet, 'what's the name of that girl you're taking in to dinner?'

'Haven't the foggiest. Why'd you ask?'

'Would you mind awfully if we swapped? I'll have Miss What's-her-name, and you have Miss Somersby.'

'By all means, Fitzy. But do get a move on or we'll be late for dinner and then we'll both be in the dog house.'

The two young men said goodnight and set off downstairs. For a while Dorothea could hear their voices echoing along the corridor.

'What's so wrong with Miss Somersby, Fitzy old chap?'

'There's nothing *wrong* with her. She's just not *right* for me. Only Mother can't see it.'

'Oho, like that, is it! Well, I think she's rather nice. Miss Somersby, that is, not your mother.'

'Are you saying my mother's not nice, you scoundrel?'

'That's not what I meant at all, Fitzy, and you know it!'

'But that's what you said.'

'I did not say that, confound you . . .'

The voices finally faded. The day room fell silent once again.

Polly was watching with a beady eye. 'Oh, Polly . . . !' Dorothea had been falling asleep over the newspaper (the story of the battle was rather long and confusing). Now she was wide awake, restless, swinging round the day room, her thoughts full of the race — just the day after tomorrow! 'What will happen, Polly? Will the BFS motors win?'

Polly shut her eyes disdainfully. There was no one else to talk to. Dorothea thought longingly of the dinner downstairs. When would she be allowed down to dine? She was nearly *fourteen*. There was less than two weeks to her birthday. Was she someone Henry would want to take into dinner? He had called her pretty but that was just his gallant way. She wasn't pretty, she knew that. Probably, when it came to it, people would try to swap her the way Henry had swapped Miss Somersby.

She sighed, returning to her supper and the newspaper. *The wind was now freshening,* she read, *and the sea, already rough, began to run very high. The fog began to lift. Togo signalled that the fate of the Empire depended on this effort and the men must do their utmost . . .*

The fate of the Japanese empire had depended on the battle; the fate of the BFS motors would depend on the race at Darvell Hall. Henry, Mr Giles and the others must do their utmost. But would the result be victory as it had been for the Japanese in the sea battle? Or, like the Russians, would the BFS motors fall to an ignominious defeat?

* * *

'Such characteristic bank holiday weather,' said Aunt Eloise drily as she got into the motor.

It was Whit Monday and it was drizzling. They were off to Darvell Hall for the race. Dorothea was sitting in the back of the motor next to her aunt. Nora was up front next to the grey old chauffeur. (Mlle Lacroix was still unwell, so Nora had been chosen to deputise; she was 'pleased as punch' to be having a day out.) Aunt Eloise looked both regal and somewhat mysterious in her long coat and veil. Even Mrs Somersby could have no complaints about Aunt Eloise's motoring clothes.

The aged chauffeur drove at a snail's pace. Dorothea's mind raced ahead, through the village, along the Newbolt Road, past Hayton Grange. (Had Lady Fitzwilliam set out yet? Henry along with Uncle Albert and the others had spent last night at Darvell Hall in preparation for the big day.) Next came Newbolt (wave to Colonel Harding in passing?), then the junction with the Roman Road. Straight on at this crossroads, arch over the canal, dive under the railway, and up, up, to the fork in the road. After that — after that her imagination failed her. She had never been beyond the fork in the road, had never cycled further than that, had never seen Darvell Hall.

The race was taking place at Darvell by kind permission of Sir Walter Milton, Mr Giles's father. Although not a speed trial — as Uncle Albert had pointed out — the competing vehicles would still be going faster than the twenty miles per hour speed limit, which made it necessary to hold the event on private land. The Miltons had plenty of land purchased with money made from coal or iron or something like that (Dorothea could not remember the details).

Looking out at the grey sky, the rain, the dripping hedgerows, the mournful flowers peeping amongst the long grass of the verges — white stitchwort, yellow celandine, blue speedwell — Dorothea found she had butterflies in her tummy. Why should it matter so much if the BFS motors were successful or not? Yet ever since the days of Eve, Dorothea had felt she had a stake in them. She had been there at the birth — just as she had with little Dicky Turner. And that meant something. You were snared. Your fortunes ran parallel, like the tracks of a railway. That was how it felt.

They came at long last, after crawling though the rain, to the turning for Darvell Hall. The gates were wide open. Bunting adorned them. A banner hung across the arch. *Darvell Hall — Fête and Motor Trial — Whit Monday — All Welcome.*

And *all* had indeed come, or so it seemed, and despite the weather. There were flocks of people on foot, on bicycles, in gigs and carts, all of them making their way up the long drive. The Clifton motor nosed its way amongst them, passed through a belt of trees — and suddenly, there was the Hall itself!

Clifton paled beside it. Darvell Hall was much more imposing, with a vast facade of pale grey stone and an ornamental parapet on top. There were windows beyond count, and two tall towers flanking a colonnaded entrance. On the steps in front of this entrance stood a white-haired figure, arms flung wide as if greeting the whole world — surely Sir Walter Milton, thought Dorothea. He looked like an illustration of Old King Cole from a picture book.

The driveway bisected a wide green lawn, smooth as a carpet. On the left was more bunting and many flags on poles. Marquees had been set up here, along with coconut shies, roundabouts, swing boats, and many other booths and stalls. Somewhere, a band was playing. People thronged the walkways.

On the right hand side there were no marquees. Here, autocars of all types were lined up, row after row. So many, thought Dorothea. The BFS machines were lost in the crowd. Men were busy, polishing the motors, checking the engines. Other men stood in little groups, talking and pointing. Nearby, some sturdy shire horses were patiently waiting.

Dorothea looked ahead as the motor swept on. The driveway divided in front of the house. They followed the left-hand branch, passing under a wooden arch with START and FINISH painted on it, before proceeding into a meadow to the left of the house itself where already many carriages, carts and autocars were parked; there were also bicycles in profusion. Horses with nosebags were tethered to a fence. Coachmen and chauffeurs in smart uniforms were standing round, chatting and smoking.

Their own grey old chauffeur found a place to stop. The engine died. Dorothea could hardly wait to get down. She held her skirts up away from the wet grass. The leaden sky pressed down on them but at least the rain had stopped now.

Birds were singing. The sound of music and many voices came faintly on the breeze.

'Oh, miss!' whispered Nora. 'Isn't it lovely! What a treat!'

Aunt Eloise sounded less impressed. 'Let us and go and find out what one is meant to do in all this pandemonium.'

They left the aged chauffeur in charge of the motor, picked their way across the soggy field and out through a gate onto the drive. Aunt Eloise forged ahead like a galleon breasting the waves. People jumped out of her way then stopped to look back — for her aunt, thought Dorothea with a rush of pride, was magnificent: immensely dignified; handsome; immutable.

As they neared the front steps of the house, a woman in a striking lime green dress and an enormous hat came bearing down on them.

'So you are here too! Isn't it extraordinary? Such a triumph for Sir Walter. Half the county is here.' It was Mrs Somersby, wildly ostentatious as always; her daughter Julia was demure at her side. 'One had wondered if . . . with Sir Walter only being the son of a — *ahem* — but . . . there are rumours that Lord Denecote himself will grace us with his presence later, which puts rather a different complexion on things. I am just going to pay my respects to Lady Milton. We can go together, Eloise. Only the select few are being admitted to the house, naturally. Come along Julia. And do try not to frown, darling, it really doesn't become you.'

Poor Julia! There was nothing *wrong* with her, Dorothea remembered, but she wasn't *right* for Henry. But nobody would good enough for Henry — not unless he married Nora or the mam'zelle. But alas, Dorothea was old and wise enough to know that some marriages would never be possible.

Aunt Eloise went off towards the house with Mrs Somersby and Miss Julia, after giving Dorothea permission to go and look at the autocars with Nora to keep an eye on her. They wandered between the rows of vehicles.

'There they are, miss!' exclaimed Nora. 'There's Mr Brannan and Master Henry and the rest. And — oh!'

Nora stopped short, went bright red. Following the direction of her gaze, Dorothea saw a young mechanic bent over one of the BFS engines — none other than Arnie Carter, she realised, looking very smart in his blue overalls, almost as smart and bright and polished as the motors themselves. But the motors! There were two of them, sleek, shiny, stylish. Her heart thumped with pride. She felt as if they were hers, her own creation.

This was the new model, Mark II. It was very similar to the old Mark I (Eve) to look at, but there was something different about their engines — some great improvement. Henry had tried to explain, but Dorothea had not been able to keep up. It all sounded so complicated. Richard, of course, with his dream of becoming an engineer, would have been rapt; but Richard—

Oh, Richard! When would she learn to stop saying to herself, 'I must tell Richard that', only to remember with a terrible jolt that she would never tell him anything ever again?

Dorothea blinked away tears as she looked at the rows and rows of vehicles. She could not mask a twinge of doubt. Would the BFS motors really get the better of them *all*? But it was so very important that they did. The order books were nearly empty, Uncle Albert said. Business was ticking over instead of taking off. What was required was a practical demonstration of just how reliable and superior a BFS motor car was.

The BFS contingent certainly looked cheerful and confident. Dorothea had never seen Uncle Albert so expansive, accosting passers-by, pointing proudly to the Mark II, engaging in banter. Mr Simcox and Mr Smith were handing out leaflets. Henry and Mr Giles were on hand, looking very dashing in their leather coats with their goggles pushed up over the caps. Along with Arnie Carter, there was another mechanic by the name of Young, at one time the blacksmith's apprentice in the village. Young had been a dab hand at knocking up spare parts for Henry. Now he was employed by Uncle Albert in Coventry, where he was involved in the manufacture of motor components. Getting hold of components had always been something of a problem, which Uncle Albert had partly solved by making his own, turning over part of the bicycle business to that end, ensuring a regular supply of a quality he could rely on.

The blacksmith had been philosophical, on the whole, about losing his apprentice. 'These young lads. They don't know when they're well off. Give up a good trade at the drop of a hat for the latest fad and fancy, and think nothing of it. I don't know what the world is coming to.'

Arnie Carter was the first to notice as Dorothea and Nora approached. He doffed his cap to Dorothea. 'Hello, miss. Remember me? It must be all of two years now since you came up to Coventry that time. I hardly recognised you, you look so grown up!' He grinned at her but his eyes kept sliding past to look at Nora. She was hanging back, oddly reticent. 'How's things in the village, miss? How's our Becky and our Nibs and the rest? It's been a while since I found time to go home, what with the new models and the race and all. But I'm getting on well, miss, earning a good wage now, and . . .' He was screwing his cap in his hands, looked suddenly anxious.

'The village is just the same,' said Dorothea. 'Becky is keeping busy and Nibs . . . well, Nibs is Nibs. But Nora can tell you more. She knows all the goings-on.'

'Oh, miss, why did you go and say that!' Nora hissed in Dorothea's ear. 'I can't think of a word, and that's the truth!'

She was as red as a beetroot, it was quite inexplicable. But Dorothea had no time to get to the bottom of Nora's and Arnie's strange behaviour. Henry came bounding over — *full of the joys of spring*, as Nora might have said if she hadn't been so tongue-tied.

'Quite a sight, isn't it, all this! And they say autocars won't ever amount to anything!'

'But Henry, there are so many! How can you hope to win?'

'We've every faith in the Mark II. Smith is nothing short of a genius. We've done our homework, too, you can be sure of that. We've worked out that there are only about a dozen serious challengers for today's prize. Do you see that machine over there with the blue bonnet? That's one of the Vesey-Lanes. A Vesey-Lane did a practice lap yesterday averaging thirty miles per hour, at twenty miles to the gallon! We're keeping our eyes on them!'

'I don't understand how this race works, Henry. What have miles per hour and gallons got to do with it?'

Henry explained. Each motor, he said, would set off at one minute intervals and do five circuits of the parkland. The winner would be the vehicle which did the best time (or had the highest average speed, which worked out as the same thing, apparently), while using the least amount of fuel. This was a competition for ordinary vehicles, he added — motors that you might see out and about on the roads — and to that end there were limits on weight and fuel. Last night, each machine had been weighed, and its tank had been filled with the allocated amount of petroleum and then sealed. Henry's job — and Mr Giles's — was to get the Mark IIs around as fast as they could without using up too much fuel.

'If we can pull this out of the bag, Doro, it will be just the ticket! The publicity will work wonders. There's a man from the *Motor News* here, and also from the *Northampton Chronicle*.'

'But none from the London papers,' said Uncle Albert, coming over. His expansive public smile had faded; his brow was now creased. 'We could do with some national coverage. That would really give us a boost. Ah well. We have to win first. Come along, child. Let's go and see the first competitors off. They're about ready to start, I think.'

Leaving Henry to his preparations, Dorothea walked with Uncle Albert towards the start/finish line. Mr Simcox accompanied them. A motor was being drawn slowly into place by plodding shire horses.

'So as not to waste fuel,' Uncle Albert explained. 'Which vehicle is that, Simcox?'

'The Wiggly Superior. If you remember, they had to resort to a cardboard bonnet to come in under the weight limit.'

'Ah, yes, so they did. I hope for their sake it doesn't start raining again, eh!'

The Old-King-Cole-figure of Sir Walter was now mounting the podium by the start/finish line. People were streaming from the marquee area, converging around the wooden arch. Sir Walter raised his hand — then dropped it. There was an eruption of applause and cheering as the Wiggly Superior with its cardboard bonnet jerked forward, its engine coughing, exhaust fumes billowing. Then it was away, negotiating the long straight in front of the house before turning a corner and disappearing into the parkland.

Uncle Albert blew out his moustache. 'Well,' he said. 'It's begun.'

The first of the Vesey-Lanes was next to go, followed by Mr Giles in one of the BFS Mark IIs. Mr Giles had Arnie Carter with him as his travelling mechanic, which was required in the rules.

'Oh, miss, isn't he handsome!' said a voice in Dorothea's ear. It was Nora, wreathed in smiles, rather breathless. She wasn't talking about Mr Giles, Dorothea surmised. 'They're bound to win, miss! I just know they'll win!'

But Dorothea wasn't so sure, and Uncle Albert was looking rather stern. Only Mr Simcox appeared unruffled, consulting his pocket watch and writing figures down in a little notebook. 'We'll get some early indication of how things are going when they come round to complete the first lap,' he said.

But the first indication came much sooner than that. There were calls for the horses, some sort of emergency. A vehicle had gone in a ditch, it was reported.

'Uncle, do you think—?'

'It won't be us, child.' He patted her shoulder. 'Milton's got his head screwed on, he won't be taking any unnecessary risks.' But his hand gripped her shoulder as the horses came back, dragging a machine behind them.

It was the Vesey-Lane. Dorothea let out a sigh of relief as she watched it, rather squashed and muddy, being moved back to the competitors' area. The driver and his mechanic looked shaken but were unharmed.

The second Vesey-Lane got under way as the first was being ignominiously towed back. After that came a flash-looking vehicle in bold red. It was long and sleek and rather larger than most of the other machines.

'The Speedmobile,' said Mr Simcox, noting down its time of departure.

'What do we know about it, Simcox?'

'Not much. It's rather been kept under wraps. Didn't do a practice run. The rumour is, it has a six-cylinder engine, in which case there's no hope of it completing the course, no matter how speedy it is — not with the allotted fuel.'

'Ah, well, good. One less to worry about.' Uncle Albert watched through narrowed eyes as the big motor car streaked away, its engine roaring.

Henry was next to go, with Mr Smith as mechanic. Dorothea waved and hurrahed but Nora obviously did not think either man handsome enough for comment.

The last few competitors set off. Already the crowd was thinning, people drawn back to the marquees, the amusements, the pie stalls and the beer tent. The band struck up a new tune. The smell of cooking began to mingle with that of exhaust fumes and trampled grass.

'Shall we take a look, miss?' Nora cast her eyes towards the marquees.

But Dorothea could think of nothing but the race, her heart in her mouth.

Why should it matter so much, she asked again. Why? And yet it did. Uncle Albert felt the same, she could tell. He gave her a taut little smile, looking rather paler than usual.

They waited.

* * *

Time passed. The guest of honour arrived. His ornate, resplendent coach created quite a stir. Watching the stooped figure of the earl being helped up the steps to the colonnaded entrance, Dorothea remembered how terrified she'd been meeting him so unexpectedly three years ago.

A small token. On behalf of my grandson. For your kindness.

But there would be no more shiny half-sovereigns; there was no one to be kind to now. Did the old earl miss Richard too, she wondered, or was the boy's death merely an inconvenience, an irritation — like unseasonal weather or his horse coming last in the Derby?

After luncheon, the earl reappeared along with Sir Walter and the other luminaries — Aunt Eloise, Mrs Somersby and Lady Fitzwilliam amongst them. Chairs had been set out for them at the top of the steps, and an awning erected to protect them from the rain (but somehow, despite the lowering sky, the rain was holding off). There was a large flock of Miltons up there, too. They let out a rousing cheer as Mr Giles came round to complete his penultimate lap. But Mr Giles was beginning to lose ground. He had started brightly, Simcox said, but was now well down the field. At least he was still going. News had been filtering back for some time of crashes and engine trouble and vehicles running out of petrol. A third of the field had come to grief one way or another. Was Henry still on course? He was due round any time now.

Mr Simcox was busy with his calculations. The Vesey-Lane was in the lead so far, he reckoned. The brilliant red Speedmobile was second, just half a minute behind and moving quickly up the rankings. But it would never last the course, Mr Simcox was certain. It must be down to its last drops of fuel by now.

At last Henry reappeared. It had been a long wait, thought Dorothea — or did it just seem that way? Simcox made some jottings in his notebook. The news was good — better than good. Henry was a minute up on the Vesey-Lane. On the last circuit he had actually taken the lead!

'Are you sure, Simcox?' said Uncle Albert with a furrowed brow.

'Absolutely sure.' Simcox tucked his pencil behind his ear, adjusted his cap. He was unflappable. A good, steady right-hand man. Perhaps that was why Uncle Albert had employed and promoted him all these years. Uncle Albert was less sanguine. Dorothea would never have believed he could get the jitters but when it was something that really mattered, like today, well . . .

A thin drizzle began to fall as people came drifting back from the marquees and attractions, gathering for the end of the race. The band reassembled by the start/finish line and struck up a cheerful number. Dorothea sheltered with Nora under an umbrella. Soon the first competitors came whirring and wheezing over the finish line. Judges bustled forward with clip boards, marking down the times, measuring the fuel.

Simcox's notebook was rather soggy by now, but as Henry drove under the wooden arch to complete the course he calculated that the Mark II had averaged 33.4 miles per hour; and when news came that the motor had finished with seven pints of fuel in reserve, there was a sense of elation in the BFS camp.

'That's a much better result than the Vesey-Lane managed,' Mr Simcox said, flicking through the pages of his damp notebook. 'A much better result. I am quietly optimistic. We just have to wait for the last competitors now.'

Events were moving to a pitch of excitement. Dorothea had butterflies in her tummy, Uncle Albert was pacing restlessly. But a shock awaited. Against all predictions, the Speedmobile had survived to reach the finish line. Soon an astonishing rumour was spreading like lightning amongst the aficionados. The Speedmobile had managed an average of 33.6 miles per hour and had nine pints of fuel left! It was no real surprise that the Speedmobile should be quicker, Mr Simcox said, but the fuel consumption for a six-cylinder engine was nothing short of miraculous. Whoever had designed the Speedmobile had broken new ground in efficiency.

A crowd began to gather around the bright red machine, the man from the *Motor News* amongst them.

'Pipped at the post!' said Uncle Albert bitterly.

'But we came second, Uncle!'

'No one will remember the name of the vehicle that came second. No, child. We have to accept it. We were beaten by a better machine.' He rubbed his arm, grimacing, as if to accept defeat was like a physical pain.

'Smith will need to pull his finger out,' said Mr Simcox, 'if he is to match an engine of that calibre. It's back to the drawing board for us.'

'The business is likely to go under before that happens,' said Uncle Albert, still rubbing his arm.

'Are you . . . alright, Uncle?' He had gone a bit grey in the face.

'Just a twinge, child. Don't fuss.'

'All the same,' said Simcox quietly, 'it wouldn't hurt you to sit down for a bit.'

He touched Uncle Albert's elbow, indicating with a nod of his head some chairs a little way off. Surprisingly, Uncle Albert didn't argue. Perhaps he really did feel off-colour, or perhaps he had too much respect for Mr Simcox. It was interesting, thought Dorothea, these little glimpses into her uncle's other life, the Coventry life of the businesses and the factory. But standing under the umbrella with Nora watching Uncle Albert and Simcox walk away through the drizzle, a sense of disappointment swept over her, as grey and heavy as the clouds. She remembered that bright autumn day two and a half years ago when Eve first arrived at Clifton Park. There had been such excitement and optimism — and now it had come to nothing. All their hopes and dreams were being washed away on a dank Whitsun Monday.

The area in front of the podium was now being cleared ready for the presentation. All the vehicles except the top three were driven, pushed or pulled back to the competitors' area. Mr Smith came hurrying over. He needed help moving the second BFS, the one that had finished some way down the field. Had Dorothea seen Giles Milton? Where were Simcox and Mr Brannan? 'I did ask that Carter boy to give me a hand, but he was too busy chatting up the Speedmobile mechanics — and the next thing I knew, they were all off to the beer tent! I expected better of Carter, I have to say. He'll be jumping ship next, I shouldn't wonder. Wants a piece of the glory, I daresay.'

'I'll go and fetch him, sir. I'll go right away.' Nora looked stung by Mr Smith's criticisms of her beloved Arnie Carter. As she turned to go she muttered, 'I thought Arnie had more about him, miss. Fancy leaving his friends to go off drinking! I'll have some words to say on the matter, you can be sure!' Could it be that the paragon Arnie Carter had finally blotted his copy book? Dorothea thought that she wouldn't like to be in Arnie's shoes. Nora had a face like thunder.

Dorothea now found herself alone on the edge of the crowd. The drizzle had petered out, so she folded the umbrella and took a look around. There seemed to be a hiatus in proceedings. The band had fallen silent but the dignitaries were still missing from the podium. Up by the colonnaded entrance to the house there was a bustle of activity. A knot of people had gathered. Someone was being helped indoors. Had the old earl been taken ill? For some reason she could not put her finger on, Dorothea felt a sense of foreboding. She began to walk towards the steps to find out what was happening but at that moment someone tapped her urgently on the shoulder. Nora she thought, back from the beer tent with news of Arnie. But when she turned round she found herself face-to-face with Arnie himself. There was no sign of Nora.

'Miss Dorothea? It's a liberty, I know, but could you possibly give me a hand with something?' He was pink-cheeked, rather flustered, as if he *had* been drinking, but Dorothea knew all about drink and its effects, and there was no smell of beer on Arnie's breath. 'I need to have a look at that Speedmobile, miss, a good proper look.'

'But why? I don't—'

'It's important, miss, real important. But they're not letting anyone near.'

It was true. There was still quite a crowd around the shiny red vehicle and its proud owners were there, strutting up and down like peacocks, keeping admirers at bay.

'Please, miss. Will you come? Will you come now? I don't have time to explain!'

He didn't really give her chance to refuse, taking her arm and guiding her towards the winning motor. Dorothea didn't know what to think. All she could focus on was the fact that she would never hear the last of it from Nora if she let precious Arnie down in any way.

'Try to cause a diversion, miss! Catch their attention, the lot of them!'

But how? Arnie nudged her forward, his pale eyes needling her. She couldn't think of anything. Her mind was a blank. But at that moment, out of the corner of her eye, she saw Sir Walter and the earl at last making their way down the steps from the house. Without stopping to think, she began jumping up and down, pointing, shrieking at the top of her voice. 'Look, look! It's Sir Walter and his lordship! They're going to present the prizes! Isn't it exciting! Isn't it exciting!'

She felt ridiculous, like a silly little girl having hysterics and making a spectacle of herself. But after the first few terrible moments when everyone turned to stare at her, it wasn't so bad. Attention shifted to Sir Walter and the earl. People began clapping and cheering, lining the route to the podium. Sir Walter was smiling and waving, stopping to exchange pleasantries with every second person. The Speedmobile's two owners stood watching, exchanging self-satisfied looks. They obviously couldn't wait to get their hands on the prize.

'Now, Arnie, now!' Dorothea turned, urging him on — but Arnie Carter had vanished!

Even as she stood there looking all round in bewilderment, she heard a scrabbling sound at her feet and Arnie came wiggling out like a ferret from under the Speedmobile. He jumped to his feet, his overalls wet from the grass. His face was grim as he took his cap out of his pocket and jammed it on his head.

'It's just as I thought, miss. The Speedmobile didn't win fair and square at all. They're cheats, miss: cheats!'

* * *

Everything happened in a whirl. Dorothea found herself pushing though the crowd in Arnie's wake. She could see in the distance — half-hidden by bobbing heads, the tops of hats — Sir Walter and the old earl ascending the podium. The band had struck up again, people were clapping and cheering. She thought she could hear Arnie, some way off now, shouting. 'Sop! Wait!' But she'd lost track of him, was caught in the crush, couldn't go forwards, couldn't go backwards.

The music stopped abruptly. There was a buzz in the crowd. Dorothea was pushed this way and that as people surged forward, eager to find out what was happening. The buzz grew louder. Dorothea began to panic. She couldn't breathe, was trapped, bodies pressing round her, crushing her. Twisting round, she fought desperately to escape, to retrace her steps, barely aware of wild rumour chasing wild rumour through the crowd.

All at once a know-it-all voice nearby rose above the hubbub. 'It's that winning motor, the Speedster or whatever it's called. That's what all the fuss is about.'

Despite her anxiety Dorothea paused, listening. People were turning towards the know-all, flinging eager questions at him. What was happening now? Why the delay? What did it all mean?

'They've tried to swindle us, that's what's happened!' cried the know-all. 'Their fuel tank has a false bottom! They had a secret supply of fuel!'

So that was it, thought Dorothea as she began to push her way through the crowd again but at a more sedate pace now, her panic subsiding. That was what Arnie Carter had been looking for. Mr Simcox had said that it was nothing short of miraculous the way the Speedmobile had managed to get round the course on so little fuel. Arnie must have guessed or somehow discovered that there was a more sinister explanation to the so-called miracle. Perhaps it had something to do with him hobnobbing with the Speedmobile mechanics, going with them to the beer tent. Perhaps they'd let something slip, aroused Arnie's suspicions. Mr Smith had been annoyed, Nora had been disappointed — but Arnie had been doing the right thing all along!

With a big sigh of relief, Dorothea eased her way out from the back of the crush, gulped in air. The crowd had broken into applause again, people were cheering. Making her way to the steps of the house, Dorothea climbed up so she could see. On the podium, Sir Walter was making a speech. Snatches of it drifted through the damp air across the heads of the crowd. '. . . a wonderful day . . . marvellous spectacle . . . outstanding success . . . the forefront of engineering on display . . . the right result — in the end . . . and now, it gives me great pleasure . . . his grace the Earl of Denecote!'

There was a little table on the podium with a large trophy and a bottle of champagne. The earl stepped forward, leaning on his stick. And then, mounting the podium, their hats in their hands, bashful smiles on their faces, Henry appeared with Mr Smith in tow. Wild applause and cheering. Henry held the trophy above his head. But where was Uncle Albert? This was his triumph as much as anyone's. Who else would have taken a chance on a stranger met so casually on a train? Who else would have seen the potential? He should be there on the podium at this moment of triumph!

She heard feet skipping down behind her and turned to see Mr Giles making his way down the steps.

'Mr Giles, Mr Giles, wait! Where is Uncle Albert? Why isn't he with Henry and Mr Smith?'

Mr Giles paused, looked at her sidelong. Didn't she know, he lisped, had no one told her? Mr Brannan had been taken ill, he'd had to be carried into the house. The doctor had been summoned.

Dorothea went cold all over. She remembered her sense of foreboding from earlier. Seeing the commotion up by the entrance, she'd thought it must be the old earl. Afterwards, when she'd seen Lord Denecote making his way to the podium, she had never guessed, had never dreamed—

Alone on the steps, she looked up at the vast, imposing facade of the house and she trembled.

* * *

It was a magnificent room, enormous, wood-panelled and gilt-edged, packed with sumptuous furniture. A huge painting dominated one wall: a warlike scene with a label saying *The Battle of Malplaquet*. Uncle Albert was stretched out on a chaise longue, his face grey and drawn. He looked somehow smaller, diminished — but Dorothea could not decide if that was the effect of his illness, or of the spacious, majestic room.

'I'm alright, child, I'm perfectly alright. I was just a little short of breath, had a pain in my chest. It's gone now, I feel much better. It will take more than a dizzy turn to throw me off my stride! Now, then. Tell me what has been happening. What have I missed?'

Dorothea couldn't for a moment speak. Making her way into the house, she had been overcome by dread. She had been thinking of Richard. It had all come back to her as if it was yesterday, the shock and the trauma and the overwhelming sense of grief. Was she now to go through it all again? To find Uncle Albert alive and — he insisted — quite well was such a relief that it took her breath away. Aunt Eloise was standing by the chaise longue, upright, like a guardian angel, watching over Uncle Albert, protecting him.

It seemed to Dorothea as she looked at her aunt through a sudden mist in her eyes that the battle scene in the background was coming to life, horses rearing, sabres flashing, smoke drifting, the cannon booming — or was that her own heart, thudding wildly inside her chest? But nothing would daunt Aunt Eloise, not even the Battle of Malplaquet. She stood stiff and straight, unyielding. Even Death wouldn't dare, even Death wouldn't . . .

Aunt Eloise took a step forward. 'If you will sit with him for a moment, Dorothea, I will see if the doctor has arrived yet.'

'All this fuss,' muttered Uncle Albert but Dorothea blinked away the mist in her eyes and nodded at her aunt vigorously. She felt as if she had just been handed something of immense value — a golden chalice, perhaps; her aunt had entrusted her with a golden chalice.

Aunt Eloise inclined her head as if in blessing, then glanced at Uncle Albert, her eyes showing momentary doubt. 'All this fuss,' he muttered again but he held up his hand and Aunt Eloise reached out too, and for a split second their fingers touched. Then Aunt Eloise was gone, sweeping regally from the room. Behind the place where she'd been standing, the scene of battle was now stilled, frozen in time once more.

'Now then, child.' Uncle Albert sat up and Dorothea found a foot stool and plumped herself down and began telling him everything that had been going on outside.

'Well, well. A secret supply of fuel, eh? Well I never!' Uncle Albert chuckled. 'Poor old Smith! He was quite convinced someone had outmatched him — quite down in the dumps about it. And young Carter: he's a lad with his head screwed on, I've always said as much.' He chuckled again. There was some colour coming into his cheeks now and a sparkle in his eyes.

Thank heavens, thought Dorothea, that it had been *good* news she had brought with her. It seemed to have worked wonders.

* * *

The doctor came. Everyone was ushered from the room. Dorothea went outside to get a breath of air and to see what was going on. It was late afternoon now but the fête was still in full swing. A raucous sound of music and many voices was drifting from the marquees and amusements. Next to the podium, the Speedmobile had gone and the BFS Mark II had taken pride of place. An admiring crowd had gathered around it. Henry and Mr Smith were being lionised.

Mr Simcox came hastening up the steps, anxious for news about Uncle Albert. He and Uncle Albert had known one another for years, Dorothea remembered. It was only natural that he should be concerned. But it was more than that, almost as if they were friends rather than employer and employee — though Simcox was never less than deferential. Having assured him that Uncle Albert was none the worse for his dizzy turn, Dorothea prompted him to tell her all that had happened while she had been in the house. Well, said Simcox, well. His worried frown lifted a little. It was all good, he reported — better, really, than they could ever have expected. Several new orders had been placed already for BFS motors, including Sir Walter and — incredibly — the earl. Lord Denecote, Simcox said in a respectful tone, had requested two vehicles and had paid in full on the spot. Meanwhile, the man from the *Motor News* was preparing a glowing report for the next number of his magazine. There was even talk of the London papers being interested in the day's events. The cheating scandal would, of course, be of chief concern but there was every reason to believe that the BFS Motor Manufacturing Company would get an honourable mention.

Leaving the lugubrious Mr Simcox to reflect on the fortunes of the day, Dorothea returned to the house. In the lavish hallway she hesitated amongst the statues on plinths and the ferns and flowering plants in earthenware pots. Voices were coming from the room where she had left Uncle Albert. One of the voices was her uncle's. The other was aged, rasping, rigid with pride. Lord Denecote, she realised with a jolt of surprise. Lord Denecote was talking to Uncle Albert.

'. . . apologise for any vexation or nuisance he may have caused. He does not stop to consider the *consequences* of his actions, never has . . .'

He, thought Dorothea, who was *he*? Was the old earl talking about his son, Viscount Lynford? Did he know that Uncle Albert had chased Lynford away from Clifton two years ago? Was he angry about it? He did not *sound* angry. His tone was as stiff and formal as ever.

'. . . only myself to blame, I realise that of course. I spoiled the boy. I spoiled them both: the boy *and* his sister. My own father, you see, was a brutal man — a brutal man. I did not want to fall into the same trap.' There was a brief silence, then a long rattling sigh. 'And so I erred the other way. I indulged them. Coddled them. I see that now. But no one has paid a higher price for that mistake than I. This, however, is of no interest to you. I merely wished to convey my regret if his behaviour in any way . . . and of course, if you find that you are out of pocket due to his . . . his—'

Uncle Albert interrupted at this point. There was no need to talk of money, he said; his grace wasn't culpable, in any case. It would be best all round if the whole episode was forgotten.

After the earl's clipped, crabbed, but precise tones, Uncle Albert sounded rather uncouth, rough round the edges, like a bear growling.

'He has always been profligate, irresponsible,' the earl resumed after a pause. 'Gambling, drinking, all manner of other habits and weaknesses. I have done my best to change him but . . . well, he may be beyond redemption, I fear. But at least his child — his heir — is now out of harm's way. I have the boy under my own protection. As for my other grandson — well, he is at peace now, but I wanted an opportunity of thanking you for all that you did for him — you *and* your wife . . .'

Richard, thought Dorothea. The old man was referring to Richard. *All that you did for him, you* and *your wife*. She recalled the terrible vision she had seen in the field in January — a mad delusion, it seemed to her now, a symptom of her illness. Aunt Eloise was not wicked. Whatever else she was, she was not wicked. For one thing, Uncle Albert would never have married a *wicked* woman. Dorothea had complete faith in her uncle's judgment. However devoted Aunt Eloise was to Clifton Park, she would never have wished Richard *dead* so that she could get her hands on it.

All that you did. And who could have done more? No one could have healed his withered leg, no one could have saved him from the ravages of diphtheria — not even the earl and all his riches.

As she gulped back a sob — thinking of Richard still made her cry — Dorothea heard a scraping, sliding sound, and a puffing of breath. She realised that his lordship must be getting ready to go, struggling to his feet.

'I will take my leave, Mr Brannan. Oh, and one last thing. Congratulations on your success today. Well deserved, I do not doubt it. Hard work brings its own rewards — something my son has never been able to grasp. I wish you all the best with your project. I hope you have a speedy recovery.'

Dorothea shrank behind a potted palm as the earl came shuffling out of the room, tap-tapping with his stick. Bent over, wrinkled, his hair thinning and completely white, his face was nonetheless set and determined, his eyes steely — as if it was the strength of his will that kept him going in his fading years, knitting his very sinews together. A terrible man, she thought hiding her face behind the waxy leaves. A good man perhaps, deep down, but terrible even so. Watching as a liveried attendant came running from a side door to help the old man, Dorothea shuddered, glad of her uncle — of Aunt Eloise, too, cold and aloof but with a heart beating inside her. She was only human, had made mistakes. Had she really fallen in love with Jonathan Huntley, for instance? Would one ever know, or was it lost in the mists of the past? But her mistakes were long ago and she had learned her lesson. She had chosen wisely since then. She had chosen Uncle Albert.

Poor, poor Richard! Such a terrifying grandfather, such an unscrupulous uncle, such a short little life! *God's will,* Mlle Lacroix called it; God would look after him now. But as she stood there in the empty hallway, Dorothea had the strangest feeling that Richard was there, just out of reach, behind one of the statues, perhaps, or concealed by the foliage. She smiled, thinking of how he would have enjoyed today if he'd been well enough to come, and how much she would have had to tell him if he'd stayed at home. What a day it had been!

* * *

It was coming to an end at last. The stalls and attractions were shutting down, the marquees were being dismantled. A stream of people, of bicycles, carts, carriages and motors, was dwindling away up the drive. All that was left was trampled grass and patches of mud. The two BFS motors departed, Uncle Albert and Henry in one, the other heading for Coventry with Mr Simcox, Mr Smith, Arnie Carter and Young the second mechanic. Uncle Albert looked completely recovered. A heart murmur, the doctor had said. It couldn't be very serious, thought Dorothea, a mere *murmur*.

Walking back to their own motor, Dorothea lagged behind her aunt, Nora beside her talking nineteen to the dozen. She'd never known such excitement, she'd had a wonderful time, she would never forget it until the end of her days. And Arnie — oh, wasn't he a hero, and so handsome too, even with oil on his face and grubby wet overalls and one too many beers inside him.

'Oh, miss! Miss! If I keep it to myself any longer I shall burst! You'll never *guess* what has happened — you'll never *guess*! He has asked me to marry him! *Me*, marry *him*! Can you credit it? Oh, miss, I'm that happy I could—'

But at that moment Aunt Eloise called on them to hurry and there was no time for further talk.

Rolling slowly homewards through the dusky lanes, Dorothea leant out of the window, the wind whirling in her face, blowing her thoughts every which way. The leafy hedgerows spun past, vanished behind them into the gloom. There were spots of rain in the air again.

'Shut the window, now, Dorothea,' said Aunt Eloise. 'It is getting draughty.'

With the window closed, the evening countryside suddenly seemed dim and distant. Dorothea sat cocooned in the motor as it jolted and jerked over the ruts in the road. The journey back seemed to be taking an eternity. Her eyelids began to droop.

And Nora, she said to herself, picking up the threads of her thoughts: Nora was getting married, Arnie Carter had asked her at last. But did that mean Nora would go away? She would have to leave the nursery, whatever happened. She would not be able to keep her situation once she was married. But would she move to Coventry — all the way to Coventry?

Dorothea's heart lurched at the idea of losing Nora. Nora had always been there, from the very first morning. Dear Nora. Why, when wonderful things happened — the BFS motor winning first prize, Nora getting married — did unpleasant things have to happen too, like Uncle Albert's illness and Nora leaving Clifton?

I wish, thought Dorothea, *oh how I wish—*

But the thought was too vast and nebulous for her tired head to encompass and she never completed it. Instead her eyes closed, her head lolled, and she slept.

CHAPTER TEN

Taking a deep breath, Dorothea opened the drawing room door and walked in — only to find it empty. She was the first one down. She let out her breath, a sigh of relief; for it would have been agonizing to have made an entrance, to have all eyes upon her. Not that she didn't think her frock — white cotton gauze with stitched mauve decoration — the most beautiful thing she had ever seen, but somehow it seemed almost *too* beautiful, as if she had a cheek to even *think* of wearing it, plain old Dorothea. There had been no question, however, of *not* wearing it. It was a gift from Aunt Eloise, made especially. It had taken an age to put on, with so many buttons and hooks-and-eyes, and the new nursery maid all fingers and thumbs, not a patch on Nora. Finding good staff was quite impossible these days, Aunt Eloise had said pointedly as she kept a watchful eye on proceedings. The poor maid! She faced an uphill task. Anyone would be ham-fisted in Aunt Eloise's punctilious presence. And no one could fill Nora's shoes.

Dorothea crossed the drawing room, aware of every rustle of material, every swirl of her skirts, feeling every inch a young lady: it was a feeling that would take some getting used to. The french windows were open. She stepped out onto the terrace.

The heat of the day was lingering, though the air felt cool on her neck, unused as she was to having her hair up. The sun was low in the sky away to the right. Shadows were lengthening. Beneath the distant boughs of Ingleby Wood dusk already lay in wait. But evening sunshine lay thick and golden on the verdant fields and hedgerows, and glinted here and there on the half-hidden canal. Dorothea breathed deeply. The air was scented with grass and clover. A perfect day, she said to herself. *Her* day. Her birthday. The seventh birthday she'd celebrated at Clifton.

Seven years! She could scarcely believe it! Time was she'd not envisaged spending one birthday here let alone seven. Her first birthday at Clifton had passed almost unnoticed. She'd still been getting used to the place, getting used to her new governess too — discovering that not all governesses were monsters. Her birthday last year had been very different, a real celebration, made all the more special because it came so soon after the triumph of the BFS Mark II motor at Dravell Hall. But even last year paled by comparison with today. And the best was yet to come, for there was to be a dinner party in her honour — a dinner at which she was to be present, Roderick too, unlike that dinner party for Roderick's birthday long ago from which he'd been excluded to his great disgust. Dorothea smiled, remembering how they had sneaked downstairs and spied on the grown-ups, and how, without warning, Mrs Bourne had come swooping upon them, driving them back to their rightful place in the nursery. In those days the green baize door had been a frontier one only dared cross at one's peril but times had changed and now the whole house was open to her. Aunt Eloise still perhaps frowned on her habit of spending too much time in the servants' areas but nowhere these days was strictly out of bounds.

As for Roderick, he was home by special dispensation. She had pleaded his case to her aunt. 'WE can't have a dinner party without Roddy' she'd insisted as Aunt Eloise drew up a tentative guest list (a line had been drawn at asking any of the Turners). 'Pleas, Aunt! Roddy simply *has* to be here!'

Aunt Eloise had seemed pleased by her entreaty, had agreed at once, had written to the school and arranged for Roderick to take time off.

Dorothea sighed, shielding her eyes against the sunset as she looked at distant Hambury Hill which reared like a dark massing wave on the bright horizon. Roderick did not engender soothing thoughts. He'd never been the easiest to get on with. His presence was always a mixed blessing. Sometimes Dorothea wondered if he was worth bothering with at all. Arriving yesterday evening, Roderick had brought with him — uninvited — a friend from school named Harrington-Shaw, a rather podgy boy who went bright red whenever anyone spoke to him. It seemed to Dorothea an unlikely friendship. But what did she know of boys and their friendships?

She had nothing against Harrington-Shaw. What irked her was Roderick's high-handedness in bringing him. Roderick did things to suit himself. This could be very irritating. Which was why she had not been in the most conciliatory of moods this morning when they'd quarrelled. The quarrel had been about Nibs Carter, as it so often was.

Dorothea sighed again. Not quite a *perfect* day, then. But what day ever was?

Leaning over the parapet, Dorothea heard faint sounds on the still air. One of the basement windows must be open — the kitchen, by the sound of it. She could hear a clatter of dishes and Cook's voice, harassed. 'Mind my bread sauce. And what in heaven's name have you done with the watercress?'

Dorothea smiled, remembering Cook's 'particular breakfast' which had been brought up to the nursery that morning with a flourish and which she had shared with Eliza so that Eliza would not feel left out. This had started the day on the right note. Mlle Lacroix had then announced there would be no lessons that day and when soon after Uncle Albert had put in an appearance it only added to the sense of occasion. He'd not be going to Coventry today, he'd said, as it was a red letter day. What did she say to a little stroll later, just the two of them? Perhaps after lunch? He'd look forward to it!

The first hint of trouble had come when she went down to the kitchen to thank Cook for her breakfast. The kitchen maid, Milly Carter, had been in floods of tears, inconsolable. Nibs had been caught stealing vegetables from the garden. He'd had been dismissed outright.

'But he wouldn't, miss,' Milly had sobbed. 'He wouldn't do a thing like that!'

Dorothea had been inclined to agree. She'd felt even more dubious about the whole affair when she learned that Roderick was involved.

'I saw him with my own eyes, Doro. He was caught in the act.'

'Are you sure? You're not just making this up to get back at him?'

'Are you calling me a *liar*?' Roderick had got on his high horse. 'Alright then, don't believe me, see if I care.'

'Why must you be such a *child*!' she'd shouted after him as he stomped off. But almost at once she'd felt remorse, wondering if she might have got it wrong. After all, on the very first occasion she'd met Nibs Carter, he'd been stealing apples from the orchard. Perhaps he hadn't changed.

Directly after luncheon, she'd set off on her walk with Uncle Albert. It had seemed inevitable that their steps should take them to the village. They had stopped briefly at Richard's grave, turfed over now, slightly sunken, adorned with only a simple headstone — but a simple headstone seemed fitting, somehow: he had not been an ostentatious sort of boy. Starlings had been chattering on the church roof; the sun had been veiled by high clouds; her eyes had filled with tears. But only a single, solitary tear had run down her cheek as she stood there, realising that she was now older than Richard would ever be. Uncle Albert had taken her hand without a word and they had left the churchyard, crossed the green, walked slowly down School Street. After four years, the jagged walls of the burnt-out cottages had been rubbed smooth at the edges by the wind and the rain and the sun. The black stains were slowly fading into the sandstone. Ivy wreathed them; grass lapped them. They seemed indeed to be slowly sinking into the greenery. Down in Wilmot's yard, smart new stables had appeared, but there was no hay rick yet this year.

Strolling up Back Lane, Uncle Albert had taken a detour down the footpath towards Manor Farm in order to call on Noah Lee in his little cottage. 'I have a new kind of ointment for his rheumatics which I want to drop off.' But Dorothea had known that this was just an excuse. Once they got going, the two men would chunter away for half an hour at least, 'putting the world to rights', as Uncle Albert said. Dorothea, leaving her uncle to his talk, had taken the opportunity to hurry on up Back Lane. She'd not been sure what good she could do even if she dared knock on the Carters' door but there'd been no need to knock, for Nibs had been at work in his garden.

He had been at his most exasperatingly obtuse. 'Well, miss, if they say I took the vegetables, I suppose I must have done.'

'Which is it? Did you or didn't you?'

'I wouldn't like to say, miss.'

'Robin Carter! You're sixteen years old! I thought you'd have outgrown this childishness by now! And stop calling me *miss*.'

'What else should I call yer?'

'Whatever you like. You don't work at the big house anymore, so please don't feel the need to be polite.' She'd winced at the sarcasm in her words but that was what he drove her to.

He'd looked at her in his deadpan way and said, 'Ah. Well. I don't call you *miss* because I have to, but because I want to. *You're* alright, miss, as I've said before. But there's others I could mention who think they're God Almighty and who need to watch their step in future.'

'Roddy, you mean?'

But he wouldn't say, just repeated over and over that he'd been taken for a muggings and he wouldn't fall for that sort of trick again.

Standing now on the terrace with the evening sun giving a golden sheen to the world, Dorothea wondered if she would ever get to the bottom of this latest run-in between Roderick and Nibs — or indeed any of their other arguments over the years. What was it all for? Did they even know themselves? She had never been given any satisfactory explanation as to how and why the feud had started. It seemed to be lost in the mists of time. Perhaps there *was* no explanation. Perhaps boys couldn't help being pig-headed and silly. Nibs went out of his way to make life difficult for himself, that was certain.

Unable to make any headway that afternoon, she had left Nibs to his own devices and loitered in the street, waiting for Uncle Albert and feeling that the afternoon had been spoiled. But then Mrs Turner had come out of her cottage wiping her hands on her apron and had called Dorothea over to her gate, wishing her many happy returns and offering her a choice of flowers from the garden to make into a bouquet or corsage.

'You may have as many as you like, miss, with my blessing, only I won't cut them now. I'll send them up later so they stay fresh. You can wear them to this dinner which our Nora says is to be given in your honour.'

All these hours later, Dorothea on the terrace fingered her corsage with a sense of pride, for Mrs Turner did not give her flowers to just anybody. Billy Turner had conveyed them from the village, had come right up to the nursery with a bunch of pinks, wallflowers and forget-me-nots in his fist.

'Mother made me promise to give them to you personal. And see, I've not crushed a one.' And in that he'd confounded his mother's expectations — for *cack-handed* wasn't the word, she'd said, when it came to their Billy. 'Seventeen, he is. A lubbery great lad. But he has a heart of gold for all that.'

Dorothea had always found him rather dour but she was willing to take the heart of gold on trust. He was, after all, a Turner.

The day room had been busy by then, Dorothea resplendent in her new frock, all the buttons and hooks-and-eyes finally fastened. Mlle Lacroix, Nanny, little Eliza had all exclaimed at the vision she made; Aunt Eloise had stood silent to one side with a contented look on her face. It had been rather an odd moment, thought Dorothea as she strolled up and down the terrace. A strangely satisfying moment, to have Billy Turner in the nursery with his clod-hopping boots and his cap in his hand and his cheeks on fire while Aunt Eloise stood there regally, not a hair out of place. Such a clash of opposites! And yet . . . and yet . . .

Dorothea paused in her perambulations, unable to frame her thoughts, unable to explain why it should make her heart beat so fast to be wearing Aunt Eloise's dress and Mrs Turner's flowers at the same time. Looking out from the terrace, watching the ponderous flight of a heron as it skimmed in the distance along the invisible line of the canal, it suddenly struck her that in all the hustle and bustle of the nursery earlier one had barely given a thought to Nanny sitting in a corner as quiet as a mouse — if one could legitimately compare so plump and solid-looking a woman as Nanny to a mouse. Thinking back in time to her first days and months at Clifton, it seemed to Dorothea scarcely credible that she had held Nanny in such dread. Over the years, Nanny's potency had diminished. Even little Eliza was not browbeaten by her these days.

Was this what it meant to grow up, Dorothea asked herself, this ability to see people in a different light, from two different vantage points?

The heron dwindled, was lost in the distance. Dorothea turned away, went back inside. The drawing room was empty and expectant. She couldn't sit still. She walked round and round, trailing her hand over the piano, peering at the delft vase on the sideboard, keeping half an eye on the door, wanting it to open, dreading it. But at least she could await Roderick's appearance with less trepidation now she had made her peace with him.

She had gone looking for him after her return from the village, knowing that Nibs's vagueness over the vegetable affair would allow her to sidestep the question of who was in the right and who wrong: the woolly thinking of a goody-goody, as Roderick would say.

She'd found him in the library, smoking.

'Smoking! You'll be in the dog house, Roddy, if Aunt Eloise catches you!'

'I'm quite safe. Mother *never* comes in here.' He'd been blasé about it, sitting with his feet propped on the desk. 'Odd, really, about Mother never coming here. I've not given it much thought until now.'

He'd blown out smoke, his eyes coming to rest on her speculatively — trying to pass himself off as older than he was, she'd thought; trying to make out he was grown up and worldly-wise. The vexing thing was, it worked. He pulled it off. One had constantly to remind oneself that he wasn't yet fourteen.

As if he could read her mind, he'd said with a mocking smile, 'And how does it feel to be the ripe old age of fifteen?'

'Why must you be so . . . so *horrible*?'

'What did I say?' All innocence. 'I only asked what it's like being fifteen. I wouldn't know, as I'm such a *child*. That was the word you used, wasn't it, earlier?'

'Well, you *are* a child. You *are*. You're horrible, too — sometimes, anyway.'

'I can't help that. It's in my nature. It's the way I'm made. Slugs and snails and puppy dogs' tails.'

'That's what you'd like people to think, but it's not true. Underneath, you're . . . you're nice.'

'*Nice*!' He'd been affronted and his voice had cracked, seesawing from baritone to treble and back again as he spoke. 'I am *not* nice at all! *Nice* people get walked on. I'd have thought you'd have learned that by now — at your age.'

She had managed to rein herself in, to smile, wise to his ways. 'I'm not going to argue with you, Roddy. I know that's what you want and I shan't do it!'

Roderick had smiled too, had given her a superior look as he sauntered over to the window to throw out his cigarette end.

Well, let him smile, she'd thought: *let him think he's superior if that's what he wants, if it makes him happy. And let Nibs sit at home without a job nursing his precious pride. I don't have to pander to either of them.*

As they left the library together, they'd run into Mrs Bourne in the corridor. It was impossible not to quail, impossible not to shrink against the wall and wait for the lash of her tongue. But the housekeeper had merely nodded and in a voice drenched with age-long decorum she had said, 'Miss Dorothea. Many happy returns of the day.' Then she had swept on her way, the sound of jangling keys fading as she went down the stairs to the basement.

If Dorothea had been astonished, then Roderick had been more so. His mouth had dropped open, he had looked at her as if she had just tamed a wild dragon. She had burst out laughing, because he looked so ridiculous — so like a *child*. But she had spared his blushes by not telling him so.

* * *

'Such a beautiful view, *Madame*,' said Mlle Lacroix to Aunt Eloise as they stood by the french windows waiting to go through to dinner. 'So very *English*. I have always thought so.'

'But it is not quite the view that was intended, Mademoiselle. The landscaping, unfortunately, was never finished.'

Aunt Eloise gave a sweep of her hand which, to Dorothea looking on, seemed to indicate not just the wide meadow known as The Park, but the whole panorama: the hedges, the trees, the hidden canal, the dark smudge of Ingleby Wood — even, perhaps, the distant mass of Barrow Hill, and the sky itself, deepening now to a dusky blue laced with thin white clouds. All this, Aunt Eloise seemed to be saying, was to have been encompassed in the unfinished landscaping of Clifton Park. And why not? What else was there? On this June evening, with the light lingering on the horizon, the heat of the day slowly fading, the air still, a hush on the land, it was impossible to think of being anywhere else. Coventry was a mirage, London a fading dream. Such a place as Stepnall Street might well never have existed except in the darkest of half-forgotten nightmares. Clifton was the centre of everything — *was* everything.

I am seeing Clifton, thought Dorothea, *through Aunt Eloise's eyes.*

'Almost no work was done on the grounds,' Aunt Eloise continued. 'The gardens as you see them now belonged to the old manor house which was demolished nearly two hundred years ago. If you notice, the house and the gardens are not quite aligned. The garden wall runs at an angle. New gardens were planned but — like the parkland — they were never set out. One must use one's imagination to see how it would have been.'

'I like your gardens as they are, *Madame*. So *parfait*. Delightful.'

'That is my opinion exactly, Mademoiselle.' Aunt Eloise bestowed on the governess a noble smile.

After all this time, thought Dorothea, Mlle Lacroix was finally being *approved* of. But it was almost too late.

This reminder of Mlle Lacroix's imminent departure filled her with dismay. The dreadful day was almost upon her. And yet Clifton Park without Mlle Lacroix was unthinkable.

Dorothea shivered, turning her back on the future, moving away from the french windows through which cool air was now whispering like a first, faint presage of the deep, dark night to come. She was no longer the centre of attention and she was glad of it. She had braved the little shocks as people came into the room, saw her, and said — oh, so many nice things, she couldn't remember half of them. But she felt like an impostor, just as she'd felt like an impostor earlier when Nanny had made her sand in the middle of the day room and turn round and round so she could be inspected from every side. 'You'll be the belle of the ball, my girl, the belle of the ball.' Nanny for once had not been irritable or put out. She'd sounded, in fact, almost wistful, as if long ago she'd once dreamed of being the belle of the ball. But Dorothea didn't want to be a belle. How could any girl want it? To be the centre of attention, to experience all the little shocks of people looking — it was a terrible ordeal! And the nice words, for all they were nice, were also like beaks pecking — pecking, pecking, pecking — pulling you apart, each person taking their portion.

Even a perfect day was not entirely perfect, as she'd realized earlier. There was always something, a twist of sadness, sharp and bitter. But, oh! If one could only draw the sting!

Here, though, was Uncle Albert on the settee, a big, solid, comforting presence. Lady Fitzwilliam was sat next to him. Dorothea lingered nearby, listening to their talk.

'Oh, don't worry about me,' Uncle Albert was saying. 'I'm as right as nine pence, in perfect health.'

'But you gave us such a fright, Albert, that day at Darvell Hall. I shall never forget it.'

'My dear Alice, that was a year ago. I'm quite recovered now. Ask Camborne if you don't believe me.'

'Is it really a whole year since the fête at Darvell Hall? How time flies at our age!'

'Our age!' scoffed Uncle Albert. 'I am in the prime of life, and you, Alice, are a spring chicken in comparison.'

Lady Fitzwilliam laughed. 'Such flattery! And you used to be such a plain-spoken man! But even a man in his prime must rest now and then, yet Eloise tells me you are busier than ever!'

'Ellie fusses,' said Uncle Albert. (Dorothea tried to imagine Aunt Eloise *fussing* and failed.) 'Ellie fusses, but in actual fact I am all but retired now. Some weeks I am in Coventry only three days out of six, if you can believe it.'

'You have your trusty lieutenants, Henry tells me, Mr Simcox and Mr Smith.'

'True, true. Simcox takes care of things at Crown Street — the bicycles, that is, and the motor components. Smith rules the roost at Allibone Road. Your son has told you, I suppose, about our new works in Allibone Road — the new BFS factory. Business is so brisk we needed larger premises. There's a new four-seater Mark II on the way. It will be launched at the Motor Show later this year. And there's the competition department. But you will know all about that. Your boy is in the forefront there.'

'My boy — as you call him — talks of nothing else.'

'Then you don't need to hear it from me. I am boring you, Alice. I'm sorry.'

'My dear Albert, *you* couldn't bore me if you tried! But here's Dorothea. Come and sit with us, my dear, there's plenty of room. There. That's it. A rose between two thorns. Tell me, how have you been spending this auspicious day?'

'She has spent a part of it with her old uncle. We walked to Hayton this afternoon, didn't we, child? Mind you, it took twice as long as I expected. The girl seems to know the whole village. Everyone we met wanted to stop and talk.'

'People talked to you, too, Uncle. And you were ages with Noah Lee.'

'Ah, so you're acquainted with *him*, are you, Albert? My late husband rather admired him on the quiet. A village character. He was, of course, an incorrigible poacher in his day. Old Harry — your aunt's father, my dear — used to tirade about it. He was a great sportsman, Old Harry, so all poachers were anathema to him. But it wasn't just poachers he fulminated against. It was the railways, too, and Gladstone. All the work of the Devil in Old Harry's eyes.'

Dorothea ventured to say, 'Noah Lee once told me Mr Rycroft was a tyrant.'

'It didn't do to cross him, my dear, that's true enough. But he was always charming to me. A real gentleman, I like to think.'

'That's what Becket says, too. Old Mr Rycroft kept the gardens spic and span, Becket says.'

'I daresay he did. Dear Old Harry. But he wouldn't have got on in the modern world. He wasn't like you, Albert. He was a creature of his time.'

'All I know is, I'm no sportsman. On our walk this afternoon we saw rabbits, pheasants, woodpigeon and I don't know what else. I felt no desire to shoot any of them. I no longer feel the need to go along with all that, even if I do live in the countryside — God help me.'

Lady Fitzwilliam laughed. 'Such an admission does you no discredit, Albert. I have never been wildly enthusiastic about that sort of thing myself. But we must look lively, my dears. I do believe it is time to go through to dinner.'

* * *

'Eight,' Aunt Eloise had said, looking at the names on her list. 'Such a small number. I could, I suppose, ask the Somersbys; or maybe the Adnitts from the village at a pinch.'

But Dorothea had been content with the list as it was. The Somersbys were not special friends like the Fitzwilliams, and the Adnitts she only really knew by sight.

Aunt Eloise had sighed. 'Very well. If that is how you want it. But it will be rather an *intimate* dinner.' She had taken her pen and drawn a line at the bottom of her list. 'Now comes the problem of who shall sit where.'

Dorothea found she'd been placed next to Roderick's friend from school. She watched him shyly out of the corner of her eye as he spooned his soup and tore up his bread roll, keeping his eyes down, his face flushing every shade of pink, beads of perspiration on his forehead. Was dinner, then, such an ordeal? She wished she had the gift of putting people at their ease the way her aunt did. Aunt Eloise made a success of every occasion, so that even virtual strangers were wont to think they'd made a conquest, talking of their 'dear new friend, Mrs Brannan'. But it was all a sleight of hand, for no one really knew Aunt Eloise at all — least of all her own family, or so it seemed. At times one caught glimpses beneath the facade but it was like trying to puzzle out the long history of the house merely by peering in at the windows.

All this, however, did not help when it came to starting a conversation with Harrington-Shaw.

'Mr Harrington-Shaw—' She blushed, feeling silly, like a little girl playing with dolls, putting words in their mouths. 'How is . . . er . . . how is school?'

School for Roderick and for Harrington-Shaw was a place called Downfield. Roderick had moved there last September after finishing prep school. Downfield was the traditional family school, Aunt Eloise said. Her brother Frederick had gone there as a boy. Aunt Eloise always spoke of Frederick in reverent tones. Handsome, clever, charming, modest, she made him sound like a *shining example*. There was never any mention, Dorothea noted, of his being a rake or rapscallion; his wild youth was not discussed.

'What is Downton *like*, Mr Harrington-Shaw?' She got very little out of Roderick, which only made her the more curious. He spent half his life at school, yet she knew next to nothing about it.

'It's . . . er . . . it's . . .' Harrington-Shaw went red as a beetroot, spilling his soup, scattering crumbs from his napkin. From the few stumbling words he got out, she understood that Downfield was very different to one's prep school, that it took some getting used to. It was, of course, one of the foremost establishments of its kind in the country, with much history and tradition, and so on and so forth (his voice trailed off into an indecipherable mumble).

That was all very well, thought Dorothea, but what actually *happened* there? Would she ever find out?

The disjointed conversation petered out. How did Aunt Eloise keep the talk flowing, where did she find the patience? Looking down, Dorothea realised her plate had been whisked away. Another course had come and gone. The lobster mayonnaise was finished. The roast duck must be on its way.

They were half way through the meal already and she could remember nothing, when she ought to be storing every detail, her birthday dinner, her first step into the world of the grown-ups. No more spying through the crack in the Dining Room door!

She began to note things down: the crease in the table cloth, the glittering chandelier, Mr Ordish discreet and inconspicuous. The cut glass seemed to shimmer in the electric light. Timms — the new John, Tomlin's replacement — repeatedly bit his bottom lip as he piled plates on his arm. And then there were the conversations weaving back and forth across the table. Dorothea dipped in to first one, then another.

'. . . and I took the bend at completely the wrong angle, skidded right round, and ended up facing downhill. Naturally I'd no chance of winning the climb after that . . .'

'. . . this is *le couteau* in French, Monsieur, and that is *la fourchette* . . .'

'. . . who would ever have imagined, my dear, that *all seven* Northamptonshire seats would go to the Liberals. Joseph must be turning in his grave . . .'

'. . . he has a ripping new cricket bat and I was wondering if I . . .'

'. . . motorised bicycles are really beginning to take off, and as for the motor components side of things — well, we can barely keep up with demand. The Crown Street works have never been busier . . .'

The roast duck came, the roast duck went; Cook's 'particular' birthday pudding slipped by too. Aunt Eloise got to her feet. Dinner was over. Dorothea folded her napkin. The ladies retired to the drawing room.

The french windows were still open. 'Very careless,' said Aunt Eloise reaching for the bell. But Dorothea said, 'I will close them, Aunt.' And Aunt Eloise said, 'Thank you, Dorothea.'

Dorothea closed one door, looked out before closing the second. There remained a glimmer of light, a rim on the horizon, far to the right, but high above stars were glinting in dark pools between the massing clouds. There was no moon: it was only one day from the new.

Dorothea pushed the door shut and turned the key in the lock.

* * *

Henry had brought his gramophone with him. They had music when the gentlemen joined them.

'A guinea a disc,' sighed Lady Fitzwilliam. 'Such profligacy.'

'But the music, Alice!' said Aunt Eloise. 'The music is enchanting!'

That is my aunt, thought Dorothea with a sense of wonder as the scratchy sound of Caruso's voice seeped from the gramophone. She'd never seen Aunt Eloise quite like this before, enthroned on the settee, smiling, dazzling, like sunlight sparkling on ice.

Henry stepped up, held out his hand. 'The birthday girl must dance.'

'Oh, no, Henry . . .'

But, yes, yes, they all said, and the table was pushed aside and she had no choice in the matter. She felt her cheeks burning as Henry took her in his arms, and then they were whirling away across the room in time to the music, to Caruso's ethereal voice which sounded as if he was singing to them from the far end of a long metal pipe. All her senses were tingling. There was a smell of soap and hair oil, and a smell of Henry himself. His bow tie was askew, there was a speck — gravy? wine? — on his collar. She could see the tiny shaven bristles on his jaw. She watched the colour flush up into his cheeks. And the whole time his eyes were shining at her.

'I shall never forget,' he said in an undertone, 'the night I first saw you, a little girl dressed in rags, crying, your curls all tangled.' He reached up, stroked her hair. The light in his eyes burned brighter. 'Only a few months later I rescued you on the Welby Road—'

'Rescued me?'

The smudges of colour in his cheeks darkened, like the reds and purples of a deepening sunset. 'That . . . that is how I always put it to myself: that I rescued you.' He swallowed, his adam's apple bobbing above his collar.

For a moment, pressed up against him, she felt stifled. She was at a loss to explain it. But of course the windows were shut, there was no air in the room. That was all it was. She could feel his arm across her back, guiding her in the dance, and suddenly she began to giggle softly, for it seemed to her that she was being driven the way he drove his motors. This was how Bernadette must have felt all these years with his careful hands on her wheel, his long, thin fingers. What a girl she must seem to him, giggling and stumbling around the room. What a girl she must seem to a man of his age, twenty-eight, so very grown up. He must be able to see through the touch of glamour — the new frock, the careful coiffure. He saw instead the girl in rags who'd sat on his knee so long ago. He saw the waif he'd rescued on the Welby Road, a waif without a penny to her name and a tam o'shanter that kept falling over her eyes.

As they swung past the settee, she overheard Lady Fitzwilliam talking to Aunt Eloise. 'Such a pity about Julia Somersby . . .' Dorothea could tell that Henry had heard too by the furrows that appeared on his brow.

'Is it absolutely out of the question?' Aunt Eloise murmured.

'I rather think Giles Milton has wrapped things up there.' Lady Fitzwilliam sighed. 'One is fond of Giles, naturally, but . . . a sixth son only . . . a boy with a lisp . . . and Henry, with all his advantages. To have one's hopes dashed again . . .'

Dorothea felt Henry's body tense up but at that moment they came to an abrupt halt. Roderick was blocking their path.

'It is my turn now,' he said curtly, setting his jaw.

Dorothea was inclined to laugh. What did Roderick know about dancing? But he looked so ferocious and determined, elbowing Henry aside, that the laughter died on her lips. What an extraordinary boy he was, so gruff and gangling, already almost as tall as Henry — and now he wanted to dance with her when he seemed to have been avoiding her all evening!

'Henry,' Roderick muttered as they began to move. His lips tickled her ear. 'That goose, that pudding-head.'

He was always the same, she thought with a twist of anger. He never had a good word for anybody. She tried to tear her hands away but he held on tight and swung her round and he whispered fiercely into her ear, 'I suppose you think you're all grown up now, don't you, Miss Ryan — Miss Dorothea Ryan!' And he scowled so hard his eyebrows met in the middle.

She had been right to doubt his dancing. He held her like a sack of potatoes, trod on her toes, stomped round the room like an angry bull. But if he wasn't exactly a grown man, you couldn't call him a child either. Who was he, she wondered, would anyone ever know? Did he even *like* her, deep down? Sometimes she doubted it. Sometimes she felt they had got no further than the first day, watching each other with suspicion in the day room.

'Don't they make a lovely couple,' said Lady Fitzwilliam, sotto voce. 'One could almost take them for brother and sister. They are really quite alike and so devoted.'

Roderick was scowling again, flushed with annoyance (why did he get so angry all the time?). She half expected him to push her away, to belie Lady Fitzwilliam's words. But instead he gritted his teeth and gripped her tighter and they went twirling and twirling as the gramophone began to slow, Caruso's voice stretching out and out along the metal pipe.

'Dear Dorothea,' Lady Fitzwilliam said. 'One has grown so fond of her. One feels one has known her forever.'

'I was thinking exactly the same thing myself,' said Aunt Eloise, her voice stiff with gravitas. 'One has to admit, one can't imagine the place without her anymore. It is as if she *belongs* here, somehow.'

And Dorothea, laying her cheek against Roderick's chest, felt her heart swelling inside her, for no one in all her life had ever paid her such a compliment before.

* * *

She was too keyed up to sleep, brimming over with so many different feelings, and music still playing in her head along with the sound of voices and sparks of laughter. But the drawing room downstairs was now dark and empty, the guests gone, everyone else in bed, the evening at an end, her birthday over.

She walked round and round the day room in the dim light from the lamp on the corner table, humming to herself, watched only by the fading eyes of the rocking horse and by Polly in her cage. It was not just her birthday which was over. So was life at Clifton as she'd known it. Richard had gone first, then Nora, and now Mlle Lacroix was to take her leave: the last of her original friends and the one who'd made most difference.

The governess had wisdom and an inner strength which always made the world seem a sunnier place.

'Oh, Polly! How will I ever manage without her?'

But Polly, inscrutable as ever, kept her thoughts to herself.

* * *

The sky was a cloudless, brilliant blue. The morning sun was hot and bright. As the motor swept along the road — the canopy down, the engine humming contentedly — the world seemed to open up around them, corn ripening, haymaking underway, flowers bursting from the tangled hedgerows, birds in profusion busy with their own affairs. But Dorothea in her mind's eye was seeing this road as it had been six-and-a-half years ago, dark and cold and lonely as she was dragged and carried by her papa from the station to a meet an uncle she had never heard of. She had today the same sense of journeying towards an uncertain end, for today was the day when the governess was leaving.

Mlle Lacroix sat beside her in the motor, buttoned into her jacket, gloves in her lap, wide-brimmed hat pinned in place. Dorothea felt as if a gap had already opened between them, as if — in spirit — the Frenchwoman was speeding south by train or halfway across the Channel or making her way down the familiar byways of her home. She was travelling alone as if it was nothing, as if she was merely taking a walk in the gardens. But the gardens would miss her after today.

It was all wrong, thought Dorothea, this bright morning with the birds singing. Rain ought to be lashing, the wind should be wailing, thunder should be booming like the drums of doom. She remembered what the nursery had been like before the governess came, the feelings of loneliness, of being in gaol. She shuddered despite the warm sunshine.

All too soon, the station hived into view. The motor pulled up into the forecourt. Mlle Lacroix got down, was handed her little case by the old chauffeur (her trunk was being sent on). Dorothea followed her up the steps to the platform. There was no one else waiting. The platform was empty, the benches still wet from the dew, tubs of flowers bright and effusive, the black-and-white sign bold and official: WELBY.

'So now, Dorossea, it is time to say *au revoir*.'

'Not yet, Mam'zelle. The train isn't here yet.'

'Very well, *ma petite*. A few minutes more.'

'Oh, Mam'zelle: why must you go?'

'I have explained why, I have told you. *Maman* is poorly. She need me. And — if I speak the truth — I have already stayed far longer than ever I intended.'

'Will we . . . will we *ever* meet again?'

'But of course! Perhaps I will not come to England a second time, but you — you will, you must, visit me! I shall be expecting you!'

Go to France? Impossible! One might as well wish to visit the mountains of the moon.

A whistle tooted in the distance, piercing Dorothea's heart. The train must already have emerged from the tunnel beneath Duncan's Hill. It would be here in a matter of moments. Already she could see the smoke of it, puffs of grey against the cloudless sky. Time was running out, the last seconds trickling away, irretrievable.

Was there anything she had forgotten to say?

Only everything! And every day would bring a thousand things more. But Mlle Lacroix would not be there to hear them.

The governess took Dorothea's face between her hands as the train came thundering into the station, kissed her on both cheeks.

'*Au revoir, ma petite!* You must be brave now! Remember all I have taught and all that we have learned together. What an adventure it has been! Remember, too, to put your trust in God. He will not let you down.' But even God had been a gift from the governess.

'Oh Mam'zelle! I don't know what I shall do without you!'

Mlle Lacroix had turned the brass handle, had opened the door, had stepped up into the carriage. Now she looked back, half in and half out. Her eyes searched Dorothea's face, then she smiled. '*Alors!* You do not need me anymore, Dorossea! My work here is done! You are a young lady now!'

The door slammed shut. A whistle blew. The train moved, uncertain at first but soon gathering speed. Mlle Lacroix waved, framed in the window. Dorothea ran after her, her booted feet striking on the wood of the platform. A mist descended — tears perhaps, or the billowing steam of the engine. Chuffing greedily, belching and hissing, heavy wheels trundling faster and faster, the train sped away. The last of the carriages flowed round a bend in the line and was gone. The noise and the steam slowly dissipated. The empty rails glinted in the golden June sunshine, curving away into the blue. A deep silence descended.

Dorothea stood on the very end of the platform. She had been left behind, abandoned once more, just like before, six-and-a-half years ago, the last time she had seen her papa. She was taken back to that first evening, looking out from the nursery window at the alien landscape, utterly alone.

You do not need me anymore . . . you are a young lady now . . . Mlle Lacroix's last words echoed in her head. It seemed impossible to believe in them. And yet when had the governess ever been known to be wrong?

Faces began to crowd into Dorothea's head, more and more of them, all of the people she knew, Roderick and Henry and Uncle Albert, Nibs and Becket and Mrs Turner, even little Dicky smiling and sucking his thumb. The names went on and on. And there was Aunt Eloise, too. Had Aunt Eloise not said, *One can't imagine the place without her . . . it is if she* belongs *here . . .*

Was it possible? Had Aunt Eloise come to accept her at last?

But it wasn't quite like that, thought Dorothea as she turned and made her way slowly back along the platform. It was more as if the *house* had accepted her — had claimed her for its own. Aunt Eloise had merely acquiesced in this fait accompli.

The stationmaster, dead-heading flowers in the boxes, nodded to her as she passed and she quickened her pace, for the chauffeur would be waiting to take her back to Clifton Park. But at that thought she stopped, poised at the top of the stairs.

No, she said to herself. Not Clifton Park. Home. It was time to go home.

Gathering her skirts, she skipped down the steps in the June sunshine while from above, cascading out of the high blue sky, came the liquid song of a lark.

THE END

ALSO BY DOMINIC LUKE

THE BRANNANS FAMILY TRILOGY
Book 1: AUTUMN SOFTLY FELL
Book 2: NOTHING UNDONE REMAINED
Book 3: DREAMS THAT VEIL

Thank you for reading this book.

If you enjoyed it please leave feedback on Amazon or Goodreads, and if there is anything we missed or you have a question about, then please get in touch. We appreciate you choosing our book.

Founded in 2014 in Shoreditch, London, we at Joffe Books pride ourselves on our history of innovative publishing. We were thrilled to be shortlisted for Independent Publisher of the Year at the British Book Awards.

www.joffebooks.com

We're very grateful to eagle-eyed readers who take the time to contact us. Please send any errors you find to corrections@joffebooks.com. We'll get them fixed ASAP.

Printed in Great Britain
by Amazon

62883306R00147